A Scottish Christmas Hideaway

ALSO BY ELLIE HENDERSON

SCOTTISH ROMANCES
Book 1: A Summer Wedding on Arran
Book 2: A Christmas Escape to Arran
Book 3: A Summer House on Arran
Book 4: A Christmas Wish on Arran
Book 5: A Summer of Secrets on Arran

ROWAN BAY ROMANCES
Book 1: A Scottish Christmas Hideaway

A Scottish Christmas Hideaway

Ellie Henderson

Choc Lit
A JOFFE BOOKS COMPANY

Choc Lit, London
A Joffe Books company
www.choc-lit.com

First published in Great Britain in 2025

Cover art by Jarmila Takač

ISBN: 978-1781899236

AUTHOR'S NOTE

Rowan Bay is a completely fictional village on the eastern shore of Loch Lomond. It is located in the iconic Loch Lomond and The Trossachs National Park. For the purposes of this book, I wanted to create a fictional village by the water without having to worry about damage to the natural environment or needing planning permission! Rowan Bay is purely a product of my creative imagination, which is one of the many joys and privileges of being a writer. The nearby villages of Drymen and Balmaha, both mentioned in the book, are very real and worth visiting, as is the St Mocha coffee shop in Balmaha.

For Dougie — Thank you for your constant support, love and belief in me.

PROLOGUE

Jessica's eyes widened in wonder when she stepped out of the taxi at her Manhattan hotel. It was early December and the whole city appeared to be sprinkled with twinkling lights and dusted with a kind of festive magic that came with this time of the year. The streets were crammed with horn-honking cabs and the wide pavements bustled with people, laden with parcels and packages. The cold air made her wince and she pulled her hat firmly down over her ears to protect against the wind chill. As she looked up at the dark, velvety sky she felt something tickle her nose. She clapped her gloved hands in delight when she realised they were snowflakes. She paid the driver and wheeled her cabin bag into the huge marble lobby. The doorman tipped his head at her just as she managed to avoid colliding with the huge Christmas tree at the entrance.

When she opened the door to her room, she kicked off her shoes, pulled off her hat and gloves then unbuttoned her heavy winter coat. She had only landed at JFK airport a few hours ago and had headed straight to her law firm's offices near the Rockefeller Center. Jessica had needed to remind herself she was there on important client business and to rein in her starry-eyed wonder as she looked at everything with a

1

childlike gaze. Now she allowed herself to finally squeal with excitement as she ran to the window and took in the view of the street below and the tall buildings in front of her. The snow was falling faster now and she hoped it would blanket the pavements for a while at least before turning to slush. Jessica had never been to New York at Christmas time — or any time at all. She smiled in delight. 'It's the most wonderful time of the year,' she said softly, finally understanding what it was that Andy Williams had been crooning about all these years. For a moment she allowed herself to be absorbed in the enchanting scene in front of her. What a *romantic* city. Then her phone buzzed, interrupting her enchantment, and she snatched it up from the bed.

Hey beautiful. See you here in an hour. Xx

Jessica sighed with anticipation, grinned and felt her stomach flip. Tim had sent her the map for a wine bar they were to meet in, just a few blocks away. When she was told, late last night, that she would have to fly to the Big Apple to see a client, she had felt a ripple of excitement, not just because she was finally being allowed to handle this senior client on her own but it meant she might be able to snatch some unexpected time with Tim, her boyfriend, who lived in Boston; he travelled frequently between New York and London, where she'd met him a few months ago. She knew she hadn't given him much notice about her last-minute trip, but just before her plane took off from Heathrow, he messaged to say her luck was in — he just so happened to be in New York. Tim was a hedge fund manager which seemed to be a high-risk, high-pressured environment to work in. Jessica was never quite sure what he actually did day-to-day as he could be vague about the specifics, but she was aware that he made a lot of money and enjoyed a fast-paced lifestyle. Their relationship was long-distance, erratic and exciting due to their hectic and often conflicting schedules, which made this extra unexpected night together even more special. The thought of staring into his dark eyes and being wrapped in his arms later was holding all thoughts of jet lag at bay.

More than an hour later, having showered and changed into a maroon woollen dress and boots, she was sitting at a small table, tucked away in the corner of the cosy wine bar, waiting for Tim. The dim lighting and candles made it the perfect place for their date. She sent him a quick text to let him know she had arrived. Warmed by a glass of red wine, she wasn't too bothered that he was late. That was par for the course with Tim. She knew what it was like to work with powerful, rich and demanding clients in her role as an employment lawyer. That was why their relationship seemed to work. They didn't have demands or expectations, although Jessica had to admit to herself that she was falling for him and she was almost giddy with excitement at the thought of seeing him any minute now. But she had to remind herself to remain aloof. She didn't want him to think she was needy. He seemed to like the fact that she was an independent career woman with her own life in London, which consisted mainly of her job. Meeting Tim was a reminder that she should be enjoying more of a balance.

As she waited for him to arrive, she quickly checked the family WhatsApp chat. Her parents had just arrived in Melbourne for Christmas, where her older brother, Murray, lived with his wife Carolyn and their baby, Lexi.

We're here! We made it to Oz!! Love Mum x

Although Jessica had been invited, she couldn't take any extended leave over the festive period and, secretly, she hoped she may be able to find a day or two to hole up with Tim if he made it to London as he had promised. Her flatmate, Kristen, was going to be away for the holidays so she and Tim would have the place to themselves. Her legs trembled at the thought of spending several days with him. She could hardly wait.

She flicked through the *many* photos of her mum and dad grinning proudly as they cradled Lexi in their arms. She had grown so much since Jessica last saw her earlier in the year when she was only a few months old. Smiling, she looked at the blue sky and sunshine in the background and her brother wearing his shorts and T-shirt. It was a stark contrast to the wind chill factor and snow that *had* now turned to mush on the streets of New York. But she knew where she would rather be. Tapping out a quick message, *guess where I am?* she attached a picture of the giant, twinkling tree at the Rockefeller Center she'd managed to quickly snap earlier. She longed to go back and look at it properly and was planning to suggest a walk there with Tim after dinner.

'Are you ready to order?' asked the waitress, forcing her to look up from her phone.

Jessica had finished her glass of wine and, glancing at her watch, saw that she'd been waiting for more than half an hour and he hadn't replied to her text. 'Hmm, can I have another glass of wine please and some olives. I'm still waiting for my friend.'

The waitress raised an eyebrow. 'Sure. No problem.'

But after another half hour, and no sign of Tim, she tried calling his phone. It was switched off with just the sound of his deep voice telling her to leave a message. That was strange. Even though he was often late, he always let her know. Why wasn't he calling her or picking up his phone? Yawning, *again*, she felt her eyelids growing heavy and knew she could do with getting some sleep after all. She had an early start again in the morning and a full day's work ahead of her before she caught her flight back to London. She paid the bill and walked dejectedly back to her hotel, all thoughts of any late-night sightseeing forgotten. Something important must have come up for Tim not to show. But she had been so looking forward to seeing him. Jessica longed to press her lips against his and feel his hand against her face. His touch was something she didn't think she would ever tire of. She felt a tear slide down her face and an ache of disappointment in her gut.

CHAPTER ONE

One Year Later

Jessica was frantically bashing away at her keyboard, trying to clear the backlog of emails that were dropping into her inbox like a steady fire of bullets. She paused when she realised someone had placed a coffee in front of her. Glancing up, expecting to see the office PA, Rachel, she moved her hands away from the keyboard when she realised it was Ivan. She gulped. Ivan, her boss, never did the coffee run and the stern expression on his face indicated he wasn't here to make idle chit-chat with Jessica about her weekend plans. This did not bode well.

'Erm, is everything okay?' she said, feeling her stomach tighten.

'Let's have a chat,' he said, gesturing towards his office.

She picked up her coffee and followed him, wondering what he wanted to talk to her about.

'Close the door please. Take a seat.'

Jessica gingerly perched on the edge of the chair.

'I've noticed you have been a bit more irritable than usual.' Ivan was always direct and to the point.

Jessica sighed. She knew she had been snappier these past few weeks. But let's face it, the legal profession was hardly a compassionate and kind place to work. Not only that but it was highly competitive too. She immediately wondered if one of her ambitious associates had said something. Was someone after her clients? Or had there been a complaint? Jessica was never stumped for words but today she couldn't even stutter a reply. Instead, she tried to casually pop the lid off her coffee cup. She took a sip of the cinnamon-dusted drink. Only then did she feel able to say, 'Oh.'

'It's been brought to my attention that you are quite stressed and have been working all hours.'

Jessica blinked at him as she listened in astonishment. She had not been expecting him to say that at all. Unless he was being sarcastic, of course. But Ivan wasn't a joker. Being a workaholic was part of the deal. They were all expected to work every hour they could, which was why they were paid so well. Never ever, in her entire career, had anyone accused her of working *too* much. She didn't think it could *actually* be done. Work was her main priority. In fact, it was her only priority. Wasn't that a good thing?

He shook his head. 'We have had a complaint. Another one.'

'Is this about Dana Matthews again? I thought we'd dealt with this already,' she said curtly. 'There was a conflict of interest.'

'No,' said Ivan swiftly. 'It's about Zander Harrison. He's just off the phone.'

She managed not to roll her eyes. So this was what it was about. That meeting the other day when the client had been completely patronising towards her. 'He was mansplaining,' she said briskly. The way he always insisted on sitting so close to her in meetings was also completely creepy, but she managed not to blurt that out to Ivan. Especially as she knew she *had* been rude to him.

Ivan narrowed his eyes and there was a faint smile on his lips, which lasted about a millisecond. 'I know what Zander is like. I know how condescending he is. But he is paying us a lot of money to get the results he knows we deliver. Remember, the client likes to think they are right.'

Jessica chewed her lip for a minute, realising that she was actually very tired of putting up with people who thought they could act in any way they pleased because they had money. She actually didn't care any more. 'Even when they aren't,' she muttered, immediately realising it was the wrong thing to say.

Ivan stood up straight and frowned. 'When they're paying us the amount they are, they are always entitled to think they are right, Jessica. There are plenty of other firms they can take their business to if our actions displease them.'

And there was the rub. If Zander Harrison wandered into the office right this minute and tried to tell her once more how to do her job, she'd probably tell him where to shove his bottomless wallet. Which didn't bode well. Maybe Ivan had a point. Had she let her professional standards slip? Was she being too prickly and oversensitive with clients? Or had she reached her limits with the job?

'Look,' he said more gently. 'I don't really know what is going on with you and it's none of my business. Unless it starts to impact on your work. I did check with HR and you've hardly used any of your annual leave this year.'

She swallowed. He was right. But the last thing she had wanted to do was take a break. Work had given her the focus she'd needed this year.

'Take some time off,' he said, which sounded like a clear directive rather than a friendly suggestion. Then his mobile started ringing and he moved away from his desk, the conversation clearly over.

She picked up her cup and returned to her own desk, sitting there for as long as she could, trying to casually drink her coffee and look at the screen in front of her. But she could feel shooting pains behind her eyes and was horrified at having to choke back a sob. She absolutely could not start to cry in here. It would be the *end* of her.

Taking a breath, she managed to hold herself together. She walked from the office to the toilets. As she dried her hands under the fluorescent lights, she looked back at her reflection in disgust. Her face was white, her cheeks hollow and her strawberry-blonde hair was dull and hung limply around her shoulders. It badly needed a colour, a cut and a blow dry. She didn't exactly epitomise the look of a top lawyer. Ivan was right to be concerned. He didn't want his reputation flawed in any way and she was hardly helping things when she looked like she'd been dragged through a hedge backwards.

The door swung open and she heard footsteps approaching. 'Hey,' said Freda, who came and stood next to her. Freda was tall and willowy and her long blonde hair hung over her shoulders in waves. Leaning into the mirror, Freda applied some lip gloss to her rosebud lips and smacked them together. In her sharp black suit, white shirt and red heels, Freda looked very much the brilliant lawyer that she was.

Jessica sighed loudly and then looked guiltily at Freda. 'Sorry. I didn't mean to do that quite so loudly. I just realised how awful I look.'

Freda turned to face her and looked at her properly through icy-blue eyes and a stare that could penetrate through the toughest of clients. But there was kindness in her eyes too as she reached over to pat Jessica on the arm. She tilted her head. 'I'm not going to lie. You do look terrible, Jess. You've not been yourself for a while. You know we're all worried about you?'

Jessica nodded, her head now starting to throb, and she gave her a weak smile. Since the beginning of the year she had started to withdraw and was much quieter than usual. She didn't always return texts or phone calls and had retreated back into work until that was all she did. She was at her desk early every morning and then didn't leave until she had worked at least twelve hours, which was fairly standard for a lot of people in her profession. But there was no respite from work at all. She had even started running into the office at

8

weekends, along the River Thames from her apartment in Putney, telling herself that it was exercise and fresh air and that she needed to check some files anyway. A quick hour in the office soon turned into several, until it became a regular habit and she was there all the time. 'Yes, Ivan has just told me to take some time off. I think I'm scaring the clients.'

'You could do with a break, Jessica,' she said softly. 'You look utterly exhausted.'

Jessica's jaw tightened. She was *knackered*. Even her bones felt old and weary. But even though she had loads of outstanding annual leave accrued, the thought of a break from her routine terrified her because that would mean she had time to think. She tried to speak but the words were swirling in her mouth and suddenly she felt as though her brain was filled with glue.

'Take a breath,' said Freda, calmly. 'You're okay, Jessica. Just take a few slow breaths.'

Jessica's heart rate quickened and she tried to breathe slowly as her eyes widened in panic.

'Splash your hands under the taps,' said Freda, gently taking her trembling hands and running the water over them. 'It's okay. Let's just take a minute before we go somewhere quiet.'

It was as though she was having an out-of-body experience as she looked at Freda and listened to her words. They sounded muffled, as though they were both underwater. After a minute or two, with Freda talking soothingly next to her, Jessica's breathing started to slow again and she watched as Freda dried her hands for her with some paper towels.

'Come on. Let's go and get a cup of tea.' She didn't wait for an answer. She led Jessica out of the toilets by the arm and discreetly towards the lift. Ushering her in, she pressed the button to take them straight to the floor the café was on. It was empty — everyone was far too busy to ever actually sit in it — and she guided Jessica to a table in the corner and fetched them both a cup of tea. She unwrapped a flapjack and pushed it towards Jessica. 'I bet you haven't eaten all day, have you?'

Jessica shook her head and then the tears started to trickle down her cheeks. She felt for a tissue in her pocket and quickly tried to stem the flow, mortified that she was crying at work.

'Oh, love,' said Freda kindly. 'What is it? What's going on?'

Jessica gulped. How could she tell her the truth? That she wasn't coping any more. And that she'd had enough. Freda had privately supported Jess throughout the ordeal of the past year. But Jessica didn't go into all the gory details. That she'd had her heart broken and smashed into smithereens repeatedly.

'We've all been worried about you . . . You're just not yourself. And haven't been for a while. And that's understandable with what you've had to deal with. But . . .' Freda sighed and leaned in. 'I always hate telling colleagues what to do. But it sounds like that was an order coming from Ivan. And you look as though you're about to hit the wall, Jessica. If you don't hit Zander Harrison first. And if that happens then you're no use to anyone.'

And just in that moment as Jessica looked at Freda, she realised what she needed to do before she was made to. 'You're right, Freda. I'm in a total state. Not just my hair,' she said in a bid to make a feeble joke. 'I need to take some time off . . . I need to go home.'

Freda nodded. 'I can take over any of your clients for the duration.'

Once upon a time she would have reacted in defence and abject horror to that suggestion. But she was exhausted and realised she didn't actually care about work any more. She didn't care about anything. She just wanted to go home to see her parents and sleep. She wanted to go home to Rowan Bay and hide.

'A few weeks away will do you the world of good. Especially at this time of year when things are kind of slowing down anyway,' said Freda firmly.

Jessica looked at her unconvinced. Things never slowed down at their firm. At any time of the year. But she simply shrugged.

Freda leaned forward and patted her arm. Even her fingernails were immaculate, painted in a bright red shade to match her shoes.

Jessica looked down at her chewed nails in comparison. She used to always pride herself on her appearance and having her nails done was always part of her routine.

'Look,' said Freda kindly. 'Have some time away from work, go to the spa and get your nails done.' She raised an eyebrow. 'But most of all, go and spend Christmas with your loved ones.'

CHAPTER TWO

A few days later, having agreed with her firm to take a period of extended leave, Jessica was packed and ready to go home to Thistle Cottage. She had messaged Kristen, who was working in Singapore until later in the month, to let her know she was going home to Scotland and that the flat would be empty. The thought of seeing Loch Lomond again and having some space to just be was already making her feel marginally better. She hoped that almost six weeks of fresh air, lots of rest and home-cooked food would be just the medicine that she needed. Though she was slightly worried at her own lack of concern over being away from work for so long. Once it would have been unthinkable. But a lot had changed and she reminded herself that this break would give her the chance to think about what she did next. When she had called her parents to tell them she was coming home, her mum had whooped in delight and then put her on speaker phone so her dad could hear.

'How long for, dear?' asked her mum.

'Um, probably until the new year.'

'That's wonderful!' said her dad. 'How are you managing to get all of that time off work though?'

'I've got loads of holiday to take,' she'd said quickly. 'I thought it would be nice to spend it with you. Especially as Murray, Carolyn and Lexi will also be home. That's if you don't mind?'

'Of course we don't, Jess. It's been ages since we saw you. It will be lovely to have you all here together — goodness, this is the best Christmas gift ever!'

Her throat had choked with emotion as she thought how sad her parents would be if they knew why she was really coming back for so long. They didn't need to know she was facing burnout from both work and her personal life. She hadn't been home since last year and she felt so guilty that she hadn't made time to visit.

As the plane took off from Heathrow, Jessica thought about how much her life had changed since this time last year when she was looking forward to celebrating Christmas with Tim. Her mind wandered to the early heady days when she and Tim had first started seeing each other. She had actually bumped into him stumbling out of the office after another long day at work. She was checking her phone, her head down, when she had walked into him not looking where she was going. 'I'm so sorry,' he'd said, catching her arm, and when she looked up at him, her eyes had locked on his. It was like a thunderbolt moment which she had never had before.

'It's okay,' she managed to stutter, unable to peel her eyes from his.

'Let me buy you a drink to apologise,' he said.

Her automatic response was to refuse. He could have been anyone. But something made her accept. Maybe it was his American accent and his dark eyes and black hair. But it was Friday night and she couldn't remember the last time she had been to a pub. And she didn't have work the next day. 'Okay, sure,' she said casually. 'Just the one though.'

A few minutes later they sat together in a crowded corner of a bar.

She gripped the glass and took a long gulp of the chilled Sancerre.

'Good?' he asked, his eyes fixed on hers.

'Very,' she replied, unable to take her eyes off his.

'Cheers,' he said, knocking his glass against hers. He was very close to her and he whispered in her ear. 'It's so loud in here. Shall we get out of here? If you want to . . .' He'd looked at her suggestively.

Jessica felt a warm sensation in her stomach as she looked up at him. He was tall and broad and wearing a navy designer suit with a crisp white shirt underneath. His hair was dark and wavy and his eyes the darkest shade of brown she had ever seen. They were almost black. She quickly finished the wine and, as she stood up, she felt slightly giddy, realising it wasn't the effect of the alcohol but being in close proximity to this man. A very good-looking man who smelled of sharp, woody and very expensive aftershave. He gently touched her elbow and guided her towards the door. As they walked along the pavement together, she felt as though a thread was pulling them closer and closer together until, all of a sudden, he was holding her hand and she was gripping it back. And before she knew it, they were somehow back at her flat.

She woke in the middle of the night almost looking at him in disbelief when she realised he was still there in her bed. He hadn't been a dream. She leaned over and kissed him on the lips. His eyes fluttered open and he gave her a sexy grin. And from that moment on she was hooked. In the months that followed, they spent as much time together as they could, which was tricky due to the transatlantic nature of their relationship. Tim had completely swept her off her feet.

Now as she walked through the brightly lit domestic arrivals hall at Glasgow Airport, her life couldn't have been more of a contrast. She scanned the rows of people waiting to collect friends and family. She couldn't see her parents and felt herself growing anxious until she heard her name.

'Jess! Over here, Jess.'

It was her dad's voice. She looked around and saw him standing with a wide smile on his face a few metres away. She ran towards him. '*Daaad.*'

'Oh, Jess. My wee Jess. It is so good to see you.' He hugged her tightly and kissed the top of her head.

Despite being thirty-two, she immediately felt like a little girl again, and as the enormity of the past year started to catch up with her, she burst into tears. Which was exactly the very last thing she wanted to do. She hated worrying her parents.

'Jess, what's wrong?' he said gently, stepping back to look at her with concern. Then he reached into his pocket and found a tissue.

Jessica took it and dabbed at her tears. Her dad, Angus, had always been tall, but as she gazed up at him, she realised he had definitely shrunk. His beard was greyer now rather than its usual salt and pepper look. He also had more lines around his eyes which made him seem older, and the tears started to fall again.

Her dad looked at her, concern so evident.

'I'm okay. Honestly,' she said. 'Just tired and emotional and glad to see you, Dad . . . Where's Mum?'

'Guess,' he said with a roll of his eyes.

'The loo?'

'Yup,' he said with a chuckle.

It was a long-standing family joke that her mum, Catriona, always made a beeline for the toilets wherever she was.

'Catriona,' said her dad gruffly with a wave. 'Over here.'

Her mum ran towards her, beaming, but when she noticed her daughter's blotchy face, she stopped smiling. 'Oh, what's the matter? Och, my darling, are you okay? I can hardly believe that you're here.' She threw her arms around her. 'Jessica, there's nothing to you. Have you lost weight? And you look so pale. Have you not been eating? We have been so worried you know.'

'Catriona, are you going to take a breath and let the girl reply?'

Her mum stepped back and Jessica shook her head, aware that her face was now probably streaked with mascara. 'I'm fine. Honestly. It's just been a busy year. And I got a bit over-whelmed when I saw Dad.'

'It's probably your hormones,' she said knowingly. 'Or the planets. Mercury is in retrograde and that can put everything into a *spin*.'

Jessica clocked her dad giving her mum a look which meant please rein it in for now. Then he looked at her and rolled his eyes as if to say, *here we go*.

'Anyway, the main thing is that you're here, darling, and you can relax and be looked after for a change. You look utterly shattered.' Mum paused. 'I am glad you're home and I promise we'll take care of you. And we have you to ourselves for a bit before chaos descends.'

Jessica smiled knowing she was referring to Murray and Carolyn and little Lexi who were due to arrive in a couple of weeks. 'It will be great to see them all. I still can't believe I haven't physically seen Lexi since she was a baby.' Her niece was now almost two years old and she did feel guilty that, since a quick trip to see her when she was born, she had only seen photos of her and waved hello when her brother FaceTimed her.

'She's a wee poppet,' said her dad proudly. 'But I suspect it will be full on when they arrive.'

'Indeed,' said Mum. 'Which is why we've made a plan.'

Jessica tilted her head, intrigued. 'What's the plan?'

Her mum gestured towards the exit. 'We'll fill you in later. Come on. We'd better get back to the car before we need to remortgage the house to pay for the parking. This way.'

'Here, let me take your bag, dear,' Dad said, taking Jessica's case from her and wheeling it effortlessly towards the exit.

'Come on, troops,' ordered Mum. She led the way as she bustled off towards the doors, her mass of grey curls trailing down the back of her cerise coat.

'Thank goodness you're here,' said her dad conspirato-rially. 'She's in full organisational mode. All I want is five minutes' peace but she is having none of it.'

Jessica chuckled. Her dad didn't need to say any more. She walked next to him as they tried to keep up with her mum, who was a woman on a mission, swiftly weaving her way through the other passengers on her route to the payment machine.

'That's an absolute outrage,' said Catriona, exclaiming loudly at the cost of the ticket.

Jessica shook her head fondly and smiled even more when the other lady at the machine also started tutting and agreeing with her. How she had missed her mum.

'I know, someone is having a laugh. Daylight robbery, so it is,' said the woman with a dry chuckle. 'Merry Christmas indeed.'

As she followed her parents to their car, Jessica felt a small weight lift from her shoulders. Things might just be okay. It was the first time she had felt a glimmer of anything like that all year. But now that she was home for Christmas she could hide away and perhaps emerge as a new woman in the new year.

CHAPTER THREE

Reuben climbed down the ladder, pulled off his goggles and stretched his arms up in the air to ease his stiff shoulders. For the past couple of hours he had been diligently rolling white paint across the ceiling of the small sitting room at Primrose Cottage. Despite his aching limbs, he was finding it strangely therapeutic, especially as he didn't have to talk to anyone else while he did it. It was nice to focus only on the direction of the roller and then dip it back into the tray of paint. He looked down at his overalls. They were splattered with an assortment of colours, and as he scratched his head, he realised that his dark hair would be sprinkled with flecks of white paint too as he'd forgotten to put on his old cap.

For the past few months, the cottage had undergone quite the overhaul and renovation. Reuben had tried to make sure the building retained its charm while opening up some of the smaller downstairs rooms to make a bright and open kitchen full of light. He had always loved the back of the house and was glad he had been able to add French doors that opened onto the private garden.

Primrose Cottage was tucked down a small lane which could be easily missed if you didn't know what you were looking for. In spring and summer, it was flanked by the greenery of trees. It was only in winter when they stood bare that the lane was more exposed. There were only four other cottages along the lane which was why it was such an appealing spot. It was private, quiet and unassuming, which Reuben realised ironically were also words that could describe him, and even more so this past year.

He walked through to the kitchen and poured himself a glass of water at the sink. As he sipped it, he looked out at the garden which was dusted with frost. The wee summer house that his friend and local tradesman Brodie had put up looked great, and he hoped Lexi would like it and maybe get a chance to play in the garden if the weather stayed dry. He should also really get a tree for the front room if he was going to do things properly this year and make the cottage festive for his guests.

Reuben didn't particularly like Christmas. Not any more. It was a time for kids who believed in Santa and had dreams and hopes. However, getting the cottage ready and painted in time had given him a project to focus on. He might even *begrudgingly* admit that he had quite enjoyed it. The painting was almost finished and, after that, he just needed to get the curtains and blinds hung. He checked himself. Organising the soft furnishings for a cottage wasn't something he had ever needed to think about. He was an architect, all about the light and maximising space. His apartment in Glasgow was very much a bachelor pad with a few bits of statement furniture, wooden shutters on the windows and polished floors. He laughed, wondering what his friends would make of him if they could see him now fretting about fabrics and finishing touches. At this rate he would be buying scented candles.

The late morning sunshine was now streaming through the windows and he decided he would go and grab a coffee from the village bakery and get some fresh air away from the paint fumes. He pulled on his old jacket over his overalls and grabbed his hat, his stomach growling at the thought of a hot coffee and a bacon roll. As he pulled the front door closed, he stepped out onto the lane and then turned back to admire the cottage from afar. He was pleased that he had painted the front door in sage green. It looked good against the brown stone of the house, and when spring came again, he knew the daffodil bulbs he had put in his dad's miniature wooden wheelbarrow planters by the door would look great.

Reuben sighed and smiled, watching his warm breath float away like cigarette smoke in the cold air. Then he shoved his hands deep into his pockets and made his way up the lane, stepping out the way and smiling when he saw Angus and Catriona Stewart, who had just turned into the lane to drive up to Thistle Cottage two doors away.

Walking down the road and towards the main street, he looked at the view of the loch, framed by hills behind. It was a view he would never tire of. Loch Lomond was a freshwater loch and the largest inland stretch of water in the UK. When he was growing up, he'd loved playing on the beach and paddling during the summer though he was told repeatedly to be careful. The water was freezing and extremely deep. He still found it hard to believe that people would willingly go swimming there all year round, but wild swimming was increasingly popular.

Rowan Bay wasn't perhaps as picture postcard beautiful as Luss, the village on the west side of the loch, but Reuben thought that made it even more appealing, as the tour buses packed with tourists keen to see most of Scotland in a day would quickly stop at Luss so people could pile off and have their picture taken at the picturesque pier. Rowan Bay tended to get overlooked, which suited him just fine as it felt more private and less of a tourist trap. It still had more than its fair share of beautiful old properties and it was no coincidence that Reuben now specialised in period homes. He loved the challenge of using his architectural skills to preserve the timeless charm of a building while also giving it a fresh look. For him it was about respecting the history of a building while making it suitable for modern living. He was always intrigued by the craftsmanship that went into original features like sash windows and ornate fireplaces. But he also liked to incorporate modern twists to his designs, such as skylights that flooded the space with natural light and underfloor heating under flagstone floors. His motto had always been quality over quantity as he wanted to ensure that each home and client got the attention they deserved.

Looking around now, as he made his way to the bakery, he never tired of looking at the different architecture in Rowan Bay. There was a mixture of houses and many of the cottages, including Primrose Cottage, were built in the nineteenth century as accommodation for workers from nearby slate quarries. There were flats above the shops on the main street and old crofters' cottages and byres for livestock which had been renovated and transformed into modern homes with minimalist décor. There were also new-builds which had been discreetly added to the outskirts of the village. As he approached the bakery, situated near the small square by the village clock, he could see that the windows were steamed up and he pushed the door open, inhaling the delicious scent of warm pastries and bread as he entered.

'Hey, you,' said the friendly woman serving behind the counter. She grinned and pointed at his hair as he pulled off his hat and raked his hands through it.

'Don't tell me. I've got the white effect?'

She nodded. 'Yes. Though only you can get away with it. Makes you look distinguished.'

'I'll take that as a compliment,' he said with a laugh. 'It's warm in here, isn't it?'

Her cheeks were flushed. 'Tell me about it. Try working back here. I'm pure sweating. Do you want your usual? Or can I tempt you with a gingerbread latte?'

'Aye, go on then, I'll try the fancy latte. How are you today, Gillian?'

She rolled her eyes. 'Och, okay. Though I was up half the night with Millie. She had a bad dream.'

He tipped his head sympathetically and tried to think of something helpful to say. 'That must be tough.'

She shrugged. 'All part of the fun and games of being a mum. I wouldn't change it for the world though.'

'You do a great job,' he said, meaning every word. Gillian was a single parent and quietly got on with things even though there was a lot she could complain about given half the chance.

'Here you go,' she said handing him a steaming cup and a paper bag with his usual roll and bacon. 'Are you rushing back to paint?'

'Nah, I think I'll sit for a minute and enjoy this before I start again.'

'You enjoy it, Reuben. Same time tomorrow?'

He nodded and grinned. 'Most probably.' He sat at the stool in the far corner of the window and wiped a bit of the window clear with a handful of napkins. With his back pressed against the wall, he could just make out a wee sliver of water. Taking a sip of coffee, he closed his eyes. It tasted amazing. Then he took a bite from his bacon roll. At that moment, his life couldn't have felt any better. He reminded himself to enjoy it while he could. He was getting better at appreciating things in the moment. For Reuben knew more than most how quickly life could change. One minute you could think that you're winning at life and everything is going your way . . . He shuddered slightly when he thought back to how smug *and* arrogant he'd been when he was on top of the world and thought he had smashed it. He'd always been slightly dismissive of those who constantly seemed to have challenges or moans. He always believed you were in control of your destiny. Until he wasn't.

Finishing the roll, he crunched the paper bag into a ball. He had been rudely reminded that anyone could be chucked a curveball and he was no different. He waved at Gillian, opened the door and headed out, realising that his late granny was right. She always said that life sent lessons to teach us and he had learned the hard way. He could still see her sitting in her chair by the window of her little house near the loch. Her eyes were always twinkling with kindness and her smile lit up her whole face — he often wondered if she had the same beam for all her grandchildren. When he was a boy, he used to think she kept her biggest smiles for him. He shook his head. God, he was a conceited wee knob.

Now he kept himself to himself, lived a quiet life and understood what his granny meant. He unlocked the door of Primrose Cottage feeling happy to be back.

CHAPTER FOUR

Jessica had nodded off in the back seat of the car on the way back from the airport and woke up to the sound of her mum calling. 'We're here. That's us home, love.' Jessica rubbed her eyes, surprised she had fallen into such a deep sleep in the car. Especially when she couldn't quite remember when she had last slept through the night in her own bed in London.

'Come on, Jess,' said her dad, opening the car door for her.

Yawning, she climbed out the car and immediately noticed the huge wreath on the front door of Thistle Cottage, studded with gold stars, pinecones and red baubles. 'I made it at a craft session in the village hall,' said her mum, looking at it proudly.

'Well done. It looks great, Mum. Very shabby chic.'

'That was *exactly* the look I was going for.' Her mum grinned in delight. 'See, Gus. At least *someone* appreciates my artistic talent.'

Her dad shook his head in confusion and tilted his head towards the house. 'I'll just put your things in your room, Jess,' he said, unlocking the door.

As she walked into the vestibule, she kicked off her shoes and felt the rough texture of the seagrass carpet dig into her feet. It was scratchy but comfortingly familiar. Then she slipped off her coat and hung it on the row of pegs by the door. She took a deep breath in. She had forgotten how comforting the smell of home was. It was a mixture of laundry powder, freshly baked cake and nutmeg. It felt exactly how it always had done. She sighed with relief, so glad to be back.

'Do you fancy a nice cuppa?' Mum said, bustling into the kitchen and filling the kettle.

'That would be great. Thank you.' She followed her mum and sat down at the pine table that was pushed against the wall. On it were various piles of Christmas cards, written and to be written, unopened mail and her mum's to-do list which was as lengthy as a loo roll. She refused to make lists on her phone, claiming she liked the sense of being able to physically cross things out with a pen.

'It's so nice to have you here,' said her mum, setting a mug down next to her and opening a large tin of fruit scones. 'Help yourself. I made these fresh this morning. I'll just get the butter.'

'Thanks, Mum.' Jessica took a sip of tea and then reached for a scone and spread it with butter then added a dod of jam.

'Now, you make yourself at home and just come and go as you please. We added you on to the car insurance in case you want to head to Glasgow to do some shopping. I expect you'll be wanting to do your own thing and have made your own plans.'

Jessica shook her head thoughtfully. 'Not really,' she said. It had been ages since she'd caught up with anyone from her childhood home. Especially as most of her friends had moved away elsewhere. She had no idea who would be around over the festive period. 'I'm just looking forward to catching up on some sleep and reading.' The thought of Christmas shopping in Glasgow held no appeal whatsoever even though it used to be a highlight when she was younger. Watching the carol singers at Princes Square used to be an annual tradition.

Her mum sat back in her chair and eyed her suspiciously but didn't say anything.

'How are *you*?' Jessica said, quick to avoid one of her mum's interrogations.

'I'm very happy to have you home, and the fact your brother is coming, too, is an added bonus. It will be wonderful to have the family all together again. Christmas is such a magical time anyway and it will be extra special this year with you all here and wee Lexi.'

'Yes,' agreed Jessica. The thought of Lexi being around was making her feel slightly more enthusiastic about Christmas.

'Your dad was waiting for you to come back so you could come with us to get the tree at the farm.'

She forced a bright smile. 'Sounds good.' She bit into the scone. It was crumbly and buttery. 'This is so delicious,' she said between mouthfuls.

Her mum raised an eyebrow. 'I'm glad you're enjoying. Tuck in.'

'Am I allowed one?' said her dad, wandering into the kitchen. He made himself a cup of tea and then sat in the chair opposite Jessica. 'You know your mum doesn't really bake any more. When I had the tin open this morning, I got a row. You would have thought I was stealing the crown jewels.'

'Hmm, that's not entirely true, Gus.'

'It is so. If you do bake, then you're usually doing it for someone else. So I can smell all these lovely things being made and then you tell me they're not for me . . . they're for the village hall or Jeannie down the road or the book club.'

'That's because you need to watch your cholesterol levels,' she said firmly.

'That's so tragic, Dad,' said Jessica with a smile. 'By the way, your jam is delicious.'

He beamed proudly. 'All made from the raspberries grown in the garden too. I was lucky and had a bumper crop this summer.'

The thought of actually growing anything and then making jam from it left Jessica bemused. She couldn't ever imagine having that much time. It was far easier to pick up a jar at Waitrose. Though she knew it wouldn't be as nice as the home-made stuff.

'Are you still baking your bread?' enquired her dad.

Jessica shook her head, remembering the joy that baking bread used to bring her. She had stopped just around the time she met Tim and then things changed. She hadn't baked any bread since. 'Nope. Not any more. I haven't made bread for ages.' Or eaten it either, she contemplated. The thought of eating carbs at work was abhorrent, especially as everyone seemed to be on some type of ketogenic diet where bread and pasta were viewed as the food of the devil.

'Well, you are welcome to make some while you're here,' said her mum. 'There's nothing better than a freshly baked loaf.' Catriona finished her tea and then stood up. 'Sorry to dash, but I promised to go and help decorate the village hall. It's the Christmas fair at the weekend.' She looked sheepish. 'I didn't want to crowd you by breathing down your neck and being around all the time,' she explained. 'And I thought you might be tired and want a wee nap.'

As though on cue, Jessica yawned. 'I will go and have a lie down if you don't mind.'

Angus reached for his glasses and unfolded the newspaper. 'You make yourself at home. I'll be down here reading the paper and then doing the crossword.'

'Just make sure you don't eat all those scones,' said Catriona admonishingly as he sliced his in two and began spreading the two halves with butter.

Jessica laughed at the way her dad pretended not to hear what she was saying. 'See you later, Mum, and thanks for coming to get me.'

Catriona gave her a smile and a wave and disappeared out the front door, closing it with a bang which caused Jessica to jump.

'I do wish she wouldn't do that,' said her dad. 'She does it every time. I keep telling her that the cottage will fall down one day. Makes no difference though.' He reached into the tin for another scone and lined it up next to the buttered one on his plate. He was clearly making the most of Catriona being out.

'You enjoy your five minutes of peace, Dad. I'm away for a nap.' Jessica smiled as she slowly plodded up the stairs towards her bedroom. The third step from the top still creaked and she chuckled, remembering how she and Murray would always avoid it if they came back from a night out later than they should. Reaching the top, she turned right at the landing. She was never quite sure what to expect when she came up here. The dark red carpet was still there and the walls were still an off-white. The same pictures were hanging on the wall. There was the one of their old golden retriever, Charlie, who had gone to Rainbow Bridge fifteen years ago, and another, a watercolour of Loch Lomond. Everything *looked* the same, but she knew when she opened the door of her old bedroom, she could be faced with anything. It could be a crafting room, yoga studio or gym. Her mum was always repurposing her room for different hobbies which changed frequently. Her brother's room was now a small library which housed her entire collection of Mills & Boon books. Jessica and her brother called it the *love* room. In fact, her mum had started calling it that too. She wondered how that was going to work when Murray and family were back for the holidays. It was hardly the appropriate surroundings for a small family with a toddler.

Gingerly, she swung open the oak door of her old bedroom; it still squeaked reassuringly. Jessica gasped when she looked inside. Her mum had indeed redecorated since she'd last been home. This wasn't what Jessica had been expecting at all. But fortunately, Mum had gone for the shabby chic look, something she was obviously embracing at the moment. The walls were a vintage pale pink, and the bedspread was white with the palest pink roses. She had strung white flower fairy lights around the bed, giving the room a warm glow. A new fabric tub chair sat at the window with its view over the back garden. Her old pine wardrobe had been stripped and repainted white, along with the floorboards. A large dusty rose rug had been added, along with a matching Roman blind to the window. It was the perfect room for her to retreat to.

Yawning again, she decided to unpack later. She lay down on the bed, pulling the blanket over her, and within a few minutes she had fallen fast asleep.

CHAPTER FIVE

By the time Jessica made it downstairs the next morning, there was no sign of her parents. It was after eleven and she was still wearing her pyjamas and fluffy socks. She opened the fridge door and idly thought about what to make for breakfast. Realising she wasn't actually all that hungry, she closed the fridge, turned and saw the handwritten note on the kitchen table. Her parents always reverted to notes when they were at home rather than text messages. 'Why would I send you a text when we're in the same building?' her dad asked in bewilderment when she'd previously suggested texts rather than notes.

She picked the piece of paper up and read it.

> *Dear Jess, we hope you had a good sleep. I kept checking on you but you were out for the count! You must be tired. Dad and I are away out on some errands. There's some broth in the pot for lunch in case you're hungry. Mum and Dad x*

She couldn't remember when she had last slept so long and so soundly. Other than a couple of trips to the loo, she'd managed to sleep for almost a day. Yet it was amazing how much better she felt for it. The morning sunshine was weak but it looked nice out, and although she was tempted to make a mug of tea and go back to bed and burrow under the covers again, she knew that a walk and some fresh air would do her good. She could hear her mum's voice saying the very same thing. Making herself go out now would mean that she'd get that outdoor box ticked and then could come back and just relax. She fully intended to spend as much time as she could in her pyjamas while she was here.

Twenty minutes later, having given her hair a quick brush and pulled on her jeans, sweatshirt and trainers, she was wishing she'd packed a more practical jacket instead of her woollen coat. She would just need to borrow one of her dad's. She spotted a warm-looking padded red jacket with a hood on the peg and slipped it on, grabbing her hat and gloves. The cool air caught at the back of her throat as she made her way down the lane. Shivering, she shoved her hands in her pockets and walked towards the shores of the loch. The sun was still shining, just about, but the sky looked heavy as though it was ready to dump lots of snow. Nothing would surprise her. Growing up in the west of Scotland, with the hills in the background, meant she was prepared for anything. She would often go to school in the morning wearing a light cotton summer dress and by the time the bell went in the afternoon it would be hailing and freezing. Her parents were always in and out the garden hanging washing only to bring it in again ten minutes later.

It didn't take her long to get to the gravel stretch of beach she was aiming for. She walked, pausing occasionally to skim a stone across the flat surface of the water. She smiled as a pebble bounced in and out three times, leaving a trail behind. It was something she never tired of as a child, especially as her brother always tried to beat her with more bounces but never could. Retrieving her phone from her pocket, she took a picture of the loch to send to him later. Although they had never been particularly close, and now he lived on the other side of the world, he was always very good at keeping in touch and checking in. She bit her lip when she thought about the number of times he'd asked how she was and she'd replied, 'fine' or 'tired'. She wasn't quite sure how he would respond if she told him she was 'heartbroken' or 'shattered' and it wasn't just work that had caused her to burn out. Her whole life was such a mess. It was going to be harder to hide the truth from him when he was actually here in person, too.

Taking in a huge gulp of air, she slowly blew it out through her mouth, trying to expel the small niggle of anxiety and sadness starting to swirl again in her stomach. It was like a shadow that followed her around. Turning to walk back up onto the road, she plodded slowly towards the high street, noticing the holly wreaths, hanging on the doors of cottages, dressed with ribbons, berries and pine cones. The shopfronts were decorated with festive lights and as snowflakes started to softly fall, she felt as though she was in a perfect postcard scene. She passed the butcher's and the cheese shop, the small Co-op, the Coffee Pot coffee shop, which looked busy with all the tables in the window taken. She glanced at the gift shop, The Bay, wondering if that was new as she hadn't noticed it the last time she was home. The Wee Bookshop was definitely a new addition and Jessica was looking forward to checking it out. She smiled to herself, feeling as though she was really noticing it all for the first time.

Then she walked past the bakery and the comforting smell of cinnamon and fresh bread made her pause. When she saw someone coming out with a takeaway coffee, she impulsively decided she would do the same. She walked towards the door just as the man with the coffee was about to close it. He was obviously a painter and decorator given the state of his splattered overalls.

'There you go,' he said with a cheery smile, holding it open for her.

'Thanks.' Jessica wondered why he was staring at her. And why was he now grinning at her? She frowned, slightly irritated. Why was he lingering? Why couldn't he just accept her thanks and get on with his day?

'Hey,' he said softly. 'How are you?'

She hovered in the threshold of the doorway, puzzled. 'Erm, okay, thanks, just taking shelter from the snow,' she said, aware that her voice was a bit clipped. Remembering she was no longer in London, she put in a bit of effort to be friendlier. 'Thanks for holding the door.'

'I think that's the snow finished for now.' He gestured at the sky. 'Nice jacket,' he said with a chuckle and then walked away. 'See you later.'

Jessica walked into the bakery with a frown. Should she have known who that was? With the overalls and the boots and the woolly hat pulled down over his ears, she had no idea. The voice was vaguely familiar but she still couldn't place him.

The woman behind the counter interrupted her thoughts. 'What can I get for you?' Her eyes widened in delight when she realised it was Jessica she was serving.

'Jessica, you're back!' she cried with delight. 'Your mum said you were coming up for a few weeks as you had loads of time to take off work.'

'Gillian.' Jessica smiled in surprise at her old school friend. They were once quite close, especially when they had played on the school hockey team together, but then had drifted apart. She hadn't expected to see anyone she knew quite this quickly or to get such a warm welcome. 'How are you?'

'I'm good thanks. Living the dream.' She chuckled and rolled her eyes. 'It's great to see you. I'm sure your folks will love having you back.'

'It's really nice being here,' she said, with genuine warmth.

'What can I get you?'

'Just a coffee please? Um, a flat white, if you have it?' Then she immediately felt guilty for making it sound as though they were in the back of beyond where instant coffee was the only option.

Gillian grinned. 'Yes, I can do that for you, no bother, and I can offer you our special Christmas coffee blend? I can even do you a cortado or a pea milk latte. They're all the rage with the mamils.'

Jessica looked at her quizzically. 'The what?'

'The middle-aged men in lycra. The cyclists,' she said with a chuckle.

'Ah,' said Jessica grinning. 'I'd love to try the Christmas blend. Now it's the start of December I may as well embrace all things festive.'

'Anything to go with it?' Gillian pointed at the baskets loaded with goodies.

Jessica shook her head, though she could feel her mouth starting to water as she looked at the array of pastries, cinnamon buns, scones and cakes on the counter. There were cute, iced snowmen biscuits and little cakes that looked like Christmas puddings.

'Go on,' said Gillian encouragingly. 'The Christmas cinnamon buns are one of our festive specialities. Available for a limited time only. In fact, you're lucky we have any left. We're usually sold out by now.'

'Okay, you've sold me,' she said, watching as Gillian reached for a bun and popped it in a paper bag.

As Gillian made her coffee, the women chatted generally about plans for Christmas and Jessica remembered that she had a little girl, though couldn't remember her name. 'Is your daughter excited about Christmas?'

'Millie is counting down the days. She is *soooo* excited,' she said proudly.

'How old is she now?'

'She's five, which I can't believe. She's growing up far too fast. And you must be looking forward to seeing wee Lexi? Your mum is beyond excited. It is so sweet.'

'Um, yes,' she said, realising that Gillian knew more about her life than she did about hers. She momentarily felt bad that she'd not made an effort to keep in touch.

'Here you are, my lovely. Hope you enjoy it. So nice to see you back.'

Jessica inclined her head in the direction of the door. 'Um, Gill,' she said, reverting to the name she used to call Gillian. 'Can I ask you something?'

'Sure you can,' she said.

'That guy sounded really familiar but I didn't recognise him.'

'Do you mean the guy who just left?'

She nodded.

Gillian chuckled. 'Yes, I suppose you wouldn't recognise him in that get up. You should have seen him the day he came in wearing his painting goggles. He'd forgotten to take them off. That was funny.'

'But who is it?' Jessica was still none the wiser.

'It's Reuben Campbell . . .'

'*Really*?' Jessica tried to hide her astonishment, but her jaw almost hit the ground. Reuben was her brother's friend from way back and for as long as she had known him, he'd always managed to annoy her. He really was the last person she wanted to run into while she was here. 'I haven't seen him for years. I had no idea it was him. Does he live here?'

'Sometimes.' Gillian looked as though she was about to say something else, but then the door opened and another few customers walked in. 'Don't be a stranger,' she said with a cheery wave.

Jessica smiled and nodded. She didn't have the heart to tell her that she intended to keep a very low profile over the next few weeks.

CHAPTER SIX

Walking back home, Jessica took a sip of coffee, grateful for the hot drink which was surprisingly nice. It really was very cold and before long the sun would start to dip again and the light would fade. It had been nice seeing Gillian's friendly face and it made her think about the lack of contact she had in the area of London that she lived in. Putney no doubt had a good community feel if you actually spent time there and were out and about and involved in the local area and then got to know people. But for her it had always been a place to rest her head. Work had always been the focus and the most important thing in her life. She realised that she hadn't given work or her clients a second thought since leaving the office last week. That was a sign she really was out of sorts. But she no longer had the energy to care. Her stomach growled and she stopped for a moment to take a bite of the cinnamon bun. Closing her eyes, she enjoyed the sugary taste of the icing, drizzled over it, with the light layers of flaky pastry. It was delicious and perhaps one of the best she had ever tasted. During her baking phase, when she once had a healthier work-life balance, she'd tried making them a few times with surprisingly good results. The thought of spending any time in the kitchen lately seemed odd. Yet it used to be her relaxation technique and a way of unwinding from her stressful job.

Then she thought about Reuben again and felt a bit apprehensive. She wondered what he was doing in Rowan Bay and how typical it would be that he was here when she was. To her he would always be her older brother's annoying best friend, who rattled their letterbox when calling for Murray, and pulled her ponytail, much to her irritation. As they got older, he was popular with all her friends and a bit of a ladies' man. The last time she'd bumped into him, which was years ago at Glasgow Airport, a glamorous woman appeared at his side, possessively looping her arm through his and looking at Jessica in disdain. Reuben had introduced her as his wife, Belinda. Reuben may have grown up and looked gorgeous in his business suit, but she was in no doubt he was the same arrogant person she knew from before.

Now, as she walked up the street and took the turning for Rowan Lane, she noticed that Primrose Cottage had been spruced up. It had a smart front door and new windows, and she frowned as she tried to remember who lived in it now. It had been Reuben's family home which was why he and her brother had been such good friends back then. Jessica always wished he'd had a sister who she could be friends with too. His mum had died quite a while ago, and she had a vague memory of her own mum telling her that his dad had been moved into a care home. Usually, whenever she spoke to her mum on the phone, she would get the full rundown of comings and goings in the street and indeed the whole village. She guiltily realised that her mum could have told her Taylor Swift or Harry Styles had moved into the village and she would be none the wiser — she didn't listen properly, always distracted, her mind elsewhere.

Her parents' car was back in the small, cobbled driveway, and she swung the front door open, kicking off her shoes as she walked in. She felt cosy in the jacket and so kept it on as she walked through to the kitchen.

'Hi, dear,' said her mum. 'I'm glad you managed a good sleep.'

'Hey, Mum. I certainly did,' she said, putting her bag and cup on the table. 'I just nipped out for some fresh air while it was sunny. I went to the bakery.'

'Oh, you'll have seen Gillian then. She's always asking after you. She was really pleased to hear you would be back for a while.'

Jessica nodded. 'Yes, it was nice to see her. How's your morning been?'

'Busy,' Mum said, sighing dramatically. 'Wee Jeannie has fallen and broken her wrist and so now they're short of helpers on the bottle tombola. It's the most popular stall at the Christmas fair and the one that earns the most. Anyway, I knew you'd want to help and so I hope you don't mind but I signed you up for it. It's on Saturday.'

Jessica's mouth fell open. *Bottle tombola at the Christmas fair?*

'It was either that or selling tickets for the sauna down at the loch.'

'Sauna?'

'Aye, have you not seen it yet? I wondered if you might have gone down that way for a walk.'

She shook her head. 'A sauna? Here in Rowan Bay?'

'Yes. It's all the rage. They're everywhere now. Here and over in Luss, too. Basically, anywhere there's a loch you'll now find a sauna. You sit and sweat in it and then cool off in the loch. It's brilliant. Your dad and I love it. It's like therapy,' she said evangelically. 'We'll need to sign you up for it. It's excellent for your mental health.'

'I didn't notice it when I was on the beach.'

'You need to walk left for a bit before you can see it.'

'Right. Where is Dad?' said Jessica, feeling as though she had walked into a parallel universe. *Saunas and bottle tombolas?*

'Playing golf. And probably on his second bacon roll now with the boys,' she said disapprovingly. 'I was just about to put some soup on. Do you fancy a wee drop?'

'Um, sure,' she said, even though she had just finished the bun.

'That jacket suits you,' said her mum approvingly. 'Red is definitely one of your colours. It matches your skin tone.'

'I was cold and didn't think Dad would mind. It's quite on-trend for him. Did you buy it for him? I can't imagine it's something he would buy for himself.'

She chuckled. 'Sadly not. It's not actually your dad's. It belongs to Reuben. He must have left it here the other day.'

She felt her jaw drop open once again. '*Reuben's?*' That was why he had kind of smirked at her and made a comment about the jacket. And to think she hadn't even recognised him but was brazenly strutting around the village wearing his coat. How embarrassing. And how *annoying*. She quickly shrugged the jacket off. 'I didn't realise, otherwise I wouldn't have put it on.'

Her mum shook her head. 'Oh, don't worry about that. I'm sure he won't be bothered but maybe he's forgotten he left it here. Do you mind just dropping it off to him?'

Her mum was making a reasonable request, so why did Jessica feel so resistant? She dug her fingers into the back of the chair she was now leaning into.

Catriona, gaily stirring the soup in the large pot on the stove, looked up. 'In fact, you could ask him if he fancies a spot of lunch too? He's been working so hard. He must be famished.'

'Mum, what do you mean? Where am I to drop it off to? What's he been working hard on?' The cogs were slowly whirring in her head as she tried to piece the puzzle together. Her mum gave one of her looks as though to say *are you okay, dear?*

'I'm sure I've told you this already. He's just a few doors down. At Primrose Cottage. He's been finishing it off.'

'Finishing it off?' she said confused. 'But what do you mean? Why?'

'Because he's the new owner,' said her mum patiently. 'He bought it from his dad when he had to move into the care home.'

'Oh . . . and is he going to live there?' Why would he want to return to live in his childhood home? He was a high-flying architect who lived in Glasgow with his glamorous wife. Wasn't he?

'I'm not entirely sure what his plans are to be honest, dear. You could maybe ask him that when you see him. But he did insist that Murray and the family stay there when they come back. That's why he's been working every hour of the day to get it all finished.'

'Murray, Carolyn and Lexi are going to stay there?'

'Yes. It makes sense, doesn't it? We thought it might be a bit of a squeeze trying to fit them all in here. I suppose you could have gone in the love room and they could all have had your room as it's bigger. Anyway,' she said with a wave of her hand, 'at least it gives them a bit more space with Lexi. And it's only down the road. When Reuben suggested it, I could have kissed him. He's such a sweetheart. Anyway, dear, if you can take his jacket back, then you could also say he's welcome to come for lunch.'

'Okay, Mum.' Reluctantly, she picked up the jacket and headed to the front door, pulling on her own woollen coat and her shoes. She walked two doors down and knocked on the front door. She waited a few moments before it swung open.

'Twice in one day,' said Reuben with a wide smile. 'Hello again.'

'Your jacket,' she mumbled, realising that she had never appreciated what a nice smile he had until this very minute. 'I am so sorry. I didn't recognise you at the bakery and I didn't know the jacket was yours. I thought my dad had been given some kind of makeover. But Mum explained. She also said you're very welcome to come for some lunch. If you want to.' She tried to get herself to stop talking, but the words kept tumbling from her mouth. 'I hear Murray and the family will be staying here soon and my mum is *so* pleased.' She didn't mean to sound quite so petulant but it appeared that Reuben was still quite the favourite in her household. It was the same when they were kids. Even though he perpetually teased her, her family loved him. He practically lived at their house. She'd sometimes wondered why he didn't just move in. But why was she acting like an awkward teenager? She hadn't even behaved like this around him when she *was* a teenager. Honestly, the effect he was having on her was ridiculous. Especially the way he was leaning against the door, grinning lazily.

'I wondered if I'd confused you with my outfit,' he said drily.

'I guess I wasn't expecting to see you in workie's gear,' she said tersely.

'Are you only used to slick city lawyers these days?'

Urgh, he was so annoying. 'No, I didn't mean that . . . you look great,' she said quickly before realising what she'd said. *Why did she just say that?* She wanted to disappear.

'You think I look great, do you?' He flashed that smile again.

Jessica felt her cheeks turn pink with annoyance. 'I didn't mean it like that and you know it. You haven't changed at all, have you, Reuben?'

He eyed her with amusement. 'And how are you, Jessie? Is it good to be back? Your mum did tell me you were going to be home for a few weeks. They've missed you. I hear you've not been home since last year.'

She stiffened at his sideways dig. Plus she had always *hated* him calling her Jessie when they were younger, and she bristled, feeling as though she was fourteen again. When she looked up at him, he was smiling mischievously at her. She felt her face flush as she noticed his strong forearms. It was like she'd had a knock to the head. He might have had old painting overalls on, but right now she realised he would look good in a bin bag. But he was still as aggravating as ever thinking he knew best.

'Yes, I'm back for the holidays. Anyway, here you go,' she said, practically shoving his jacket at him, desperate to get away. 'What shall I say about lunch?'

'Say thanks to your mum but that I'm on a roll at the moment with the painting, so I'll just crack on. Maybe another time though, eh?' He raised an eyebrow at her.

'I'm sure you'll be invited again, given how *popular* you are with everyone.' She realised she sounded sulky but couldn't help herself. She mumbled goodbye and walked down the path. Turning to close the gate, she gave Reuben a tight smile — he was watching her.

'Bye, Jessie.' He raised his hand and waved.

The less she saw of that man the better. He may well have grown up to be handsome and full of charm but he was as infuriating as he had been when they were kids.

* * *

As Reuben closed the door he couldn't quite believe Jessica was back. She had always been his best friend's annoying little sister. And she still was, as far as he could tell, as she was practically stamping her foot at the idea he was welcome at her family home. But she had certainly grown up and there was no denying she had a spark about her *and* was gorgeous. He smiled to himself, realising having her back in the village could be fun.

CHAPTER SEVEN

Jessica had been home for four days. It was Thursday and she woke up to the sound of banging and clattering downstairs. It was still dark, and when she picked up her phone on the bedside table, the illuminated screen said it was a little after eight. Pulling the covers up around her shoulders, she thought about life in London, just last week. If she was still there, she would be sitting at her desk by now, with a bucket of coffee next to her. It was strange to be tucked up in bed in her childhood bedroom. For a fleeting moment, she felt as though she was falling, with no idea where she might land. For years, her focus on her career had kept propelling her through life. But now, as she rolled onto her side, Jessica acknowledged that she wasn't missing work in the way she had assumed she would. Once upon a time the thought of taking an extended period of leave would have horrified her, and when she was on holiday, she would have kept her phone on and dealt with any problems with clients. That was the expectation if you wanted to make partner and rise up the ranks. And she didn't mind as her job had always been *everything*. She worked and studied hard to get to where she was, and her career had validated her. Since the events of last Christmas, she was grateful that work had given her purpose and focus and a reason to get up in the morning. On many occasions she had told herself how lucky she was. She had somewhere to go each day and something to do. She had people who needed her. In fact, they *relied* on her. What would this past year have been like if she hadn't had work? She shuddered when she thought how desolate she would have been. Knowing she needed to get up and face the day each morning had definitely helped to keep the feelings of dread and doom at bay.

She closed her eyes, hoping she could turn over and go back to sleep for a little while. But then the clattering started again. What on earth was going on? She lay for a few more minutes wondering if her mum had taken up plate smashing, before realising she was emptying the dishwasher. *Very* noisily. She could hear the drawers closing and shutting as Catriona threw in the knives and the forks and spoons. Jessica wondered if she was standing at the front door and launching them from there. It was making an absolute racket. Then the radio was switched on. Sighing, she threw back the covers. It was no use. She may as well get up. She wouldn't be surprised if the blender was switched on, too, for good measure. She laughed and shook her head. No chance of a lie-in this morning. Pulling on her dressing gown, she padded downstairs.

'Good morning,' said her dad in surprise. He smiled warmly. 'You're up early, dear.' He was sitting at the kitchen table tucking into a bowl of porridge, and he put his spoon down.

'Hi, Dad. Yes, I could hear you were both up and about . . .' She raised an eyebrow.

'Oops, sorry, Jess,' said her mum, standing at the sink. 'Did we wake you? We keep forgetting that not everyone is an early riser. We're so used to our own wee routine. And you must have slept through it every other morning. Maybe it's a sign you're getting back to your old self and ready to be up with the lark?'

Jessica laughed and sat down next to her dad. 'Hmm, maybe.'

'A wee cup of tea?' asked her mum, automatically pouring it anyway without waiting for an answer. She placed the mug in front of Jessica.

'Thanks.' She wrapped her hands around it, enjoying the feel of the warmth, and then took a sip of the liquid. She had forgotten just how much she loved the taste of tea at home. The water here was so much softer than the hard water in London, which left a murky film around the mug and the kettle full of limescale. She yawned as she considered whether to head back upstairs with her tea and disappear under the covers again.

'So what's the plan today, love?' asked her mum.

She shrugged. 'I'm not sure. Just chilling I think.' Her dad gave her a look as though to say, *good luck with that*. Sitting down for more than five minutes had never been a family trait in this house.

'Seeing as you're up, do you fancy coming . . .'

She inwardly groaned. This could go anywhere. What was her mum going to suggest? The sauna or her craft group or another new hobby she hadn't yet mentioned. 'Hmm . . .' She felt her stomach sink then took a deep breath and reminded herself her mum was trying to help.

Her dad threw her a sympathetic look. 'It is quite early, Catriona, and she is meant to be here for a rest. It's still dark out.'

Catriona regarded her for a moment. 'True. But I didn't mean right this minute,' she said huffily. 'I was just trying to make a plan. Okay, go back to bed for a while,' she said, clapping her hands together. 'You can come and get the tree with us later.'

Phew, thought Jessica. 'Okay, you have yourself a deal, Mum.'

'We'll head off about ten . . .'

Jessica forced a jovial nod, and then went upstairs with her tea. The thought of going to buy the Christmas tree would once have excited her. But as she lay back down on her bed, her mind started to race as she thought about last Christmas again. She picked up her phone and scrolled through her Instagram feed. It was rammed with uplifting and cheery reels and pictures from people fully embracing the festive season even though it was only the start of December. Throwing it down on the bed, she was again reminded that, although she knew plenty of people, how many real friends did she have?

She pressed her lips together as she thought about her last close friend from university, Lana, who had ended up sleeping with the long-term boyfriend she had before she met Tim. Which was why she struggled to open up and talk properly with friends. She hadn't spoken to anyone about what had *really* happened with Tim and that was part of the problem. At the time, she had told her flatmate, Kristen, some of the story. Although Kristen had been sympathetic to start with, she had then started travelling a lot with work and was hardly in the flat. Which had suited Jessica as she had been able to pull on her 'really, I'm fine' mask in the brief times they were together. And work had been an excuse for leaving early in the morning and staying late at night. But then something had happened at work which meant she'd had to share some of what had happened with her colleague, Freda. She knew she should really talk to her mum and that it would most probably help. But she didn't want to worry her parents any more than she already was by being back home. She was thirty-two years old and supposed to be a successful independent career woman. She just needed to get on with it. Although she didn't know what *it* was any more. She had forgotten who she was and where she was going.

After last year she had vowed not to celebrate Christmas again. In fact, she now hated Christmas, and the 'h' word was one she didn't use lightly. Her friends had always described her as being a three-quarters full kind of person, which said a lot about her, having worked as a lawyer and living in a world where everything was either black or white. It was fair to say she had seen the absolute worst side of humanity and more. Yet she had always managed to find a positive gloss. Not any more though. Which was sad, as she had always loved Christmas and what it meant to her: As a child, the smell of her gran's Christmas cake; her mum's crumbly mince pies; the trip to Princes Square in Glasgow to see the carol singers; hot chocolate and ice skating in George Square. Then, as she got older, the brisk winter walks up Conic Hill and admiring the view across Loch Lomond were among the highlights at this time of year. She had even managed to embrace the magic of Christmas in London. Despite her pressurised job, she loved seeing the lights glittering as she walked home from work, enjoyed ice skating at Hampton Court Palace, and on *that* trip to New York she had loved seeing the lights and window displays as she walked down Fifth Avenue. But that was then and this was now. It was amazing how quickly things could change.

Being back home was supposed to rejuvenate her or recharge her batteries. She reminded herself she should be making the most of this enforced break from the office. There was no point in lying in bed and feeling sorry for herself. She needed to get up and keep moving.

* * *

Just over an hour later, showered and dressed, she went downstairs to find her parents ready and waiting.

'Aha, there you are,' said her dad, pulling on his coat and gloves. 'It's cold out so make sure you wrap up. This will be fun.'

Jessica couldn't help shaking her head fondly. She felt as though she was a little girl again and a vivid memory of her dad taking her sledging floated through her mind. She smiled at the thought.

'You haven't eaten anything,' said her mum with a frown. 'Shall I make you some toast before we go?'

She shook her head. 'No, thanks, Mum. I'm fine. Honestly. Don't fuss.'

'But you need your energy, Jess. There's nothing to you.'

She patted her mum's arm. 'I'll eat something later. I promise. I just don't have a big appetite in the morning.' Or anytime, she added silently, though she had definitely made the effort to eat more since being home. Pulling on her coat and slipping on her boots, she followed her dad out to the car.

'Where are we off to then?' asked Jessica, strapping herself in. 'I thought you normally went to a garden centre to get your tree.'

'There's a place we've been going to the past few years. I'm sure I must have told you about it.'

Jessica felt the twinge of guilt. She was sure her mum would have told her but she didn't remember.

'You actually get to cut your own Christmas tree. Did you bring the gloves?' she asked Angus suddenly, who nodded. 'So yes, as I was saying, you get to choose the tree that you want and cut it down.'

'Oh. That's a bit different,' said Jessica, not ever imagining that she would be doing this with her parents at her age. But she told herself this could be fun. This could help her to recapture the sparkle and optimism of Christmas.

'It's quite the trend,' said Catriona. 'Especially at the weekends, with hot chocolate and food vans. Hopefully it shouldn't be too busy today, with it being during the week, but you just never can tell.'

Jessica looked out the window, admiring the scenery they drove past, the loch on the left and fields on the right. There was something mesmerising about just staring at the stretch of water and then over at the patchwork of varying shades of brown and green. It was frosty out and the road shimmered. There was a slash of blue sky amid the clouds and the sun was trying to break through.

'How does it feel to be home?' Her mum turned to look at her in the back of the car.

'Hmm. Strange. Familiar. But nice.' She was aware her voice was flat and she tried to inject some enthusiasm into it. 'It's so peaceful here, isn't it, and just what I need, Mum. Thanks for asking me to do this with you.'

'It will be lovely and it will be so good to have the house all ready and decorated for when Lexi gets here. I know how much you used to love decorating the tree when you were younger. That's why I left it until you got home. I didn't think you'd mind.'

Jessica smiled at her mum.

'Here we are,' said Angus, indicating right and turning into a small track with a sign advertising the Christmas trees.

A few moments later, they had parked, and her dad strode ahead, keen to lead the way on the tree hunt. Her mum walked more slowly today and linked arms with Jessica.

'Dad and I have been so worried about you. We are very glad you're home with us.'

Jessica felt tears smarting in her eyes and another flash of guilt that she hadn't been home for so long. 'I know you have and I'm sorry. But honestly, I'm fine. Just a bit fed up with everything.' She couldn't keep this up. At some point her mum would want to know more.

Her mum looked sideways at her as they walked along. 'You know if you need to chat you can. I would hate you to think that you were on your own and couldn't tell us. It doesn't matter what age you are, Jessica. We're always here for you, dear.'

Jessica sighed and closed her eyes briefly, wondering if she could open up and tell her mum what had happened. Part of her longed to be a little girl again, who would run to her mum in tears, knowing she would make everything better again. 'Work has been tough this year and it's all just kind of got on top of me.' She shrugged. 'There have been some problematic clients.'

'It's a stressful job, isn't it? And you do work all the time, dear. There's not much fun for you.'

That was so true. When did she last feel joy? She remembered the fizzing excitement she felt in New York last year when she got out the taxi at the hotel, and then the bubble

49

of anticipation as she got ready for her date with Tim. Even during the walk to the bar she had been brimming with excitement. Then she remembered, all too viscerally, the disappointment and shock and utter heartbreak that came afterwards.

'Och, will you look at him?' said Catriona, tilting her head in the direction of Angus. 'Looks like he's trying to land an aircraft the way he's throwing his arms around there. *Honestly*. What is he like?'

Jessica looked up as they walked through the trees and towards her dad, who was waving his arms wildly at them. She managed a small chuckle. 'He's taking it all very seriously.' Then she turned and looked at her mum as she took one of Jessica's hands in hers and gave it a squeeze.

'Honestly, Mum. I just needed a break from London and from work.' *From everything*, she said silently.

'Well, you know it's okay to feel sad at times. You don't need to feel happy all of the time. It's okay to talk about your feelings. You're only human after all. We all are.'

Jessica was grateful that her parents had always been open with their feelings — but perhaps *too* open. It had the opposite effect on her. She had always been very private.

'Will you two hurry up?' shouted her dad. He was still waving his hands at them. 'I've found the perfect tree.'

'Come on, we'd better up the pace,' her mum said, pulling at Jessica's hand. 'There is no need to bellow, Angus. We can hear you and see you. In fact, I think the folk on top of Ben Lomond can probably hear you as well.'

'Stop exaggerating. Anyway,' he said, his eyes sparkling in triumph, 'this is an absolute beauty and someone else might get it.'

'Who's going to get it? You're holding onto it for dear life and it's still got its roots in the ground. And the place is empty,' said her mum, throwing her palms in the air in exasperation.

'Oh, Dad,' said Jessica. 'I am so glad you've not lost your competitive spirit.'

'I will have you know that last year I found the perfect tree. It was an absolute belter. The perfect height and shape.'

He looked almost dreamy as though he was describing a lost love. 'Then that wee numpty captain from the golf course steamed in and cut it down in front of me because you had the gloves and were taking so long.' He threw Catriona an accusatory glance.

'Okay,' said Jessica as smoothly as possible, drawing on her best mediating skills. 'It looks like we are the only folk here, Dad, so I think it will be fine. I don't think you need to worry about it happening again. Mum, did you bring the gloves from the car?'

She clasped her hands over her mouth and gasped dramatically. 'No, I forgot.'

'Och,' muttered Angus in disgust. 'See what I mean. And it looks like a bus load of folk have just arrived.' He jerked his head back towards the car park.

There were only two more cars than when they had parked ten minutes ago. Her dad had always been prone to exaggeration.

'Angus, I'm winding you up. You would think you'd know that of me by now. We've only been married for forty years.'

Angus looked as though he was about to retort, but Jessica glanced at him and shook her head. Fortunately, he clamped his mouth shut, realising it was better to say no more.

'Right, here you go. Here are the gloves, dear,' said Catriona sweetly, handing them to him.

Jessica watched as he pulled the gardening gloves on as though he was about to perform life-saving surgery in a hospital theatre. Catriona glanced beyond Jessica and grinned. 'Oh, look who's here. He's made it after all. Marvellous. Cooee. Over here!' she yelled loudly.

'Hey, guys,' said a voice behind them.

Jessica groaned. *Seriously?* He was the last person she wanted to see. But as she turned, she felt her cheeks flame as she took in the sight that was Reuben. He wore black jeans and boots and an *actual* lumberjack jacket which would usually have had her chuckling as it was so clichéd for the setting. But he looked *extremely* good in it. Red and navy were obviously his colours, and he looked as though he was modelling for an outdoor clothing company. She half-expected him to have his axe with him for chopping wood. Why did he have to be so . . . *manly*? She managed to drag her eyes away from him before he clocked her staring.

'Hi, Jessie,' he said with a grin.

'Isn't this lovely? I'm so glad you made it.' Catriona turned to Jessica. 'I did offer to get a tree for the cottage as well but Reuben said it was on his to-do list today anyway.'

'Oh,' said Jessica, nodding and trying to look relaxed and nonplussed by his presence.

He nodded at the group and grinned at Jessica before turning his attentions to Angus with a chuckle. 'Don't worry, Angus. I can see that one is yours. I'm not going to cut it down and take it from you. You can stop holding onto it as though you're about to take it for a jig.'

'I'm taking no chances, pal,' he said jokingly. 'Not after last year.'

'Please don't start with that again,' said Catriona, rolling her eyes. 'Now, Angus, let's crack on and get the tree sorted before you raise your blood pressure any more. Jess, maybe you can help Reuben get the tree for Primrose Cottage?'

Jessica's eyes widened in horror at her mum, who was now busying herself with her dad. Annoyingly, her mum had always had a way of making friendly suggestions that you knew were a directive, and there was no arguing with her. But the last thing she wanted to do was be left alone with Reuben. She just knew he was going to be as annoying as ever. She tried to catch her dad's eye, but he was seemingly fascinated by the pine needles on his prized tree that he was now stroking. Hesitating for a moment, she swivelled her glance to Reuben. He was looking at her, with a look she couldn't quite fathom but which quickly switched to amusement. 'Er, okay, if you feel you need help?' she said drily.

'Absolutely. I would love it if you could come and help me choose a tree, Jessie. It will be fun.'

Her mum looked on approvingly. 'Wonderful. It's just like old times.'

Jessica managed not to shake her head in disgust. *Old times*? When they were younger she had frequently wanted to batter him.

'Right you two, off you go. We'll see you back at the car.' Then her mum turned away to help Angus.

'Let's find a tree you think your wee niece will absolutely love,' said Reuben.

'Sure.' Jessica was trying to keep her voice steady. 'Lead the way. But before we do, can I ask you something?'

'Anything,' he said, raising an eyebrow.

'Please *stop* calling me Jessie.'

CHAPTER EIGHT

It had been ages since Reuben could remember enjoying himself so much. Jessica had been a bit stand-offish with him to begin with, which he assumed was because her mum had forced her to do something she clearly didn't want to. He could see the dismay in her eyes when Catriona had suggested that Jessica help him out. He couldn't believe this was the Jessica whose ponytail he always used to tug when they were kids. She had certainly changed and he couldn't help stealing quick glances at her when he thought she wasn't looking. She wore dark jeans and boots and a black coat, which looked as though it belonged to her dad. Her hair hung loose over her shoulders and she wore a red hat. She was beautiful. Although she seemed confident and funny, there was also something vulnerable about her. As though she had a protective shell around her. Then he checked himself. If Murray could see him now, checking out his sister, he would probably want to clobber him.

'I think this is the perfect one,' she said, pointing at the branches of a huge tree.

He crinkled his nose. 'Isn't it a bit big?' He walked towards a row of smaller ones and gestured towards one. 'Is this not better?'

She tutted. 'That wee skinny thing? Don't be ridiculous. It will topple over as soon as you drape a bit of tinsel on it. And it will look lost in your front room which I'm assuming is still the same and like my parents'? You want something that will be the centrepiece.'

He scratched his head. 'It will take over the whole room. I'll need to move the furniture out.'

Jessica rolled her eyes at him. 'Don't be so dramatic. Trust me,' she said tugging at the branches of her tree. 'This will look perfect.'

'Okay,' he said. 'If you insist.'

She grinned at him triumphantly and he couldn't help but laugh. 'You always did like to be right.'

She shrugged and he could feel her eyes on him as he cut it down and hoisted it over his shoulder.

'That's because I am right. I promise it will look amazing in the cottage,' she said firmly.

They walked towards the exit, where Reuben paid for the tree as it was netted. 'Do you want to come and see the cottage and advise me on where you think it should go?' he said as he secured the tree on the roof rack of his car.

Her cheeks were tinged pink by the cold air and she looked at him almost shyly from beneath her hat. 'Um, this is the part where I should say I'd better go and ask my mum and dad.' She burst out laughing.

He pulled a face as he looked across the car park. 'Well, I don't like to break it to you, Jessica, but it looks like they've already left.'

She spun round in shock. 'Oh my God, so they have. That is *outrageous*.' Her eyes smiled now. 'They've actually left their child behind. I don't believe it.'

'Just as well I'm here then to give you a lift home. Otherwise, it would be a long walk back.' He grinned at her and opened the car with a click of his key.

Inside, he turned the heating on high to warm them up from the outside chill factor.

'Thanks,' she said, rubbing her hands together. 'I am so cold. I keep forgetting how much colder it is up here.'

'Now that you're a soft southerner,' he joked.

'Yup. I am clearly too used to the balmy London temperatures.'

'I agree though, it's chilly out there. Much colder than it has been. I wonder if it might even snow,' he said, looking at the sky.

'Maybe,' she said.

They were immersed in comfortable silence as they drove back towards Rowan Bay, Reuben's eyes focused on the winding road ahead.

Then Jessica spoke. 'I didn't realise you had moved back to the village.'

'It's not really a permanent thing. I still have my flat in Glasgow. I've been dividing my time between them until I figure out what to do.'

'What made you buy the cottage from your dad then?'

'He needed full-time care and so we had to sell his home to pay the care home fees.' He paused and glanced at her. 'My dad has dementia, and although I had carers coming in to help him every day, he got to the stage where he couldn't be left on his own. I wanted to know he would be safe so moving him into the care home seemed the best solution.' It didn't matter how many times he explained the situation, he still felt guilty about it. 'I hated the thought of someone else living in the cottage.' He brushed his hand across his jaw. 'That's why I decided to buy it.'

'Ah, I see. That makes sense. I guess it's good you've been able to do that . . . and how is your dad?'

He frowned, realising he wasn't used to people asking after his dad. 'He seems settled enough. And I'm glad he's safe there. But I still feel guilty.'

'Why?'

'I feel I should have done more for him.'

'But what else could you have done, other than moving in with him and being his full-time carer?'

It was the first time he had spoken about this in a while and he hadn't realised how much it had been playing on his mind. He could feel his voice tremble as he spoke. 'It's just been hard, you know.'

'I don't think your dad would want you to feel bad,' she said gently.

He looked across at her. 'I know you're right. It's just been difficult. Doing the right thing isn't easy.'

She nodded sympathetically. 'And do you think you'll rent it out when Murray has gone back to Australia?'

He shrugged. 'I don't know. I haven't thought that far ahead yet. I haven't really thought about where my home will be.' He could tell she was looking at him, and he turned briefly to meet her quizzical gaze.

He shrugged, not really wanting to get drawn on where home was right now. 'I don't know yet and I work remotely anyway so I can be flexible about where I'm based. How about you? What does it feel like, being back in the motherland?'

She cleared her throat. 'It's a bit strange. But then it also feels very normal. Does that make sense? It's so far removed from my London life but in a good way. Part of me feels like I've never left. Being back made me realise what a great place it was to grow up in.'

He nodded in agreement. 'Yes, we were lucky having so much space when we were kids. And the loch . . .'

'I know. I miss the water too. I live near the river in London but it's just not the same.'

Reuben wanted to ask more about her life in London but he didn't want to intrude and he was struggling to think how to ask more about her life without sounding nosy. Catriona had mentioned briefly that she was exhausted and coming home for a rest. He wondered if she had burnout because of her job or whether there was more to it. Catriona had never mentioned whether she had a partner or not, and if he asked, surely that would be a bit weird? 'You'll be looking forward to seeing your brother?' he said eventually.

'Yup, it's been a while,' she said. 'I can't wait to see Lexi. She's at such a cute age.'

'Yes,' said Reuben. 'It will be good to catch up properly with him. It's been ages. I still can't quite believe he's a dad. Seems crazy.'

'What about you?' said Jessica.

'What do you mean?'

'How's married life?'

'Complicated,' he said, his voice curter than he intended it to be. He would have thought Catriona might have filled her in on his marriage breakdown. But she seemed completely unaware.

'Oh. I'm sorry,' said Jessica.

'Don't worry,' he said, keen not to talk about it any longer than he had to.

Just then, as they neared the village, Jessica's phone buzzed, and when she looked at it, she tutted and slipped it back in her pocket. She didn't say anything or give an explanation, but she became quiet. 'Everything okay?' he said, trying to sound concerned rather than prying.

'Yes,' she said distractedly. 'It's nothing important.'

'Here we are,' he said, trying to sound cheery although he now felt anything but. He felt bad for cutting her off when she'd asked him about his marriage and wished he could turn the clock back just a few minutes to when they were chatting like old friends.

'Thanks for the lift,' she said, unbuckling her seat belt and jumping out the car.

'No problem. Looks like your folks are back now too.' He reached up and started untying the tree from the car.

'Let me help you,' she said, her voice now subdued.

Reuben knew her mind was elsewhere, and he wondered if he had upset her, given how quickly the mood had shifted. He had enjoyed her company today but he certainly didn't want her to feel obliged to stay. This was why he was better off on his own, he reminded himself. It was far less complicated.

'Thanks, but honestly, it's fine. I'll manage from here. I'm sure you have loads of other things to be getting on with.'

She looked at him for a moment, but he couldn't quite read her expression. 'Well, if you're sure.' She rubbed her hands together and shivered, looking towards Thistle Cottage.

'Thanks for your help,' he said trying to sound grateful. 'But on you go, get inside. It's Baltic out here.'

'Right. I will. Thanks then,' she said, now avoiding his gaze. 'Okay, well see you around then.' She turned to walk away. 'Thanks for the lift.'

'Thanks for your help, Jessie,' he said, knowing it would annoy her yet saying it anyway. It was as though his teenage self had inhabited his body again. What was wrong with him?

She threw him a look and then spun on her heels and strode towards Thistle Cottage.

He was left standing there, knowing she was annoyed, but he couldn't help himself from grinning. Having Jessica home could make this Christmas a lot more interesting indeed.

CHAPTER NINE

Jessica opened the door and stamped her icy boots on the mat. 'Hello,' she called rather crossly. *Jessie! Nobody* called her that. Not even her parents.

'Hi, dear. Just in here.'

'What happened to you two? You abandoned me and left me behind at the Christmas tree farm.'

Her mum shook her head and laughed. 'Away you go. You were having a grand old time with Reuben. We saw you laughing together and you wouldn't have appreciated it if we broke up the party. We knew he would give you a lift home. Did you get a tree for your brother?'

'Yes,' Jessica said and shrugged.

'Are you not going to help him decorate it?'

She shook her head vehemently and huffed. 'I think he can manage it himself.' She clocked her mum raising an eyebrow at her dad.

'You can help us if you'd like, Jess.'

Her phone buzzed again and she pulled it from her pocket in irritation. 'Um, yes, okay in a minute. I just need to go upstairs and deal with this.' She pointed at her phone. 'It's a work thing,' she muttered.

'Oh, okay, dear. *Alexa* play Christmas songs,' ordered her mum loudly. Within seconds the sound of Wham's "Last Christmas" filled the room and Jessica wanted to scream. As she walked up the stairs, she felt the well of tears rising. She was annoyed at herself for breaking her vow and momentarily letting the magic of Christmas find its way back into her life. Her mum was right — this morning with Reuben *had* been fun and she was reminded of her old self when she used to always be positive and see the sparkles in life. She had obviously hit a raw nerve when she asked how married life was. She shouldn't have been so nosy. But as she closed her bedroom door, the tears started to slide down her cheeks. For it wasn't Reuben who had upset her. It was the text message she'd received. Her phone buzzed again.

Please call me. I just want to talk.

Why wouldn't they just leave her alone? It didn't matter how many times she ignored them, the texts and pleading messages still kept coming. But there was nothing else Jessica could add to what she had already said. She switched off her phone and threw it on the bed then curled up on the seat by the window, watching the fading light dance across the garden which was still covered in frost. She dabbed at her eyes with a tissue. She was home for a rest and the fewer people she saw the better, and that included Reuben, no matter how much *fun* he was. Especially when she had asked him specifically not to call her Jessie and he still had. He's an arse, she thought crossly. And *he's married* she reminded herself. A *married arse*. Which made him exactly the same player he had been at school because there had been moments when she had felt like he was definitely flirting with her. Was she the only one who saw Reuben for what he was?

Jessica soon became mesmerised watching the birds hop around the lawn, leaning forward to get a better view. She had no idea how long she was sitting there but a gentle knock at the door interrupted her thoughts.

'Hi, darling,' said her mum. 'I thought you might like a cup of tea and one of the first batch of mince pies. I've made it with Granny's recipe.' The light in the room was gloomy now and her mum reached across to turn on the lamp. 'It gets dark so quickly,' she said. Setting the tray down on the desk, she walked over and squeezed Jessica on the shoulder.

'Thanks, Mum,' she said brightly. 'Sorry if I was grumpy earlier.'

'You don't need to apologise, my love. It's fine. This is a strange time for you being back home. I get it.' She sat down on the edge of the bed. 'How did you get on with Reuben?'

'Fine.' She gave a small smile. 'Until he started calling me Jessie again,' she said tightly.

Her mum chuckled. 'I'm sure he does it just to wind you up.'

'Well, it certainly works.'

There was a silence for a moment.

Jessica tilted her head. 'What's the story with Reuben and his wife?'

She didn't reply straight away and a look of concern flitted across her face. 'Have you asked him about it?'

Jessica nodded. 'Yes, I just asked him how married life was and he said it was *complicated*. I didn't want to ask anything else in case he thought I was prying.'

Her mum reached forward and touched her hand. 'She lives in Dubai. I'm sure he will tell you about it when he's ready. In the same way that people won't ask you about what's happened in London as they don't want to be intrusive.'

'I told you work has been crazy.'

'Remember that I'm your mum and I know you, love. And I know that whatever is going on isn't just about work.' She tilted her head, her eyes full of concern. 'And I can tell you've been crying,' she said gently.

Her mum had a fair point, and as she sat there, curled up in the chair, she tentatively began to share. Biting her lip, she took a deep breath. 'You're right. Of course you are. You always are. It's not just about work, Mum. It's everything.'

Catriona nodded and waited for her to go on.

'This time last year I thought I was in love . . . I *was* in love,' she said sadly, rubbing away another tear that slid down her cheek.

'This was when we were in Australia?'

Jessica nodded. 'Remember those photos that I sent you from New York? That work trip I was on?'

Her mum nodded. 'Yes, I do,' she said softly. 'We were in Australia and you were having a magical time in New York. Was this where this special person lived?'

'No, he lived in Boston mostly but he travelled a lot with work to New York and to London — that's where we met.' Her mind wandered to those amazing early days and she was quiet for a few moments as she thought about Tim.

Her mum coughed softly, pulling her from her thoughts. 'You're miles away, love.'

'Sorry. I was just thinking,' she said, dragging her mind away from the memories she had carefully collated and stored away.

'What happened then to this new man of yours?'

'Tim. His name was Tim,' she said quietly.

Her mum nodded. 'And I'm assuming he is no longer on the scene, hence your broken heart?'

Jessica looked at her mum in the soft bedroom light, her face full of concern. If only she knew what a loaded question that was. 'No, he's no longer around,' she said quietly.

Her mum tipped her head to one side. 'What happened, love? Was it a really bad break-up?'

Jessica gulped, scarcely believing that she was going to have to say the words out loud. 'Tim is dead.'

CHAPTER TEN

'Oh, Jessica,' she said, throwing her arms around her. 'Why didn't you say anything before now? What on earth happened?'

Jessica melted into her mum's embrace, grateful she could let go of the huge burden that she had been carrying all year. The tears slid down her face as she sobbed again over the man she thought she had loved and then lost in such a devastating way. On more than one occasion she tried to pull herself out of her mum's arms, ready to tell her what happened. But each time she tried to talk, her body shuddered and the tears continued to stream.

'It's okay, Jess, everything will be okay. Sssh,' said her mum, stroking her hair soothingly. 'Just let it all out.'

Eventually, after Jessica had cried all the tears she had left, she sat back and looked at her mum. 'He died when we were in New York. But I didn't find out until afterwards . . .' Her eyes dropped to the floor and she fumbled with her hands as she remembered when and how she eventually found out that Tim had died. 'Even though he hadn't appeared for our date that night, I was annoyed but not too worried as that was the nature of our relationship. Things cropped up all the time.' She knew her mum was looking at her curiously. 'We had busy jobs,' she said as a way of explanation. 'Busy lives . . .' she said trying not to sound bitter.

There was a long silence as she tried to gather her thoughts and her mum nodded encouragingly at her.

'The following day at work I was absorbed in back-to-back meetings and could only check my phone when I managed to take a quick loo break. There were no messages from Tim, which was unusual. Normally he would have sent an apology as soon as he could if he'd had to cancel plans. It was strange that he hadn't contacted me at all.' She thought about how low she had felt later that night as she boarded the plane, her feet dragging. She'd stowed her cabin baggage on the plane and sat down at her seat, quickly sending another text letting him know her flight was about to take off. She had tried her best to get some sleep on the journey as she was going straight into work when she came off the flight. However, she was fidgety and worried and ended up half-watching one of the in-flight movies, only managing to doze.

'Even when I landed at Heathrow there was still nothing from him, which was weird.' She couldn't work out why he was ghosting her. 'I kept trying his phone a few times but his phone was switched off.' She wiped away a stray tear which was at the corner of her eye. 'For the next few days I functioned on autopilot at work, grateful that things were so busy to keep me occupied. I was so confused and exhausted and my mind was going round in circles about what had gone wrong . . . Had I imagined our connection? Had I read too much into our relationship if that was even what it was?' She wished she could let go of the bitterness that had gnawed away at her in the weeks that followed her trip to New York. How she wished he had been honest with her and told her the truth rather than just cut her off. Being ghosted by him was horrendous, and as her colleagues chatted excitedly about their Christmas plans and what they were doing over the festive break and who they were spending it with, she retreated further and further into herself. She had managed to cobble a story together about spending Christmas with friends in Surrey. But it was a lie. And now as her mum looked at her with such love and kindness in her eyes, she knew there was no need for her to spell out to her mum how miserable she had been. With Kristen away, she spent Christmas alone, wearing her pyjamas and watching Christmas movies and nibbling on cheese sandwiches, which was all she could stomach. Who knew the heartbreak diet was so effective.

'Do you feel like telling me what happened to him?' said her mum gently.

Jessica nodded. 'Okay. But I think it would be easier to walk and talk if that's okay? Moving helps me to think. And I could do with clearing my head.'

'Yes, of course.' Her mum stood up. 'I'll go downstairs and get organised. Come down when you're ready.' She leaned over and gave Jessica another hug. Jessica squeezed her mum back, grateful that she was there.

She washed her face and went downstairs ready for some fresh air. Her dad was nowhere to be seen as she and her mum pulled on their coats, hats and boots.

'He's away to Drymen to collect something for me,' said her mum, reading her mind.

They walked towards the high street and followed the glow of white lights that were wrapped around the lampposts casting pools of light onto the street.

'This is the first time I've even noticed these lights,' said Jessica, looking up at them.

'These are the winter lights that get switched on at the start of November. I quite like them, especially as the days get shorter and gloomier. Then the Christmas lights will be switched on this week after the Christmas fair. They bring the colour and sparkle to the high street. The team have done a good job with them.'

They stopped briefly to glance in some of the shop windows and she knew this was her mum's way of making sure she understood there was no rush to talk. She was grateful for the distraction and for a few minutes lost herself in the cheerful glow of the different festive displays. The new bookshop had a twinkling scene with sledges full of books and small snow-dusted trees. The gift shop had glistening baubles and paper snowflakes strung across its window, with a pile of bright and cosy scarves artfully arranged with matching gloves.

Even though it was dusk, she knew the walk like the back of her hand and felt a sense of peace as they headed onto the gravelly beach. Jessica stopped to look back at the village and took in the outline of the buildings and the church tower, dark against the dusky sky. It made her think how surreal it was that this time last year she had been in Manhattan, crammed with people and a skyline full of buildings, and full of optimism and excitement for the future, especially a life together with Tim.

'If you go that way,' said her mum, pointing in the opposite direction, 'that's where the sauna is.'

Jessica turned to look and could just make out the dark shape of a cabin about one hundred metres away. She nodded. Aware her mum's gaze was on her, she walked along for a few moments and then started to talk. 'It was just before Christmas that I found out what happened,' she said, shaking her head as she remembered the disbelief she'd felt at the time. 'I had called and called and left messages and there was nothing.' She shrugged. 'I just assumed he had decided he'd had enough of me and was no longer interested.'

'Why would he not just be upfront with you though?' asked her mum.

'That's what happens these days when you're dating, Mum. It's quite normal just to ghost you and not reply.'

'That's just rude, though.'

They kept walking, their feet crunching on the stones. Part of her wanted to head back to the safety and cosiness of Thistle Cottage and sit beside the roaring log fire. But Jessica knew she needed to talk about this even though it was extremely uncomfortable. She had tried to push away all the feelings around it for so long.

'He wasn't ignoring me though, Mum. He had a massive heart attack and collapsed as he went for the subway. I think he was on his way to meet me . . .' Her voice wobbled as she thought again how if it wasn't for her then, perhaps, he would still be here. For a long time she had felt so guilty and responsible for his death.

'Oh dear, Jessica. What a shock that must have been.'

She nodded. 'I still can't believe it. I'm not sure that I'll ever get my head round any of it. In the weeks that followed I felt completely confused.'

'What an awful thing to have happened. How old was he?'

'Forty-five.' She paused, wondering if her mum would make a comment about the age difference.

'That's still so young . . .' Her mum's voice trailed off. 'But how did you find out what had happened?'

'I called his office. I decided I needed to know one way or the other why he was ignoring my calls. I thought if I could just speak to him, then I would know what had happened and I could try and move on.' She swallowed as she remembered the phone call that she'd made and the horrible sensation in her stomach as she waited for the call to be transferred. The woman she spoke to had come back on the phone to tell her, very gravely, that he wasn't available to talk. 'When will I be able to talk to him then? When is he due back in the office?' she asked tersely, determined not to be brushed off.

She glanced at her mum. 'Then she transferred my call to one of his colleagues who informed me that Tim had sadly passed away a few weeks ago and could he help me with anything instead?' She remembered how his words sliced through her. A moan had escaped her lips as Jessica dropped the phone in horror. Dead? None of it made sense. How could Tim be dead?

Her mum's eyes widened. 'I am so sorry. Oh, Jess, I can't believe you've been carrying this burden alone for so long. I wish you had told us.'

Jessica paused, now feeling completely drained. She didn't think she could say anything more right now. Shivering, she nodded her head back towards the village. 'I'm glad I have now.'

'Let's get you home, dear. You're frozen. We'll get you by the fire and warm you up.'

She cleared her throat, realising her mum's eyes were rimmed with tears. 'Thanks for listening, Mum.' There was so much more that she wanted to say. But telling her about Tim's death was at least a start.

CHAPTER ELEVEN

Reuben smiled as he flicked on the fairy lights which were now draped around the Christmas tree. It had always been a family tradition when he was growing up that the lights didn't work no matter how carefully his dad had stored them away in the loft each year. He briefly wondered what his dad would make of Primrose Cottage now and he hoped he would be proud of what he had done with it. He had chosen warm white stars which gave the tree a comforting glow and went perfectly with the red and gold baubles and tinsel that he had found in the attic. Who knew that decorating a tree could be such an enjoyable process. He hadn't bothered with a tree in his flat last year at all and it hadn't even occurred to him to get one this year. There seemed no point when he was hardly there. But knowing that wee Lexi would be spending Christmas here in Primrose Cottage had given him a focus. He wanted it to be magical for his best friend's daughter.

As he stood admiring his handiwork for a moment, he saw the outline of two women pass the front of the window. He could just make out Catriona and Jessica and gave them a wave, unsure of whether or not they could see him as it was dark outside. They didn't wave back so he guessed not.

Jessica had been right in encouraging him to get a bigger tree. It looked perfect in the room. He smiled thinking about the spark in her eyes when he called her Jessie. She was still so easy to wind up.

He turned and surveyed the rest of the room, pleased that it looked so cosy. The stripped and polished wooden floorboards were covered with a charcoal-coloured rug. He had chosen a mustard L-shaped sofa, and a dark grey bat wing chair to go by the fire. The large watercolour on the wall, of Rowan Bay beach, looked perfect in its new home and he was glad he'd decided to splurge on it when he saw it in the window of the local art gallery. It was the perfect room to relax in.

Earlier he had briefly thought of asking Jessica to come in and see it, to stay and have a drink. He could picture her relaxing on the sofa here and laughing the way she had at the Christmas tree farm . . .

Determined to distract himself from all thoughts of Jessica, he thought about his flat in Glasgow and the loose plans he had made to drive there tonight to meet up with friends in a new bar in Byres Road in the West End. The idea really didn't excite him at all, and when he glanced at his watch and saw the time, he realised it was already getting late. He was tired and hungry and wasn't in the mood for being in a noisy pub tonight. Or any night now that he thought about it — how anti-social he had become this past year. Pondering only for a moment, he sent a message on WhatsApp apologising that he wouldn't make it. He silenced his notifications so he didn't feel guilty about the inevitable replies that would start to come in, ribbing him about his elusiveness. He had made too much of a habit of bailing out of social plans with his friends.

Twenty minutes later he walked into the bar at the Rowan Bay Inn and was given a warm greeting by Lily, the manager, who immediately led him to his favourite table in the corner by the fire. It felt different tonight, perhaps with the Christmas decorations draped around the bar and the tree by the fireplace.

'How's things?' asked Lily, her wide smile reaching her eyes. 'It's been a while since we've seen you.'

He nodded at her. 'Yeah, I've been busy with the renovations. But they're almost finished. I thought I would treat myself to dinner out.'

'Quite right. It's the week before Christmas that your guests arrive, isn't it?'

'Yes,' he said. 'So we have a bit of time. Just a few last-minute wee things to sort including getting some fairy lights for the garden . . .' He hit his hand on his head in a dramatic gesture and chuckled. 'Listen to me,' he said self-deprecatingly. 'Going shopping for fairy lights is not something I ever imagined I would be doing.'

Lily chuckled too. 'I don't know if that's necessarily a bad thing,' she said and winked.

Just then, a man walked into the bar and waved at him.

'Ah, the very guy I need to talk to,' said Reuben.

Lily looked over and grinned. 'Brodie. Nice to see you.' She glanced back at Reuben. 'What can I get you in the meantime?'

'Just a pint of Loch Lomond please,' he said.

'I'll bring it over in a mo with a menu.'

Reuben placed his jacket on the back of his chair, keen to linger by the warmth of the fire but also wanting to chat to Brodie. 'Hey, how are you?' he said, walking across to the bar.

'Good thanks. Unbelievably busy though. This used to be a seasonal job but you would not believe how many people want work done in their gardens in the winter. It's bonkers.'

Brodie was a talented landscape gardener and man of all trades. He'd moved to the village three years ago when he realised that he wanted to live near the water having had enough of life in Glasgow. He also painted and was a trained joiner, so it was little wonder he was always in demand. No job was too problematic and he quietly got on with things, always striving to do his best for customers. Reuben had hired him to do the garden at Primrose Cottage and he'd done an incredible job of landscaping it, adding decking and the small summer house. He was hoping he might be able to help him with some last-minute things he couldn't do himself. But it sounded like he was up to his eyes.

'Can I get you a pint?' he asked as Lily placed his beer in front of him at the bar. 'Thanks, Lily.'

'Sure,' Brodie said with a grin. 'I'll just have what he's having please, Lily. Why do I get the feeling you have an ulterior motive though?'

Reuben kept his fingers crossed that the bribe of beer would be enough. 'I was hoping that you could maybe find time to do a wee window seat in one of the bedrooms upstairs?'

Lily swiftly poured the pint and put it down next to Brodie.

'Cheers,' said Brodie, clinking his glass against Reuben's. 'Um, when do you need this done?' He took a drink of beer.

'Any chance you could do it sometime next week?'

Brodie put the glass down on the bar and laughed. 'For you, yes, but don't tell anyone else. I can't keep up with demand just now.'

'Thanks, mate,' said Reuben with a grateful smile.

'No worries. Always happy to help you out if I can. I'll give you a shout and pop in. Will you be around?'

He nodded. 'I definitely won't be far away. Murray and his family arrive the end of next week so it's just a case of doing the last bits and pieces.'

Brodie narrowed his eyes as he looked at him. 'Then what will you do? You'll need to find yourself another project.'

He nodded. 'We'll see. I'll need to get back into the day job which has taken a bit of a back seat this year. I've a couple of design projects to get on with in the new year.' He paused. 'Look, do you fancy joining me for some dinner? I'm famished. I've not eaten all day.'

Brodie looked longingly at the table by the fire where Reuben's coat was. 'I would love to. But . . . I should really get on. I've got loads to finish before the holidays.'

Reuben raised an eyebrow. 'Go on. I'm sure I can tempt you with a quick burger. My treat.'

He pulled a face. 'Okay, okay, no need to bribe me any more. I've said I'll come and do the window seat.' He laughed and followed Reuben over to the table.

'What can I get you guys?' said Lily. 'Are you ready to order?'

'I'll have the cheeseburger,' said Reuben, realising he was hungry and weary and ready to collapse.

'Sod it,' said Brodie. 'I'll have the same. I'm so easily led.'

'I'll bring them out when they're ready.'

It didn't take long for Lily to appear with the burgers and when Reuben bit into his he realised that his hunger and tiredness made it taste like the best meal he had ever had.

Brodie smacked his lips as he dipped a chip into ketchup and sighed. 'Just what the doctor ordered.'

'Indeed,' said Reuben before he took another mouthful of burger. They chatted about work and then inevitably the conversation turned towards football and how their favourite team was doing. They both supported Partick Thistle.

'I couldn't believe I missed the last match,' said Brodie, shaking his head. 'We had a shout just as I was about to leave for the game.'

Reuben was surprised to learn that Brodie was a member of the local lifeboat crew. 'You kept that quiet,' he said. 'I didn't know you could save lives on the water as well as all the other stuff you do.'

Brodie shrugged.

'I guess it makes you popular with the ladies?'

He gave a short laugh. 'Not really. My last girlfriend dumped me because she thought I was more dedicated to the rescue boat than her.'

'Ouch,' said Reuben.

'Which is why this Christmas I'm not hanging around.'

'What do you mean?'

Brodie grinned at him. 'I'm off to Costa Rica.'

'Wow,' said Reuben. 'I wasn't expecting you to say that. Tell me more.'

'I've not had a holiday all year and decided now was as good a time as any. So while you're eating your turkey, I'll be hanging out with sloths and screaming monkeys and enjoying paradise.' He looked very pleased at the thought.

'That does sound good,' said Reuben. Brodie definitely had the right idea. Some winter sun sounded very appealing.

'How about you?'

'Just the usual,' said Reuben with a shrug. 'A quiet one. Visiting my dad . . .'

'Any women on the scene?'

He thought fleetingly about Jessica and their trip to the Christmas tree farm. The way her eyes flashed when he called her Jessie and the pink flush on her cheeks he'd noticed when she was nervous. He sighed and firmly shook his head. 'No. I'm keeping a low profile and staying out of trouble.'

Brodie studied him for a minute before speaking. 'You know you don't have to stay hidden away forever, Reuben. Just because of what Belinda did.'

Reuben frowned. 'I know. But at the moment the thought of dating anyone is far too much hassle.'

'Cheers to that,' said Brodie.

'Cheers,' said Reuben, lifting his glass and knocking it against Brodie's. The last thing he wanted or needed was any more stress in his life. It was far better to be single. That way he could suit himself.

CHAPTER TWELVE

When Jessica opened her eyes the next morning, she knew that coming home had been the right decision. She could hear her parents downstairs in the kitchen, the radio playing in the background. As she lay there for a moment, she felt surprisingly lighter now that she had told her mum what had happened to Tim. And as she took deep and slow breaths in and out, she realised that she felt more at ease. Not completely calm though. This would be about taking one step at a time. But she was definitely more relaxed than she had been for months. She sighed and allowed herself a smile of relief. She wasn't going to allow herself to dwell on that part of her life any longer. She had ruminated on Tim and what might have been for too long. And she would never get all the answers she wanted or needed because the only person who would tell her the truth was dead. Today was a new day. It was time to move forward and part of her plan also involved some damage limitation.

A couple of hours later, she strode down the lane and stopped at Primrose Cottage, rapping on the door sharply. After a few moments the door opened.

'Good morning, Reuben. I just wanted to say thanks for the lift home yesterday and I'm sorry that I rushed off and didn't stay to help you decorate the tree. I'm off to the village and wondered if I could bring you back a coffee?'

Reuben was back in his painting overalls again and he pulled off his baseball cap and scratched his head. He looked slightly puzzled and didn't reply immediately.

She tipped her head to the side. 'What people would normally say is, *yes thanks, Jessica, that is really kind of you. And by the way, it's me who should be buying the coffees and apologising for calling you Jessie when you asked me not to.*'

Reuben paused. 'Sorry, I'm expecting a delivery. I didn't realise it would be you.'

'Sorry to disappoint. I would have called but I don't have your number. Anyway . . . What kind of coffee can I get you?' She suddenly felt nervous and hoped he would start saying something, *anything*, relatively friendly in the next few seconds. Maybe she had misread this and he was annoyed with *her* for some reason? A slight niggle of doubt lodged itself in her mind. She had to keep telling herself this was Reuben. Her brother's oldest friend, and now, it seemed, a friend of the family. It was perfectly fine for her to call in and offer to get him a drink especially when he was working so hard to help out her brother. She just had to ignore the fact he was so good-looking.

But then Reuben smiled at her and raised his eyebrows. 'You are right. I owe you an apology and I'm sorry. I will try harder from now on in to call you by your proper name. Jessica not Jessie.'

She nodded, trying to ignore the happiness she now felt that he was being himself and was okay. That *they* were okay. 'Apology accepted. Now what kind of coffee can I get you?'

'A latte would be wonderful please. And you can have my phone number if you'd like.'

Jessica pulled out her phone, ignoring Reuben's smirk and quickly typed in the number as he shared it with her, then dialled it. 'There,' she said. 'Now you have mine in your phone too.'

'Great. And thank you for thinking of me with the coffee
. . . Jessica.'

'You're welcome. I'm off for a wander, so I'll be back in
about an hour or so. Does that fit in with your timings?'

He glanced at his watch. His sleeves were rolled up. Those
forearms, she thought again. Never before had she considered
forearms sexy. But his definitely were.

'Perfect.'

She pulled her eyes away from his arms, smiled brightly
and walked away, feeling oddly excited to know that she
would definitely be seeing him again very soon. Then guilty.
He was her brother's best friend.

This time as she walked the high street she went at a more
leisurely pace, looking in the shop windows properly. Jessica
had done zilch Christmas shopping and it was starting to dawn
on her that she might like to make a start. It had been years
since she had been shopping in Glasgow and she idly wondered
if she might go there one day after all to have a mooch around
Buchanan Street. In the meantime she was going to embrace
shopping locally as much as she could. Stopping at the small
gift shop, The Bay, her eyes spotted a beautiful pair of earrings
in the window. They were cerise-pink and silver hoops and she
immediately thought of her sister-in-law, Carolyn, who loved
anything pink. They always teased her that it was lucky Lexi had
been a girl who actually liked pink. The earrings were perfect
for Carolyn and she decided today was a day for being decisive.
Pushing the door open, she walked in and gasped in delight
when she got inside. It was a complete treasure trove.

'I'll be right with you, dear,' said the woman behind the
counter, already helping some other customers.

'No rush,' said Jessica, glad of the chance to have a browse
and see what else she could find.

As she wandered around the shop, she saw a delicate
necklace with a blue pendant, perfect for her mum. Then she
spotted a stylish red tweed tartan purse, which immediately
made her think of Freda, whose favourite colour was red. She

picked it up and decided she would buy it and post it to her for Christmas. They didn't usually exchange gifts, but then she had been so supportive this year. If it hadn't been for Freda insisting she take a break from work, who knows what state she would be in. She would probably be lying in a crumpled heap underneath her desk.

Jessica had always been so busy that she didn't have a chance to look for perfect gifts — resorting to Christmas shopping that could be done online or on the hoof. The last time she had been home to celebrate Christmas, two years ago, she had rather swiftly picked up some gifts for her parents at Selfridges as she'd passed on her way back from a meeting and had a case of champagne delivered to Thistle Cottage before her arrival. She now realised how much she was enjoying just taking her time to browse and actually give the gifts she wanted to buy a bit more thought. While she was looking, she found a light silk scarf that would match the necklace for her mum. Then she saw a candle in an orange Irn-Bru tin which made her laugh out loud. She picked it up to smell it. How weird. It did in fact smell like the national soft drink. A weird combination of citrus and bubble gum and sweeties.

'You either love or hate those candles,' said the woman as she waved off the other customers and walked over to Jessica.

'The person I'm thinking of will love it,' she said. Carolyn, who was from Edinburgh, adored Irn-Bru, especially after a late night out, and she knew she would appreciate having it to take back to Melbourne as a wee reminder of home. Freda on the other hand would have been horrified as she thought Irn-Bru was an absolute crime against fizzy drinks. Not that she ever drank any type of soft drink. The only soft drinks she had seen Freda drink were water and black coffee, and the only bubbles to pass her lips were those in a glass of champagne.

'How're you getting on? Can I help you with anything?'

'You've got some lovely stuff in here,' admitted Jessica, 'but I'll take these things for now and maybe come back. My dad and my brother will be the challenges.'

The woman pushed her glasses back on her nose and laughed. 'Well, if you need any help, just pop back in. We're open all day and every day right up until Christmas Eve.'

'I'm in the village for a few weeks actually,' said Jessica. 'Staying with my folks. Catriona and Angus.'

The woman looked at her again and narrowed her eyes. 'You must be Jessica? It's so nice to finally meet you,' she said with a beam. 'I know your mum from the crafting classes. She's been so excited about having you and your brother home. Sorry, you must think I've lost the plot chatting away like a daft old woman. I'm Moira.'

'Nice to meet you, Moira. And what a brilliant shop you've got here. I can't believe I've not been in before.'

The woman smiled, clearly delighted at the praise. 'Thanks, dear. There you go,' she said, handing her the bag of gifts.

Jessica tapped her card against the machine. 'Thank you. That's made my shopping to-do list a whole lot easier.'

'You live in London, don't you? I bet you've got some great shops there.'

Jessica considered the question for a moment and realised Moira was right, but she never had the inclination to go shopping. 'This has been a far nicer experience, Moira. Thank you.' She waved bye, opened the door and walked past the art gallery, which had some beautiful pieces hanging in the window.

The watercolour of Loch Lomond caught her eye. The artist had captured it perfectly using just the right shades of blue and green. As she stopped to study it, she found herself transfixed. It was as though she was actually inside the frame and she was reminded of everything she loved about home. The colours, the scenery, the sounds, and the smell of fresh, crisp air. She was almost tempted to go in and buy it. But just as she reached for the door handle, a thought struck her. Where would she hang it? Although the room at Kristen's had been the ideal solution for Jessica when she had broken up with her ex, she didn't think she would still be there several years later. She had saved a lot of money over the years and was in the process of viewing property to buy when she'd met Tim. After he died, sticking with the status quo was just easier. She couldn't face any more upheavals or change. She turned away before she changed her mind and made an impulsive buy.

Glancing at her watch, she saw she was just about on time to take Reuben back his coffee. She walked the few steps along the road to the bakery. Pushing the door open, she joined the queue. Gillian spotted her immediately and gave her a smile. Normally, Jessica had no patience waiting for anything but she noticed that she didn't mind so much. It was warm and there was a heavenly aroma of burnt sugar and coffee. It made her realise how much she was always rushing around. She never stopped to smell the coffee or the cakes. Speaking of which, there was a mouth-watering selection to choose from. The festive range was well and truly on show and there were new Christmas cupcakes with green icing and Smarties which made them resemble trees, and mince pies dusted with icing sugar which looked like they had been sprinkled with snow.

'Hello again,' said Gillian, grinning from ear to ear. 'Nice to see you, Jessica. What can I get for you today?'

'Hi, Gill. Can I have two lattes please? And . . .' She looked at the cakes and treats and then the cinnamon buns. There were two left. It was surely a sign.

'Two buns?' said Gillian suggestively.

'I'm taking Reuben a coffee,' she said by way of explanation, even though she knew she didn't need to expand.

Gillian gave her a look. 'Mm-hmm?'

'Just trying to be neighbourly,' she said, trying not to sound flustered. Even when they were younger, Gillian had a knack of seeing right through her.

'He does like a bun,' she said knowingly.

'Two buns it is then, please.'

Gillian added the pastries to a paper bag and turned to make the coffees, which she put in a recyclable cardboard holder to make it easier for Jessica to carry. 'Oh, listen, before I forget. Do you fancy meeting me and my friend, Lily, for a drink sometime? She's the manager at the inn. I think you'd like her?'

Jessica was momentarily stunned. 'That sounds, er, nice,' she managed to say. Then more decisively she said, 'Thanks. I would like that. Just text me?'

'I don't have your number,' she said. 'But Reuben has mine. Ask him for it when you make your home delivery.' She winked at her.

'Will do,' said Jessica. 'Thank you. I'll see you soon.'

Clutching the coffee cups and buns, she walked back up the street towards Rowan Lane, now feeling slightly nervous. When she reached Primrose Cottage, she set the drinks holder down on the doorstep and knocked on the door. Her heart started to beat a bit faster and she wondered if it was too late to run away.

CHAPTER THIRTEEN

'Perfect timing,' said Reuben, swinging open the door. He pulled off his cap and ran a hand through his hair, suddenly conscious of what a state he looked.

Jessica smiled at him tentatively and handed him his latte from the drinks holder. 'I've brought you a cinnamon bun too.'

'How did you know I was in the mood for one?'

'A hunch,' she said with a shrug.

'You're an angel, Jessie,' he said with a grin. 'Oops, sorry, Jessica.' He didn't think she would be very amused to know that he had just saved her number on his phone under Jessie. 'Do you want to come in and have your coffee with me? I could do with taking a break anyway. And it would be nice to have someone to talk to.' He laughed. 'I think the birds in the garden are getting bored of my chat.'

'Sure,' she said, raising her eyebrows at him.

He held the door open as she brushed past him and made her way into the cottage. He'd forgotten what a tight space the doorway was and tried to push away the rush of excitement he felt as her hand grazed his. These were unfamiliar feelings which he wasn't quite sure what to do with. He gulped as he tried to regain some composure. 'Come through to the kitchen.'

'Should I close my eyes until it's all finished,' she said, handing him her coffee while she slipped off her shoes and set down her bag of purchases from the gift shop at the door.

He grinned. 'It's up to you. This room is finished, though you can come back and get a proper tour. I've thrown dust sheets over everything as I'm still doing some sanding upstairs and it seems to get everywhere.'

'It looks great,' she said, looking around the sitting room. 'Your tree looks perfect in the window there too.'

'I'll give you the proper tour of the cottage when the dust sheets are away. And even show you my Christmas lights,' he said with a chuckle. She gave him a look. Had he said that too suggestively? Did it sound like innuendo? 'Um, the kitchen is a bit of a mess with all my stuff and more dust sheets but you should see a change. Come on through and have a seat.' He led the way.

'It's so bright,' she said enthusiastically. 'What a great space.' She looked around taking it all in.

'Here,' he said, pulling out a chair at the table. 'Have a seat.'

She sat down and picked up her cup and took a drink.

Reuben was suddenly lost for words as he looked at her. He realised there was nowhere he would rather be right now other than sitting in this kitchen drinking coffee with Jessica. It was such a weird sensation. This was *Jessie*. Murray's younger sister. She pulled off her hat and looked at him quizzically, before opening the paper bag containing the buns. 'These are so good,' she said, passing one to him. 'Oh, you might want a plate or a napkin. They're quite sticky.' She took a bite and he had to restrain himself from reaching out to dab away the trail of icing on the side of her mouth.

Realising he was verging on being weird, rude or both, he quickly said the first thing he could think of. 'You did well to get any. People come from all over for these cinnamon buns.

The bakery is famous for them.' He inwardly groaned at himself. *Really*? Was that the best he could manage?

'We were lucky — they were the last two. It's a great place, isn't it? Such a good local resource. Is it awful that I don't even know where my local bakery in Putney is?'

He took a drink of his latte, relieved she had responded. 'Putney's a nice spot.'

'You know it?' she said surprised.

He nodded and gave a small chuckle of amusement. 'Yes, believe it or not, I have made it to London a few times. I've a good friend who lives in Fulham, and whenever I visit, we tend to walk across the bridge to Putney. There's a great Spanish restaurant there.'

She dropped her gaze for a moment and bit her lip. 'You probably know the area better than I do. I can't remember the last time I went out in my own neighbourhood.'

He tilted his head and looked at her curiously. 'I'm sure that's not the case. You've lived there for years, haven't you?'

She exhaled deeply. 'Yes. But I am embarrassed to say that over the past few years the most of London I've seen is the District line and the river path.' Jessica shrugged. 'I sometimes run to work.'

'Where is your office?'

'Hammersmith bridge.'

He widened his eyes in astonishment. 'Seriously?'

She nodded. 'Yes. Why?'

'I know that area well too. In fact, I was down earlier in the year and had a meeting with a client near there.' It was strange to think that they had been so physically close yet until now they hadn't really been on either's radar for many years. But then why would they be? He had been a happily married man.

'I didn't realise you worked in London too. I thought you were just based up here.'

He nodded. 'I am, mostly. But this was for a client I'd worked with before. He's got a holiday home near Gartocharn and wanted me to take on another renovation project for him, down south. But when I realised what a huge job it was, and that I would need to be based there for a while, I referred it to one of my friends, someone I knew could be trusted to do it well.' He took another sip of his coffee, keen to learn more about her. 'And how is work with you? It's employment law, isn't it?'

She rolled her eyes. 'Mm, I used to love it. Especially when I felt like I could help people and make a difference. Not so much lately. I thought I would miss it, you know, being up here. But I don't.'

He nodded and waited for her to go on.

'I think I've become a bit too cynical.' She smiled. 'It looks as though you've had a bit of a role change.' She gestured at his overalls.

Reuben chuckled. 'Yes, a change from the days I always wore a suit. I decided to take on fewer projects this year so I could focus on the cottage and the renovations. I've some other things lined up in the new year though.'

'And which do you prefer?'

'Good question,' he said. 'Probably the slower pace of life. It's amazing how therapeutic painting has been.' He was silent for a moment. 'It's the simple things that matter.'

Her gaze held his and in that moment something unspoken seemed to pass between them. He suddenly had an urge to reach over and kiss her. But the moment was broken when his mobile phone, on the table next to him, rang. He glanced at the caller ID. 'It's the care home,' he said. 'I'd better take it.'

She nodded and stood. 'I'll leave you to it. I'd better go anyway.'

He gave her a smile and a nod as he answered the call and watched her slip out of the room. Seconds later, he heard the front door close.

CHAPTER FOURTEEN

Jessica woke up the next morning and groaned — it was the day of the Christmas fair and the light switch on. She had promised her mum she would help and it was the least she could do, especially after everything she had shared with her and how supportive she had been — and she didn't want her parents worrying about her any more than they already were — but she suddenly felt a bit overwhelmed at the thought of being in a hall with lots of people she hadn't seen for a while and who might ask her lots of questions.

Giving herself a shake, she reminded herself that it was better to get out and about and do stuff than stay at home. She had felt so much better yesterday when she made the effort to go out. She smiled as she thought of Reuben and how nice it had been to sit and have a coffee with him. Who'd have thought the annoying best friend of her older brother would actually be good company! Maybe it was possible for them to be friends. As long as she could stop herself from looking at him in *that* way. She sat up in bed, shaking all thoughts of Reuben and his muscular body away. She stretched, had a quick shower, dressed and went downstairs.

Her parents had told her they'd be away first thing and that she could walk along when she was ready. That was as long as she was there on time to help get the stall set up.

She hastily pulled her coat and boots on and looked at herself in the hall mirror. At least her face had a bit more colour in it now. It was her hair that could do with some attention. She really needed to make an appointment to get her hair cut. She would phone the local salon later and try to get a slot with Agata who always did her mum's hair. In the meantime, at least it was long and she could scoop it into a ponytail.

As she walked down the high street, she admired the festive displays in the shop windows. She stopped for a moment to admire the small nativity display outside the local church. Then she decided to stop at the bakery and bought a special Christmas blend coffee from a harassed-looking Gillian.

'Is everything okay?' Jessica asked her in concern.

'Um, yes,' she said, distracted. Her curly red hair was pulled back from her face and tucked under a net, but a few tendrils had come loose and her cheeks were flushed.

'You sure?'

Gillian bit her lip and sighed. 'It's just been one of those mornings. I could do with crawling into a dark room and hibernating for a month. Alternatively, a month solo in the Caribbean would be nice.'

Jessica frowned. Gillian was usually so perky and chatty. It was strange to see her so down in the dumps. She looked at her questioningly. 'Is there anything I can do to help?'

Gillian glanced over her shoulder and lowered her voice. 'Can you bake bread, do the accounts, sort out a festive window display and work a miracle here?'

'Oh,' she said in surprise. 'Are things that bad?'

She pursed her lips together and nodded. 'You wouldn't believe it.'

Just then another few customers came into the shop.

'Look, I'd better leave you to it but maybe we can catch up later? I'm due to help at the fair just now and my mum won't be impressed if I'm late. She's signed me up to help at the bottle tombola, which I believe is the top earner.'

Gillian gave a small chuckle. 'Gawd, that's a huge responsibility. I don't envy you that. People get quite *frenzied* at that one. And look out for the vintage bottle of Babycham that seems to reappear every year. I'm coming with Millie later if I can get away on time.'

'Look out for me,' Jessica smiled. 'Maybe we could have a chat if that would help?'

Gillian looked at the queue that had now formed and nodded. 'Thanks, Jessica. I'd like that. See you later.'

The bell on the door tinkled behind Jessica as she pulled it shut and her mind was a whirl of thoughts as she made her way towards the hall. Suddenly she had images of herself at the bakery helping Gillian. She pictured herself making batches of bread, maybe even special festive limited editions, and contributing to something useful. She was already trying to picture what a festive window display might look like. Was she being ridiculous? Would it be a good idea? But the more she thought about things, the better a plan it seemed, until she was sure that having a focus might actually help her. Reconnecting with her home and doing something, instead of hiding away, was suddenly no longer something to dread.

Before she let her thoughts run away with her, she reminded herself to focus on the job at hand — and she found herself mesmerised by the winter wonderland that greeted her on walking through the doors of the hall. What a transformation! There was a huge Christmas tree by the door which had the most wonderful scent of pine. The market stalls, draped with twinkling fairy lights, were arranged as though they were at a proper Christmas market. She could see a chocolate fountain opposite and smell the heavenly aroma of cinnamon and nutmeg. She wasn't expecting it to be quite so festive. It was magical. Then she heard her mum call her name.

'There you are, Jess. Am I glad to see you.' She waved at Jessica and gestured for her to come over to the stall that had been formed from two tables, now covered with a Christmas tablecloth and various bottles of wine, beer, juice, washing-up liquid, laundry detergent — and the bottle of Babycham that Gillian had mentioned. 'Right, love. Iris here will tell you about the ticketing system and how it all works. Iris, do you remember Jessica?'

Iris, a petite, older woman with twinkling eyes and grey hair styled in a pixie cut, looked up at her and beamed. 'Of course I do, pet. You were one of my best pupils in your sixth year.' Iris's soft Highland lilt was still as soothing as it was when Jessica was at secondary school. Iris had moved from Inverness to the west coast when she got married and had lived in Rowan Bay ever since.

Jessica laughed. She had taken Iris's fashion and textiles course in her final year at school, not because she was particularly interested in fashion but because the class had filled a gap in her timetable. Turned out that she really enjoyed it because Iris made it such fun. 'It's nice to see you, Iris. You are looking as stylish as ever.' Jessica pointed at Iris's purple pinafore made with patches of tartan, lace and corduroy. She also had a garland of gold tinsel around her neck.

'Thanks,' she said, beaming. 'Just a wee number I rustled up with some scraps from my fabric bag.'

'It looks great on you,' Jessica said, now genuinely glad she had come to help. This could actually be fun. 'Now tell me what I need to do.'

'Well, I do hope you've had a good breakfast this morning,' she said, nodding at Jessica's coffee cup. 'This stall is not for the faint-hearted. You need *stamina*.'

Jessica chuckled, assuming she was joking. She thought it would be quite relaxed as people milled around and sipped on their cups of hot chocolate. But an hour later, she realised that Iris had been completely serious. The queue at their stall hadn't waned all morning, with Iris feverishly barking orders at Jessica when the table needed restocking and the bucket of raffle tickets needed another shake. Iris had demonstrated, rather vigorously, how to give it a 'good old jiggle' and raised an eyebrow as she warned her to watch out for people who clutched more tickets than they had paid for when they shoved their hand in the bucket. Jessica couldn't remember her being this fierce when she was a teacher. So much for the soft voice. That was a ruse. It was as though she had inhabited a different personality now that the fair was in full swing and busy. Retirement and voluntary work had clearly toughened her up and given her an edge.

The hall was warming up now and Jessica shrugged off her coat, wishing that she'd worn a lighter jumper underneath instead of the thick woolly one, complete with a snowman on the front, which her mum had left out with instructions to wear to the fair. It was currently making the sweat drip down her back. She tucked some loose tendrils of hair behind her ears and puffed, feeling as though she had just done two back-to-back spin classes rather than help at a community fair. There was a lull in the queue and she was glad of the break before the next rush began. Then her stomach did a little flip when she saw Reuben walking across the hall to where her mum was manning the home-baked stall.

'He's a good-looking fella, isn't he?' said Iris, with a mischievous giggle.

'Hmm, I hadn't noticed.' Jessica blushed, hoping she hadn't been staring too obviously.

Iris gave her a knowing smile. 'Don't worry, it's not just you. It's you and every other woman in here. He makes a refreshing change from the usual old faces in the village. And he's so kind. Nothing is ever a problem for our Reuben. He helped me with my TV when I wasn't sure what to do with the Fire Stick my granddaughter sent me for my birthday. And he looks like that big Italian hunk off the telly.'

'Which one?' said Jessica, wondering who exactly she was referring to.

'Vito from *Strictly*.'

'Ah. I see.' Although she didn't as she hadn't watched that programme for years. She would definitely need to look him up now, intrigued to see if there was a resemblance.

Iris sighed. 'He's such a nice chap. He'll make someone very happy one day, someone who deserves him.'

Jessica frowned. There was certainly something going on with Reuben's marriage. But he hadn't shared it with her, so he obviously didn't want her to know.

Iris looked at her inquisitively. 'How about you — is there a special someone?'

Jessica shook her head. 'No. I am happily single.'

'Well,' she said, glancing back towards Reuben, 'keep your options open. You just never know what's round the corner.'

She couldn't quite believe this was her old teacher talking this way and didn't quite know how to respond. 'Oh,' was all she could manage to stutter. 'I will do. Thanks for the advice.'

'He reminds me of my Frank,' she said dreamily. 'He was a looker back in the day, with his brown curly hair and his dark eyes.'

Jessica smiled kindly at her. She knew that Iris was a widow, but she had never heard her talk about her late husband before. 'He sounds like he was quite the catch.'

'Oh, he was.' She sighed. 'But I'm lucky I've got Scrumpy and Sidney to keep me company now.'

Before Jessica had a chance to ask who they were, Iris clutched her hand. 'Don't look now, dearie,' she said in a sing-song voice. 'Reuben is making his way over here. Remember, stay calm and collected.' She winked at her. 'Play hard to get.'

Jessica was speechless as she looked at Iris in bemusement. She also felt as though her feet were stuck in buckets of syrup. She wanted to move to the side and serve anyone else but Reuben, given the way he seemed to reduce her to a wobbly mess when he was in close proximity to her, but she was rooted to the spot. Why was Iris encouraging her to flirt with him? Had she missed something?

'Hi, ladies,' he said with a grin.

Jessica became completely tongue-tied knowing that Iris was watching her.

Iris cleared her throat loudly and then nudged her. 'Do your sales spiel, dear, come on.'

'Oh, okay.' She rolled her eyes upwards and then steadied her voice. 'Hi, Reuben. Would you like to buy one ticket for a pound or six tickets for a fiver?' She tried to sound breezy.

'A complete bargain,' added Iris knowingly and folded her arms while she waited for his reply.

'Go on, give me six for a fiver,' he said, reaching into his pocket and pulling out a note which he handed to her.

His hand brushed Jessica's and their eyes connected for a second more than was necessary. She really hoped he didn't think she had done that on purpose.

'Thanks for the chat yesterday,' she said, her voice slightly shaky. 'Sorry I had to go. Was everything okay with your dad?'

He nodded. 'Yes, the care home was just calling about some paperwork . . . You should come back over and see the cottage and the tree properly, in its full glory.'

'Yes,' said Jessica, 'that would be nice.' *That would be nice?* She sounded like his ageing auntie.

'I managed to get some of your mum's date and walnut loaf and famous tablet before it all sold out.' He put down a large bag of the confectionery on the table. 'My dad always loved it and I thought I'd take some in when I visit him.'

Jessica nodded. 'That's good.' *That's good?* Seriously, was that all she could say. 'Hopefully he'll enjoy it.'

He nodded. 'And if not then I will. Your mum makes the best tablet I've ever tasted.'

'I know. It's hideous to think how much sugar she puts in there. There are about three bags of the stuff in it. I swear everyone needs fillings after eating her tablet.' There was an awkward pause as she desperately tried to think of something witty to say. She couldn't. Then she noticed the queue that had formed behind him. He was quite the crowd puller, but then he always had been.

'Right, Reuben, come on, you're holding everyone up,' said Iris matter-of-factly. 'Get your tickets and see what you've won. That's if you've won anything. Then we will need to move you on. There's a queue of folk waiting their turn. But if you don't win this time, worry not, you can always join it again.' She shook the bucket vigorously at him and he raised an eyebrow at Jessica.

'Crikey,' said Jessica with a grin. 'You'd better do as you're told and hurry up.'

'Okay. Let's have a look then.' He reached his hand in, pulled out his tickets and started to unfold them. With the help of Jessica, he matched up some of the winning tickets to the bottles.

'Oh, will you look at that,' he said with a laugh. 'I've actually picked some winners. Normally the ones I get are all duds.'

'There you go. Just what you've always wanted,' she said chuckling. 'A bottle of washing-up liquid, some Nozeco . . . Oops, looks like you've won the Babycham too!'

Iris gave a hoot of laughter. 'Well someone has to win it. Better luck next time.'

'Oh, you're not quite finished. Looks like it's your lucky day. You've also won a bottle of champagne,' said Jessica.

'Hey, not bad going at all,' he said, pleased with his haul. 'I will pop it in the fridge as a welcome gift for Murray.'

'Or you could share it with a special someone,' suggested Iris innocently and looking across at Jessica.

'Anyway,' said Reuben, ignoring her comment, 'nice seeing you both. Hope the rest of the day goes well. I'm away to see my dad now.'

There was a fresh surge of customers towards the stall and before Jessica was able to say bye, he had turned and disappeared out the hall. She couldn't help feeling disappointed that he had gone.

'I think we'll be finished with this lot within the hour,' said Iris, pointing at the diminishing number of bottles on the table. 'We don't have much more to shift.'

'It's been fun,' said Jessica honestly. 'I've really enjoyed it. Thanks, Iris.'

'Hey,' said Gillian, who had just appeared behind Jessica, clutching the hand of a little girl.

'Hello,' Jessica said with a smile having swung around. She sank to her knees. 'And you must be Millie. I'm Jessica. It's very nice to meet you.' She held out her hand to shake Millie's.

Millie smiled shyly at her and hid behind her mum's legs. Her hair was curly like her mum's and she had a gap-toothed smile. Then she stuck out her hand and clutched Jessica's, giving it a shake.

'I see the Babycham is away then,' said Gillian drily.

'Yes, Reuben just won it.'

'Oh dear. I'm sure he loved that.'

'Do you want to have a shot?'

'Sure. Millie, do you want to get the tickets from the bucket?'

Millie reached in and chose six different coloured raffle tickets and waited to find out if they would match any of the bottles. 'Have we won anything?'

'Yes,' said Jessica excitedly. 'You have won a bottle of bubble bath. And your mum has won a bottle of wine.'

'Oh great,' said Gillian, perking up a bit. 'We don't usually win anything. Bath bubbles and wine sound like the recipe for a good night in if you ask me.'

'Hey, let me know if you fancy that coffee sometime?' said Jessica.

'That would be nice,' said Gillian. 'Though only if you're sure.'

'Of course I am. When suits you? I can be totally flexible.'

'Well, the bakery is shut on a Monday. We could go after I drop Millie at school?'

'Sounds like a plan,' said Jessica.

'Mummy, come on,' said Millie, tugging at Gillian's hand. 'Can we get our faces painted now?'

'Okay, love.' She pulled a face. 'I promised she could be a reindeer.'

'Have fun. And I'll see you Monday,' said Jessica.

Gillian smiled. 'Great. I'll meet you in the Coffee Pot just after nine. Does that sound okay?'

Jessica nodded. 'See you then. Bye, Millie.' She couldn't help but feel pleased when Millie turned round, grinned at her and waved. Then she glanced down at the table and saw Reuben's bag of tablet. 'Oh no,' she said. 'Iris. I'm just going to see if I can catch Reuben. He bought this for his dad and he's left it behind.'

Iris winked at her. 'Take your time. You know he's single again, dear? He split from his wife last year.'

Jessica wasn't sure what to say. Is that what he meant when he said it was complicated? And what on earth had happened to her sweet, old teacher?

CHAPTER FIFTEEN

As Reuben walked away from the village hall and towards his car, he definitely felt a little lighter in his step than he had earlier. He couldn't take his eyes off Jessica and hoped he hadn't been obviously staring at her. Although she seemed slightly harassed, her hair pulled back from her face in a messy ponytail, her face glowed and she did seem pleased to see him, which was a relief. He had managed a few surreptitious glances at her when she was speaking to other people and laughing with Iris. She had the most beautiful smile which lit up her whole face. He wondered why it had taken him this long to notice how pretty she was. He racked his brain, trying to remember the last time he'd seen her. It must have been that day at the airport a few years ago. That was in the early days of his marriage when things with Belinda were good. He wouldn't have noticed how Jessica looked then. But he noticed now and couldn't take his eyes off her.

Since the breakdown of his marriage, he hadn't looked at anyone else. He just didn't have the emotional capacity or strength to commit to another relationship again. Which made him wonder why his feelings were suddenly all over the place whenever Jessica was anywhere near him. He wondered if he should have told her about his marriage properly when they were tree shopping that day, rather than closing the conversation down. But the last thing he wanted to do was offload on her. To her, he was her brother's oldest friend. Nothing more.

'Reuben. Reuben, wait!' called an anxious voice.

He turned round in surprise to see Jessica running towards him. 'What's up? Is everything okay?' he said, urging himself to stay cool. But his mind whirred with thoughts. *Was she missing him already? Did she feel the connection too? Was he losing the plot?*

Her eyes twinkled in amusement. 'No, it's not,' she said, brushing her hair away from her face. 'I'm glad I caught you.'

It was only then that he noticed the paper bag she was clutching. 'Ah,' he said, pressing his hand against his forehead. 'The tablet.' *She was just bringing the forgotten bag to him. There was no ulterior motive.*

'I saw it on the table and, well, I know you got it especially for your dad. I didn't want you to forget it. Here you are.' She thrust it at him.

'Thanks,' he said, unable to stop looking at her very kissable full lips. He was finding it harder and harder to remind himself that she was actually his best friend's sister.

'Anyway, I'd better get back inside before Iris sends out a search party,' she said, wrapping her arms around herself. 'She is taking it all very seriously. Gosh, it's cold out here,' she said as her teeth started to chatter. 'Mind you, it's really hot in the hall.'

'Yes, I know. It's like a furnace in there. But you'd better go back in before you get a chill and a row from Iris.' He desperately wanted to slip off his jacket and wrap it around her shoulders. 'And thanks for the coffee yesterday. I'm sorry it got cut short.'

'No problem at all,' she said with a nod. 'I'm just glad everything was okay. I hope your visit goes well.'

'Thanks . . . look if you're not busy later then come over for the proper tour of the cottage I promised.'

Jessica smiled. 'It would be nice to see it so I can tell Murray what a fabulous job you've done. I'll see you later.'

As Jessica turned and walked back towards the hall, Reuben realised he had been holding his breath. This wasn't a date. So why did he feel as if he'd just scooped first prize in the Christmas raffle. It was only when she reached the doors and glanced back over her shoulder that Reuben realised he was still staring after her. He gave her a wave and then walked towards his car. *What had happened to him? Why was he behaving like a love-struck teenager?*

The care home was a thirty-minute drive away which gave him the chance to collect his thoughts and try not to think about Jessica, although she was providing pleasant distraction. He always found these visits really hard and the feelings of dread began as soon as he started the journey. He knew that feeling guilty about the decision to move his dad into the care home was a normal emotion to feel. But it didn't make things any easier.

He thought back to this time last year when it was clear his dad wasn't safe to live on his own any more. Although he had tried to support him at home as much as possible, Reuben had found it a huge strain, especially as he had been dealing with it on his own. It was times like this he wished he wasn't an only child. He thought back to the night when he wasn't there — he had been dealing with the fallout from his marriage. Angus had phoned him to say he'd found Dad in their back garden, wearing just his pyjamas with nothing on his feet. He had been shivering. Angus and Catriona took him home and put him to bed, sitting with him until the carer arrived in the morning. It was the final straw of a long list of incidents which meant he was no longer safe living alone.

Reuben still felt awful when he thought about the day he took him to the care home. His dad was so sad and distressed. The staff had been really kind and reassured him that they would look after him. Everyone kept telling him he had done the right thing — and the next time he visited, his dad had settled in and seemed happier. But this past year his dementia had deteriorated and he didn't always recognise Reuben when he visited. He knew his dad was still there inside, but he felt so alone when he left him and bereft. He talked to Murray when he could. He was the only friend that knew his dad, but it was hard with him in Australia. People were generally well-meaning, but their comments didn't always help so it was easier to not talk about it and tell everyone that he was *fine* if they did ask. Except for Catriona and Angus, who had been so kind and also went to visit his dad when they could.

He pulled into the gravel car park of the care home, which was a large, renovated Victorian mansion. Then he took a breath, grabbed the tablet and geared himself for seeing his dad. Buzzing the door, he was met by the manager, who always had a cheery smile on her face. 'Nice to see you, Reuben. Come in,' she said.

'Thanks. How is he today?'

'He's actually been really good this week. We persuaded him to come down and take part in some of the activities. He seemed to really like the Scottish songs.'

'Really,' said Reuben in surprise.

'I know, I didn't know he was such a fan. It was great to see him taking part and enjoying himself. He seemed to really like "Bonnie Glenshee" and "I Belong to Glasgow". We've got a new member of staff who is very enthusiastic *and persuasive* and she seemed to talk him into it.'

He smiled. 'Good for her. I'll go and see if he wants to tell me about it. Thank you.' He followed the corridor along until he came to his dad's door which, this morning, was open. 'Hi, Dad,' he said, walking in and seeing him sitting at the window.

'Hullo,' he said. But he kept his eyes on the large garden.

'How are you today, Dad? I hear you've had a busy week.'

His father looked at him, his eyes a rheumy blue, and gave a weak smile.

'I believe you've been busy singing?' He didn't know any of the words to the first song the manager had mentioned but he slowly started to hum the music from "I Belong to Glasgow". Then added the words he could recall. 'I belong to Glasgow . . .' He watched his dad, whose eyes were on him, and he waited.

His dad started to tap his foot on the floor. 'Dear old Glasgow town . . . well, what's the matter with Glasgow.'

Reuben grinned as his dad continued to sing. It was the first time in months that he had looked so engaged and there was now a spark in his eyes. Reuben watched and listened in astonishment as he sang the song in its entirety. It had been the greatest number of words to leave his father's lips for the longest time.

'I can hear some lovely singing coming from here,' said a care assistant, doing her rounds with the tea trolley. 'That is wonderful, Mr Campbell,' she said with a smile.

He grinned at her, clearly appreciating the praise.

'Now, gentlemen, can I offer you a cup of tea?'

They both nodded and his dad turned again to look outside. 'Look what I brought you, Dad. Remember Catriona's famous tablet?' He unwrapped one of the small packages from the paper bag and broke a piece off, putting it next to his mug. He picked it up and examined it suspiciously before putting it in his mouth. He closed his eyes for a minute as he chewed, then opened them again. 'Catriona?'

'Yes, our neighbour, Catriona. She lives at Thistle Cottage. She made it and sent it in.'

His dad nodded at him but didn't say anything else for the rest of the time that Reuben was there. But he didn't mind. He couldn't believe what a transformation he had seen in his dad today. If the best way for him to communicate was through music, then that was good enough for Reuben.

As he drove away from the care home, he felt as though a huge burden had been lifted from his shoulders. He needed to talk to someone and tell them. There was a time he would have talked to his ex, but suddenly he felt the urge to speak to Jessica. It was a long time since he'd wanted to share with anyone and he liked the feeling he had at the thought of talking to her.

CHAPTER SIXTEEN

The Christmas lights switch on was at five o'clock and started with a small procession from the village hall. Jessica had managed to grab an hour at home, to decompress from the intense bottle tombola experience earlier, while her parents went to the Rowan Bay Inn for a late lunch, early dinner or 'linner' as they liked to call it. They had arranged to meet her at the hall just before five.

It was a cold night and as she left Thistle Cottage, Jessica was glad to be wearing her warmest clothes. She still had her Christmas sweater on underneath her thick coat, tights under her jeans and a woollen scarf, gloves and hat on. Her boots crunched against the thick frost on the pavement and she shivered as the chilly air nipped at her nose. It was a clear night and the dark sky was scattered with twinkling stars. As she reached the high street, she was surprised at how many people were bustling around. Families were out, with children all wrapped up and babies cosy in their buggies. Laughter and chatter filled the air, and seeing everyone enjoying themselves made her smile. She hadn't realised that the event was such a big deal. She didn't remember it being like this when she was younger. Back then, people tended to congregate around the small square in high street to watch the Christmas tree lights be switched on. But that was about as exciting as it got. As she neared the hall, she spotted her parents in the crowd and made her way over, slipping into place beside them.

'It's about to start,' said her mum excitedly pointing at the doors of the hall which had just opened.

There was a murmur of anticipation as the steady and low sound of bagpipes began. Everyone quickly quietened down and turned their heads towards the hall as the piper stepped out. Dressed in his kilt and a thick woollen coat he gave the event a sense of ceremony as he began playing "O Little Town of Bethlehem". Jessica felt goosebumps on her arms and she gave a small shiver, though she wasn't sure if it was from the cold or the moment itself. Then as the piper moved, leading the procession behind him, Jessica could see that children were following, holding lanterns that glowed like tiny stars. Their excited faces made her smile. As the piper's tune faded, the carol singers following behind the children began to sing. Their voices were gentle and harmonious as they sang "Silent Night", and Jessica watched and listened, letting it all sink in. It felt as though the whole village had gone quiet as they listened to the familiar melodies which felt so comforting.

'It's so nice you're here with us for this,' said her dad gruffly.

She linked her arm through his and nodded. 'It's quite the event. I'm impressed.' With a small flicker of guilt, she realised she couldn't remember when she was last in the village in the run up to Christmas. She normally arrived on Christmas Eve and was only back for a couple of days.

'Here comes the man himself,' said her mum, pointing at Santa who was at the back of the procession on a large tricycle decorated with tinsel. 'It's a shame that Lexi isn't here yet. She would love this.' He waved and grinned as he passed by. As the sound of the choir started to disappear, the piper struck up a lively version of "We Wish You a Merry Christmas" and the crowd started to follow the procession towards the high street. Jessica felt a flutter of excitement in her stomach as she walked along with her parents, looking up at the lights draped from lamp post to lamp post ready to be switched on.

The procession stopped by the small square, beside the village clock, which had a large Christmas tree made entirely from strings of sparkling lights. This was the moment everyone had been waiting for. Jessica's breath caught in her throat as there was a collective countdown from the crowd. 'Ten, nine, eight, seven, six, five, four, three, two, one.' Then Santa stepped forward and pressed a button. There were loud gasps and cheers from everyone as the tree burst to life with all its twinkling lights and the brightly coloured Christmas lights flickered for a moment then lit up the street in shades of red, blue and green. Jessica smiled, feeling as though Rowan Bay had been sprinkled with magic. She looked around as she wondered if Reuben might be here. She scanned the faces in the glow of the lights, hoping to see him. She waved and smiled when she saw Gillian with Millie, but Reuben wasn't there, at least not that she could see. Her parents were now deep in conversation with Iris and another woman.

'I'll see you back at home,' she said, lightly touching her mum's arm. She turned and slipped away, walking back up the high street towards Rowan Lane. Now seemed like the perfect time to go and see the new and improved Primrose Cottage and have a look at what Reuben had done to it. She was genuinely intrigued to see it free of dust sheets. And if she was being honest with herself, it would be nice to see him. The fact he had invited her over earlier was perfect.

CHAPTER SEVENTEEN

Jessica walked up the lane and knocked on the door but there was no answer. Then she tried it again, tapping slightly harder this time.

'Hullo,' said a bleary-eyed Reuben, opening the door. 'I must have nodded off. Sorry, have you been standing there for a while?'

'I'm sorry I woke you,' she said, mortified.

He shook his head and smiled. 'Don't be daft, come on in.' He gestured for her to go through to the front room.

'Thanks.' Jessica followed him in, noticing his low-slung sweatpants and hoodie that he must have changed into after being out earlier. 'I was at the lights switch on and thought I would knock on the way back.' He raked his hands through his hair and stifled a yawn.

'Your hair is fine,' she said jokingly, telling herself to speak to him as though she would speak to her brother. He was just Murray's old friend and if she could remember that then it would make all of this easier. Except he wasn't her brother. He was a six-foot hunk with the sexiest smile she had seen in years. 'Don't fluff it up on my account,' she managed to say lightly.

He smiled warmly at her. 'Just as well it's just you and not someone else. Otherwise, I would feel the need to change. This is my *loungewear*.'

Jessica appreciated the way he seemed to relax in front of her, as it meant she felt less on edge too. Even though she couldn't help but think how good he looked fresh from a nap. She pushed the thought away. 'You look fine. Though next time I'll expect you to have your suit on with waistcoat and tie.'

He smirked. 'As if.' He gestured around the room. 'Well, this is it, Jessie. Welcome to the new and improved Primrose Cottage.'

'Wow, look what you've done in here,' she said, not even flinching when he called her by his nickname for her. There was genuine admiration in her eyes as she looked around. 'I love it. And I can actually see the furniture now.' She laughed. 'It's so stylish but really cosy too. Like a room you could properly relax in. The sofa looks super comfortable.'

He smiled as he rubbed his hand across his jaw. 'I hope Murray and family are as enthusiastic as you.'

'They will love it, Reuben. And look at your tree,' she said, walking over to it. 'You've done a fine job of decorating it. I didn't get a chance to appreciate it the last time I was here.'

Reuben bent down to flick on the lights and they stood for a moment as the fairly lights glowed then flickered on and off. 'You can also do disco mode if you want,' he said, pressing another switch, and the lights started to flash erratically.

'Hmm, nah, I prefer the way you had it before.' She chuckled. 'That's a bit full on. Feels like we're in a dodgy nightclub.'

'I agree.' He flicked it back to the more subdued effect. 'Do you want to see the rest of the cottage?'

'I'd love to,' she said, slipping off her boots and leaving them by the door. 'Lead the way.'

Reuben led her through to the dining kitchen and she gasped. What an improvement on yesterday when the place had been full of his decorating gear. He really had done a remarkable job with the space. It was so different to how she remembered it with his parents' old wooden kitchen units and orange walls. It had always seemed a dark space when they were younger and now it was filled with light. He'd created such a welcoming room and she walked across to the doors which opened out onto the garden. 'This is incredible, Reuben. I wish you could persuade my folks to do this with their kitchen.' For a split second she thought she could see him blushing. 'Honestly, you've done such an amazing job in here. You are so talented.'

He dismissed her comments with a wave but she could tell he was pleased. 'Thanks. I wanted to make the most of the space and create a special home . . .'

As his voice trailed off, Jessica wondered if his comment had been slightly loaded. Had he originally been planning to live here with his ex-wife? And why did she care so much?

'Come on, I'll show you the rooms upstairs,' he said, interrupting her thoughts.

He led her up the staircase to a large and bright hallway. 'This is the bathroom,' he said, opening up the door to a room that was far bigger than their small bathroom at Thistle Cottage. 'I knocked through to the box room,' he said, as way of explanation.

It was bright and white and modern with chrome fittings and plush grey towels. 'I love it,' she said.

'And the bedrooms,' he said, turning round and walking across the hall. 'The main one is in here.' He opened the door and put the light on.

The walls were painted a pale and chalky shade of grey, the wooden floors had been painted white and there was a fluffy dark rug along with a grey Roman blind and a woollen throw across the bed. He had even managed to fit a neat chaise longue into the window. She had a sudden vision of herself curled up next to him on the bed and could feel her cheeks colour. 'Did you say you were an architect, Reuben, or an interior designer?'

He laughed. 'Maybe I'm both.'

'I love the picture,' she said, pointing at the print on the wall. It was Conic Hill in Balmaha and one of Jessica's favourite walks. 'Did you take that?'

He nodded.

'It's amazing. What a brilliant shot. Reminds me how much I love that walk and how long it's been since I've walked there.'

'We should go sometime while you're home,' he said casually. 'I've not been there for ages either. There was that bad storm earlier in the year and loads of trees came down and for a while it was blocked off.'

Jessica looked at him, feeling that unfamiliar glimmer of hope again. Then she reminded herself not to get drawn in any more than she already was. Being neighbourly was fine, but going out for walks with him was something entirely different. 'Yes, it will be good to do with Murray when he's home. He loves that walk too.' Saying that felt like a safer option.

His eyes lingered on hers for a moment, then he turned away. 'Come on and I'll show you the room for Lexi.'

She watched as he strode to the room next door and pushed the door open. Jessica gasped. The walls were painted in a gentle lemon colour. There was a child's bed in the corner, with a bright yellow rug on the floor and a small table in the corner with little chairs at it. Each one had an animal painted on it. 'Oh,' she said, the words coming out in a gasp. He was looking nervously at her.

'Do you think it's okay? Will she like it?'

'Reuben,' she said, feeling her eyes misting up. 'She will absolutely love it.'

'I did check with Murray that she'd be okay in the wee bed and he said she would be. I managed to pick that and the furniture up for next to nothing. I just wanted to make it perfect for her.'

For a moment, he looked completely unsure of himself and she couldn't stop herself from reaching over to give him a hug. 'Honestly. This is wonderful,' she said, then stepped back blushing. She hadn't quite meant to initiate physical contact with him but he looked like he needed a hug. And she was very aware that he had hugged her tightly back. 'They are going to be so pleased,' she said, every nerve in her body now tingling. 'It's, erm, it's so sweet that you've gone to all of this effort for them.'

Reuben looked bashful. 'It's not that big a deal. It's kept me busy, you know. It's been good to have a project to lose myself in.'

Jessica looked at him quizzically for a moment, clasping her hands firmly together to stop herself from reaching out to touch his face. She knew she was being weird, but she couldn't stop herself from imagining what it would be like to kiss him. She should really get out of here sooner rather than later, before she did something she regretted.

'I'll show you the final room. It's not quite finished yet but I'm almost there,' he said, opening the door of the final upstairs room. The walls were a soft green and there was a purple sofa bed in the room and not much else. 'I've got someone coming to put a seat in there,' he said, pointing at the space underneath the window. 'Just need to get some blinds up and a wee rug and that will do for now.'

'It's a really lovely space and very tranquil. I'm impressed,' said Jessica.

'Have you got time for a cup of tea?' he said, nodding downstairs. 'I know I could do with one.'

Jessica knew the right thing to do would be to go straight home and have a cold shower. Being in the same vicinity as Reuben was making her feel light-headed. 'Sure,' she said, trying her best to sound relaxed.

'I'll put the kettle on.'

She followed him into the kitchen and sat at the kitchen table as he busied himself filling the kettle and sorting out mugs. 'How was your dad when you saw him?'

He looked over at her. 'Actually, he was really good. A lot better than he has been in ages. I couldn't believe the change in him.'

'That's good news,' she said, feeling a surge of compassion for him. She had no idea what it must feel like to be responsible for your remaining parent who was now unable to look after himself and cognitively impaired. She was reminded again how lucky she was that her parents had, touch wood, been very healthy. Aside from her dad's knee replacement surgery a few years back, that had been their only hospital stay. She couldn't imagine what it must be like to see your dad failing, both physically and mentally. 'And what had changed? Did something happen to make him seem better?' She knew her words were clumsy but she thought it better to be curious and ask rather than say nothing else at all.

'Music,' said Reuben, placing a mug in front of Jessica. 'Sorry, do you take milk or sugar?'

'Just a splash of milk,' she said as he passed her the bottle, his hand brushing against hers. 'Music?' she said, trying her best to focus on what they were talking about.

'Yes.' A faint smile played on his lips. 'There's been singing with the residents at the home and he seemed to really enjoy it.' He moved and sat next to her and took a sip of tea. 'I didn't realise until today how much I've been worrying about him.'

'It sounds like you've been dealing with a lot.'

'What else can I do other than try and do the best for him?'

There was something about his expression that made him look vulnerable and Jessica again desperately wanted to reach out and touch him. She quickly tucked her hands beneath her thighs. But as he looked at her, in that moment, something passed between them and the only sound in the room was their breathing. *Jessica*, said the sensible voice inside her head, *this is dangerous*. 'Um, so is your wife due back from Dubai soon?' She said quickly.

Reuben shook his head, not moving his eyes from hers. 'No. She lives there permanently now. We've actually been separated for some time.'

The tension was palpable and Jessica found herself lost for words, as she pulled her hands free from beneath her legs.

Reuben moved towards her and, cupping her face in his hands, he gently brushed his lips against hers. *Wow.* Her legs quivered at the jolt of electricity she felt between them. He looked at her with a heat in his eyes she hadn't seen before as he moved to kiss her again. Suddenly there was a loud knocking on the front door.

He pulled back and frowned. 'Who's that? Unless it's your folks. I did say to them to pop down and have a look. They wanted to wait until it was all done.' There was another impatient bang at the door, and with a lingering look at Jessica, he stood up and went to investigate.

Jessica stared out the window into the dark garden beyond. She felt completely dazed by that kiss. It was better than anything she could ever have imagined. All she could think about was kissing him again and again. Her cheeks flamed as she thought about what else she would like to do to him. She hoped he would quickly get rid of whoever was at the door.

The swell of admiration she had for Reuben grew as she glanced around the kitchen again. He really had worked his magic on this cottage and transformed it, at the same time as worrying about his dad. Just then she saw Reuben's reflection in the window as he walked back into the kitchen followed by someone unfamiliar. It was a woman. Jessica turned round to see Reuben looking grim-faced. 'Hello,' said Jessica politely, and then her jaw nearly hit the ground as she realised who this groomed and immaculate woman was.

'I'm Belinda,' she said to Jessica, reaching out her manicured hand.

Mortified, Jessica shook the woman's hand. Apart from the fact she still hadn't had a chance to attend to her unpainted and chewed nails, which Belinda looked at in disdain, this was Reuben's wife. And just moments ago, she had kissed him. Or had he kissed her? It didn't matter, they had kissed. She stood up, clumsily knocking her mug over. The only saving grace was that it was empty. It was time for her to make a swift exit. The woman, in her stiletto boots, towered over her. She wore black leather trousers and her black fluffy jacket looked as though several ostriches had been sacrificed to make it. Her hair was expertly blow-dried — of course it was — and she had a mahogany tan. But it was her large cartoonish eyelashes that fascinated Jessica most. They made her look like some kind of bug-eyed creature. Surely, they had to be false. She looked over at Reuben, who now looked distinctly uncomfortable. So he should too, thought Jessica. Belinda was here, which meant one thing — he wasn't as single as he'd made her believe. And she felt ashamed for allowing herself to get caught up in his kiss. She needed to remember what he was like. Once a ladies' man, *always* a ladies' man. 'Nice to meet you again, Belinda,' she eventually managed to say.

'Have we met before? I don't remember,' said the other woman dismissively.

Jessica clenched her jaw but managed to smile sweetly at her. 'At Glasgow Airport. But it was a while ago. Anyway, I'd better get home. I just live up the road. I'll leave you guys to it.'

'Yes. Thanks, if you don't mind,' said Belinda. 'I'm sure you probably have somewhere to be.'

Sadly not, Jessica thought, her heart now sinking as the heat and longing she felt when Reuben had kissed her drained away.

'You don't have to rush off,' Reuben finally said.

Belinda folded her arms and gave Jessica a look.

Jessica stared back at her, then looked at Reuben. 'It's fine. I was just leaving anyway,' she said curtly.

'Good. Because there is a lot I need to discuss with my husband.'

Reuben frowned. 'I'll see you out, Jessica.'

She gave Belinda a small nod, grabbed her coat and then walked into the front room and to the door where she had left her boots and quickly pulled them on. 'Thanks for the tea, Reuben. And great job with the house.'

'Erm, thanks for popping by,' he said with a shake of his head. 'Sorry about this.'

Reuben looked as if he was about to say something else and then his eyes moved down to her lips. Why was he still looking at her like he wanted to kiss her? From what everyone said, Belinda was his ex but she was still in the next room. Jessica desperately tried to think of something smart to say. But what *could* she say to him? None of it was any of her business. The last thing she wanted to do was get in the way and Belinda was clearly a woman on a mission. 'Don't worry about it.' She pressed her lips together to stop herself from saying anything else that she might regret. The safest option was to leave, pronto.

'Bye then,' called Belinda, now standing with her arms crossed in the doorway of the kitchen. Her words had a definite undertone of *please bugger off now*.

'See you later,' Jessica said as casually as she could to Reuben who now looked as though he had regained the weight of the world on his shoulders.

CHAPTER EIGHTEEN

Reuben couldn't believe that Belinda had turned up out of the blue. He hated to think what Jessica must be thinking now. Especially after what had just happened in the kitchen.

'Who was that?' Belinda said, her voice dripping with disdain when he returned to the kitchen.

'My friend, Jessica, who also happens to be a neighbour, like she told you,' he said. 'There was no need to be so rude.'

She raised a beauty-parlour shaped and tinted eyebrow at him. 'Really? Do neighbours always look disappointed when wives turn up. Did I interrupt something?'

Reuben shook his head at her. Jessica wasn't the only one to look disappointed. He could still smell the scent of coconut in her hair and the subtle smell of her floral perfume. He had wanted to pull her back into his arms and not let her go. Aside from the physical attraction, he had also really appreciated having the chance to talk to her about his dad. And she had actually been listening to him. Her eyes hadn't glazed over and she hadn't tried to change the subject. Which was Belinda's speciality. 'Why are you here, Belinda?'

She smiled at him, lowering her lashes. 'Come on now, that's no way to talk to your wife.'

'Belinda, you aren't my wife any more. We've been separated for a while now. You are very much my ex-wife.'

'Oh, that's harsh,' she said perching her bottom on the kitchen table. 'Technically we are still man and wife.' She flicked her hair over her shoulders and pouted at him.

He looked at her in astonishment, again wondering why on earth he had married this woman. And what on earth had she done to her eyes? Her eyelashes looked as thick as the tassels on his granny's old sofa. Had she always been so vain and self-absorbed? And he just hadn't noticed? Or had their very different lifestyles exacerbated the fault lines that were always there? She had always taken care of her appearance and liked spending money on clothes and jewellery. Reuben hadn't really bothered about her lavish spending to begin with — some of his friends had told him their wives were exactly the same. But after they had been married for a couple of years, she just seemed to want more and more and Reuben felt as though nothing he ever did would ever be enough. It was as though she had a God-sized hole that she would never be able to fill. Whether it was clothes, jewellery, trips away, expensive meals out, she was always on to the next thing. Her salary didn't match her expensive tastes and his income had taken a bit of a bashing too. It was awful to admit, but he had actually felt a sense of relief when she was offered a job working for a large marketing firm in Dubai. Reuben had refused to move there. His life and work were very much rooted in Glasgow. She said there was no way she was turning the job down, and so they reached an uneasy truce when they agreed to try their marriage long-distance. Belinda said plenty of people had long-distance relationships but Reuben knew in his gut that it wouldn't work. And it hadn't.

She smiled at him. 'I take it you haven't changed your mind about coming over to Dubai then?'

Was she having a laugh? What was going on with her? Why was she here now? She must have known that wasn't an option. When Reuben had gone out to visit her, eighteen months ago, he quickly knew there was no way on earth he would ever live there. Lots of people loved the way of life in Dubai but it wasn't for him. They had spent all of his visit socialising with Belinda's work colleagues, whose idea of a good time was partying on yachts, drinking champagne and eating out in overpriced restaurants. It just wasn't him at all. Reuben had never been more relieved in his life to get off the plane — in fact, the flight had been the highlight of the whole trip — and take gulps of fresh, cold Scottish air. It was never going to work. Belinda positively loved that kind of lifestyle and all it brought with it, and he absolutely hated it. All he wanted to do at the weekends was be outdoors, whether it be walking in the hills, or messing about down at the loch, or having dinner in a cosy pub. She'd refused to visit him in Glasgow and so they'd reached a stalemate. Until she then told him, over FaceTime this time last year, that she had been having an affair with one of her colleagues and their marriage was over. He hadn't seen her since. Until now. He felt her hand on his arm, reminding him that she was still there and standing in his kitchen. 'I think it's fair to say that will never happen, Belinda. Are you going to tell me what you want?'

'Have you missed me?' she purred.

He pulled a face. 'No, Belinda, I haven't. Not at all. Please just get to the point and tell me why you're back?' He moved away from her to create some distance.

'Well,' she chided, looking a bit put out that her charm hadn't worked. 'I was back in the country for a few days and I was in Glasgow,' she said with a shiver of distaste. 'I was planning on trying to catch up with you and knew you were down here.' She looked around the cottage, bemused. 'I bumped into some of the boys at the pub the other night in the west end,' she said in explanation. She dramatically placed her hand on her heart. 'So I jumped in my car and decided I would just come straight down and see you. It's always better to chat in person, don't you think?'

Reuben inwardly groaned. 'You should have called to let me know you were back.'

'Oh,' she said, clearly not impressed. 'Well, anyway, now that I'm here, we may as well chat. I wanted to see you because . . .'

As her voice trailed away, he looked at her again as objectively as possible, realising how once upon a time he had been absolutely devoted to her. He would have done anything for her, aside from move to Dubai. Now, he really just wanted her to leave. 'Because?' he said impatiently.

'We were good together, babe.'

Babe? She had never once called him that when they were married. And he certainly didn't want her to start calling him it now. Had she been watching too much *Love Island* or was that the lingo over there with the crowd she ran about with in Dubai? 'That was then, Belinda, and things have changed now.' His stomach sank when he realised it had started to snow outside.

'But, Reubs . . . I think I made a mistake. I still love you.'

He looked at her now, incredulous that she was bringing this up after a year of being separated. 'You had an affair, Belinda. This time last year you called me to tell me you were seeing some bloke from work. And that our marriage was over.' He paused, watching her brow furrow and the seductive smile disappear from her face. 'Let's face it,' he said, trying to make sure his voice was a bit gentler, 'we weren't meant to be together. We wanted different things.'

She chewed her bottom lip for a moment, suddenly looking unsure of herself, but the look quickly passed. She walked over to him, placing a hand on his chest and then letting her finger trail down it. He hated the way his body responded to her touch, a memory of what they once had.

'How about we give it another go,' she said, leaning closer to him. 'Don't you remember how great we were together?'

Reuben remembered the good times they'd had together when they were first married. But that had been fleeting and he also reminded himself of the hurt Belinda had caused him. Then he thought about Jessica and how good it felt to be with her and to kiss her.

Belinda smiled seductively at him, like a cat who knew it had caught its prey, and her hand lingered on the waistband of his sweatpants. 'For old time's sake at least,' she said suggestively.

But he cleared his throat and gently pushed her away. 'No,' he said firmly. 'Our marriage is over, Belinda. In fact, I think we should get on and make plans to finalise our divorce.'

She looked as though he had slapped her. It had obviously been a while since anyone had knocked her back and he was reminded again of how nasty she could turn if things didn't go her way. Narrowing her eyes, she shook her head and threw her shoulders back. 'If that's what you want, then fine.' She looked over his shoulder and out the window. 'But look, Reuben, it's snowing outside.' A smirk crossed her face. 'You can't possibly expect me to drive back to Glasgow in that. The roads will be treacherous. You know how long it takes anyone to get out there and clear them or grit them. It will be hellish. Surely you don't want me to take any chances?'

And she was right. He wanted to actually scream when he turned to see the snow falling thicker and faster. He couldn't let her head off when it was snowing so heavily. He silently prayed that the snow would stop, pronto, and pulled out his phone to check the weather forecast. But it didn't look like it was due to stop for another hour or so. 'It might well clear up.' His voice was brisk.

'And if it doesn't?' she said suggestively.

'Let's hope it does.' Reuben couldn't bear the idea of being stuck indoors with Belinda this way. 'If it doesn't stop snowing, then . . .' He took a very deep breath. 'Then, of course, you can stay here.' He added quickly, 'I'll sleep on the sofa.'

She beamed, her eyes triumphant. 'That sounds like a deal. How about we get some takeaway for dinner? I also brought some champagne with me.' She brandished the bottle she had pulled from her bag. 'We could make a night of it.'

'No thanks,' he said brusquely. Sharing champagne with his estranged wife was the absolute last thing he wanted to do. 'I don't think that's a good idea.'

'Can I have a glass of water then, please?' she said shrewdly.

'Sure.' He filled her a glass at the sink and took it over to the table where she sat. He walked over to the cupboard and pulled it open. 'If you're hungry, let me see what I can rustle up. Something on toast. Beans or grilled cheese perhaps?'

Belinda didn't answer. Reuben heard the pop of a cork. When he turned round, she had filled the tumbler with the fizz. She looked at him defiantly, drained the glass and then poured herself another.

CHAPTER NINETEEN

It was just after ten the next morning when Jessica and her mum walked past Primrose Cottage. The sun was hiding behind a dense bank of grey cloud. Jessica tried to hide her utter dismay when she realised that Belinda's car was still parked on the road. She had obviously spent the night with him. Jessica knew she had no right to feel anything at all — what Reuben did was none of her business. But she couldn't help feeling a stab of jealousy at the thought of them together. She reminded herself that she had no right to stake any claim over Reuben, especially when he and Belinda were still married. He may have told people they were separated, but clearly Belinda had a different idea on that.

'Penny for them?' said her mum as they made their way onto the high street. 'You're awfully quiet.'

She forced a yawn. 'Just sleepy still. It's quite early to be up and about at this time on a Sunday morning.'

'Well, you'll feel brand new in about an hour. I promise. Trust me,' said her mum with a chuckle.

'Hmm,' she said, unconvinced. 'I'll take your word for it. I still can't believe I've agreed to sign up to this.' She had eventually been broken by her mum's enthusiasm and agreed to give the loch-side sauna a go. Her thoughts drifted again to Reuben and yesterday. They seemed to have connected on some level when he opened up to her about his dad. That's what friends do, she reminded herself. *They talk to each other.* But she also knew friends didn't look at each other in the way that they had. Just before Belinda had knocked on the door, it was as though time had been suspended between them. After leaving Primrose Cottage, Jessica had curled up on the sofa at home and watched a movie, trying to put all thoughts of Reuben out of her head.

'Did you know that cold water therapy is a thing,' said her mum as she walked briskly towards the beach. 'It's definitely helped me feel calmer. Ask your dad.'

Angus had politely declined the invitation to join them, saying he was quite happy reading the paper by the fire. Jessica had a feeling that he was making the most of her being home. It was giving him a rest from her mum's busy schedule. 'I do believe you, honestly. I know wild swimming is all the rage now. It's funny to think that people actually choose to go and swim in the loch or in the sea, especially at this time of year.' Her boots crunched over the frosted pebbles on the beach. 'Saunas are springing up everywhere.'

'Come on, this way,' said Catriona, pointing towards the large wooden cabin at the far end of the shore. As they neared it, she noticed the panoramic windows stretching along its entire length, with views right across the loch. This could actually be better than she had thought. She followed her mum's lead as she went into the small, covered area at the back of the sauna for changing.

'Hi, Emmet,' her mum said, waving at the smiling man who had just come out of the sauna.

'Morning, Catriona. Nice to see you again. I was just checking the temperature and all is good to go.' He was very cheery and dressed from head to toe in moisture-wicking sports gear, with a bandana wrapped round his head.

'Super,' she said. 'Meet my daughter, Jessica.'

He extended a hand. 'Nice to meet you. Your mum talks about you all the time.'

Jessica shook his hand. 'I hope it's all good,' she joked.

She couldn't help noticing how enthusiastic he was when he spoke. He was what she would describe as a double-guns type of guy.

He laughed. 'Of course.' He pointed at the small wooden office that sat back from the bay. 'I'll be in there. Shout if you need me. And enjoy. It's a wonderful way to start the day.'

'Will do. Thanks, Emmet.' Her mum turned to Jessica. 'Just leave your stuff here and take in your towels,' said Catriona, who quickly pulled off her jogging bottoms, trainers, sweater and coat. She'd come with her swimming costume on underneath. 'And here are some flip-flops to put on.'

Jessica groaned. 'It's cold though.'

'Tsk, come on. Once you're in the sauna, you'll be nice and toasty, and in fact, you'll be desperate to get in the water to cool off. Honestly,' she said briskly.

Jessica begged to differ. But she did as she was told and pulled off her clothes, glad she had followed her mum's instructions to come wearing the costume she had lent her. Then she slipped her feet into the flip-flops and followed her mum into the sauna. The scent of fresh warm wood immediately greeted her and she sat down, transfixed by the view across the water, which this morning was as still as a pond. 'It's just like glass,' she said, nodding towards it.

'Isn't this so peaceful and therapeutic,' said Catriona. 'It's a bit of a treat, too, when you get the place to yourself like this. Sometimes the sessions are fully booked and you can bump into all sorts in here. The other week it was rammed. But there were quite a few people from the Christmas fair committee and we managed to get some things done.'

'That sounds interesting.' Jessica pulled a face.

'Let's just say it was a meeting with a difference. I never thought I would be sitting in here with Iris chatting strategy. Goodness knows what the other folks must have thought.'

Jessica shuddered at the idea of a work meeting in a sauna. Although she knew it was all the rage in Scandinavia. Some of her colleagues had recently visited Finland on a business trip and after dinner they had been invited to enjoy a sauna and dip in the lake afterwards. Evidently, Ivan had been horrified when he'd had to strip and sit naked opposite someone he had just been discussing strategy with. She chuckled as she remembered Freda telling her about it and swearing her to secrecy. Ivan would have been mortified if he knew his state of undress was the talk of the office. Freda had, of course, relished it and been more than happy to sit completely starkers with the other women who had been debating a case with her in a boardroom an hour earlier. She chuckled at the thought.

'It's nice to see you smile, Jessica.'

Now they had been sitting in the sauna for at least ten minutes, she could feel the tension ease from her shoulders. 'Well, Mum, I have to say that this is better than I thought.'

'It's far nicer to do something like this in the outdoors than be crammed in a gym like hamsters on wheels.'

Jessica agreed. Although there was a gym at work, which was open twenty-four hours, it was windowless and the bright lighting always gave her a headache. She much preferred running outside along the river. Although she had packed her running things, she hadn't felt like going out since arriving home. Maybe her mum's suggestion of trying the sauna and going in the loch would be more refreshing and an easier way to boost her endorphins. She was about to find out as her mum had just clocked the timer on the wall above her head.

'Time to cool off,' said Catriona. 'That's our fifteen minutes up. Come on, Jess.'

Seconds later they were both immersed in the freezing loch.

'Remember to take slow breaths and that will help you feel less panicked.'

Jessica tried it. Her mum was right. It definitely helped calm the fear of being in the baltic water. 'Can we go back in now?' she said after she'd managed to count to about forty in her head.

'Of course. It will be easier the next time. I promise.'

Jessica wasn't convinced. Back inside, she was grateful for the warmth again and the sweet smell of cedar. 'Belinda came by to see Reuben last night,' she said suddenly, curious to see her mum's reaction. 'I was there getting the tour.'

'Oh,' she said, pursing her lips. 'That's strange. She works in Dubai. They've been separated for a while. Maybe she's back for a flying visit. Let's hope so. Tell me about Gillian — how is she doing?'

Jessica noted her mum's change of topic. She clearly didn't want to linger on the subject of Reuben and Belinda. Jessica had briefly mentioned she had run into Gillian at the fair. But that was all she had told her mum. 'We're going to go for a coffee in the morning and catch up properly. She seems a bit stressed.'

Catriona nodded. 'She has a lot to deal with — her own mum, wee Millie and being on her own and juggling all she does at work. She has poured a lot of her time and energy into that bakery.'

Jessica pondered for a moment and tapped her feet excitedly on the wooden floor. Whenever she thought about the bakery, she got a ripple of excitement. She wanted to help Gillian, and the thought of doing something positive for the community was actually making her feel enthusiastic. It was a feeling she hadn't had for such a long time. 'It's got me thinking that I may try out my bread-making skills again,' she said. 'I'd love to be able to help out and volunteer. Even if it's just a short-term thing.'

Her mum arched her eyebrows. 'Hmm, yes that could be interesting.'

'In fact, if it's okay with you, I'll have a wee play around in the kitchen this afternoon.'

'Sounds good to me, dear. And I think we should have everything you need in the cupboards.'

'I suppose I need the sourdough starter . . . which will take a while to make. But I'll just see how I go today with what you have. It's just an idea. I can talk more to Gillian tomorrow.'

'Sounds a good plan, dear. Gosh, I'm hot,' she said, wiping the back of her hand against her forehead. 'Time for another dip.'

This time, Jessica breathed slowly as she entered the water and stayed in longer than the last time. She managed to count to eighty. Her mum was right. This *was* exhilarating and she could feel the endorphins start to take effect. What a lovely way to spend an hour. By the end of the session, she felt calm but also invigorated. 'You were right, Mum,' she said as she quickly got dressed. 'That was wonderful. I feel like I've had a really long workout.'

'I told you that you'd feel amazing! But I'm glad you liked it,' she said, pulling her hat on. 'It's a great way to start the day. Especially when you go home and have a nice warm shower and a tasty breakfast.'

They walked back to Thistle Cottage in a companionable silence. Then her stomach started to grumble, reminding her she was looking forward to tucking into her mum's pancakes with bacon and maple syrup. As they turned into their lane, she watched a robin hopping along the fence towards Reuben's cottage. It was almost as though it was trying to talk to her. It stopped just by the door of Primrose Cottage. Jessica smiled at it and realised how relieved she was that Belinda's car was now gone.

CHAPTER TWENTY

Reuben had hardly slept a wink. After drinking enough champagne to make sure she wasn't fit to drive, Belinda's vision for the evening had come true. Well, at least part of it. She had spent the night at Primrose Cottage in Reuben's bed. However, she had gone to sleep alone. Despite her best attempts to suggest he join her, he had slept on the sofa bed next door. But he tossed and turned for most of the night, not because it was uncomfortable, but because he couldn't believe she had put him in this position. Belinda had clearly thought she could waltz back into his life, click her fingers and have everything her own way again. He could still picture the shock on her face when she realised he was turning her down.

Reuben had made Belinda grilled cheese on toast but she had picked at it, instead refilling her glass with champagne as she told him about Dubai and the real reason she was there. The affair had been short and her eyes filled with tears as she told him that the man she had had an affair with had subsequently fired her from her job when he'd lost interest in her.

'Sounds like a right charmer. I hope he was worth it.'

Her cheeks flushed. 'I know, I know. I've been so stupid. I realise that now and I'm sorry. What can I do though about my job? He's the boss and it's his company . . .'

'It's against the law, Belinda. He can't do that.' Much as she was frustrating the hell out of him, it sounded like this guy had taken full advantage of his position, and her, then pulled the plug when he got bored.

'He's a powerful man. Who's going to side with me?' She sniffed and blinked, her lashes streaking against her face.

'Let me make you some coffee,' he said, standing up and walking over to the stainless-steel machine which he had only used a couple of times. He much preferred getting coffee in the village bakery. He hoped he could remember how to use it. He thought about her situation as he frothed some milk, making them both a strong coffee. 'There you go,' he said, putting it in front of her.

'I'll be up all night,' she said, but she picked it up and sipped it anyway. 'Thank you. I know I am a terrible person for what I did to you. It's a mistake I will always regret.'

Reuben shrugged, realising that, although, yes, it did hurt at the time, he had actually moved on. There was no point in hanging on to anger and a wounded ego — but what he could do was try to help Belinda move on properly too. 'Are you planning on returning to Dubai?'

She nodded and reached for a tissue from her bag. 'Yes, my flight is booked for next week. I've got some interviews lined up. Which is why I can't make a big deal of being sacked. You know what it's like. It's a small world and news travels fast. It doesn't matter whether he's acted badly or not. People don't care. They will think it's my fault.'

Reuben couldn't argue with her. Despite apparent moves to make the workplace fair and eradicate bullying and inappropriate behaviour, it seemed that it was as rampant as ever. His friends were always telling him about the eye-watering things that had happened at their workplaces. He sighed. He was so glad he was self-employed and didn't have to answer to anyone. Although he realised he was also lucky to be a man.

Belinda had rolled her neck and sighed loudly. 'I just need to get on with it. I love living in Dubai and I'm sure I will find another job.' The coffee seemed to be sobering her up.

She lifted her head and looked at him. 'I'm sorry for landing this all on you, Reuben. It's just that you're so easy to talk to and I can't share this with my friends at home.'

Reuben wanted to tell her that they couldn't be very good friends then, but he forced himself to keep his mouth clamped shut. Belinda seemed determined to go back and she had to make the decisions that were right for her.

Now, as he pulled on his jeans and a sweatshirt, he hoped that she would wake up soon. Padding lightly down the stairs, he decided he would be better making a bit more noise, and he stomped more loudly. It was almost ten o'clock and he could do with getting on with the day. Aside from anything else, he had to pop back to Glasgow to check on his flat and pick up some mail. As he busied himself in the kitchen, emptying the dishwasher and putting things away, he felt very at home, even though it had been years since he'd lived at the property properly. Flicking on the radio, he smiled. He'd created an environment far cosier and more welcoming than his bachelor pad in Glasgow. When they got married, he had rented the flat out, and he and Belinda rented their own place in the Merchant City. But he had never felt at home there, which wasn't a surprise, and had returned to his own place after they separated.

'Good morning,' said Belinda airily, appearing at his side.

'Hey there.' He turned to look at her. Her face was pale, she had removed the ridiculous eyelashes and her hair was pulled back from her face, which was quite a contrast to how she had looked when she arrived last night.

'Um, thanks for everything. And I'm sorry again.'

He smiled kindly. 'There's no need to keep apologising, Belinda. I get it. This is a really difficult time for you and I'm glad you told me what's been going on.'

She glanced at the door. 'I should really get going.'

'Have a cup of coffee first, I've just made some fresh.'

She sat down gratefully at the table and ran a hand over her face. 'I've made a mess of things.' She groaned. 'I am so sorry. I feel really stupid. I shouldn't have drunk that champagne. I should have gone back into Glasgow last night.'

Reuben sighed. Although what she'd done to him was wrong, she didn't deserve to lose her job. He watched her as she wiped away a tear. 'Come on now,' he said, passing the box of tissues to her along with a mug of coffee.

'Thanks,' she said smiling at him.

'Take a step at a time. It no doubt all feels shit at the moment. You know, I really don't think you're a bad person.'

'Really?' She blinked at him. 'I've hurt you, had an affair and now don't have a job because of it.'

He leaned against the kitchen worktop and sipped his coffee, contemplating for a moment. 'And you've apologised. But look, our marriage was my responsibility too. You don't need to take all the blame. I didn't want to move to Dubai. Our lives were already moving in different directions.'

She bit her lip nervously. 'Thanks, Reuben.'

'You just need to pick yourself up and keep moving, Belinda. Don't let this creep win.' His mind was whirring. 'In fact, I think I might know just the person who may be able to help. Leave it with me.'

She sighed. 'I don't deserve your kindness. But thank you.'

Reuben stared at the woman he'd once loved and knew he had to do the right thing by her despite everything. That was why he needed to talk to Jessica.

'And can I suggest that you don't wait too long before seeing your pretty neighbour again. I saw how disappointed she was when I arrived and the way you looked at her.' She paused. 'Reuben, don't let another woman get away.'

CHAPTER TWENTY-ONE

The next morning, Jessica found a small table at the back of the Coffee Pot café and kept her eyes on the door for Gillian. She sat for a moment, enjoying the scent of coffee and listened to the whirring machine and the sound of the milk being steamed. It was another chilly morning, though at least it was dry, and she appreciated the warmth of the cosy shop. As she waited, she checked her emails and texts. She was relieved that, aside from a friendly checking-in message from Freda, the office was leaving her alone. Her stomach clenched when she saw the trail of texts that had been steadily arriving and which she had continued to ignore. And a tiny flicker of something inside reminded her that she would have to deal with this sooner rather than later. The thought of returning to work did not excite her in the least. It was strange to feel a bit displaced and uncertain about what would come next, but for the first time in her life she felt okay about it.

Her mind momentarily wandered to Reuben and Belinda. She noticed Reuben's car hadn't been there since yesterday afternoon, and in her mind she had him shacked up somewhere with Belinda in Glasgow. But then she pushed the unhelpful thoughts away. Instead, she focused on the positive day that yesterday had turned out to be with the sauna experience with her mum — they had already booked their next slot for later in the week — and then the afternoon of baking bread and cakes. Her dad's eyes had almost popped out his head when she suggested he come into the kitchen and be her taster.

'Delicious,' he'd said as he chewed a slice of bread, fresh from the oven. She'd then cut him a square of date and walnut loaf and his reaction had been very positive. 'You have a talent for baking, that's for sure.'

Just then the café door opened and Gillian came in wearing a royal blue padded jacket and a bright red hat, which she pulled off her head, allowing her mass of red curls to escape.

'I didn't think I'd ever make it here. I need a coffee, pronto,' she said without stopping to take a breath. 'What a morning. What are you having?'

'You sit down,' said Jessica kindly. 'Let me go and order. What kind of coffee would you like?'

'A flat white please.'

'Anything to eat?'

'Um, yes, I'm starving. I haven't eaten breakfast yet. Maybe just a croissant please. Or a scone. I don't mind. Anything will do. But here,' she said, reaching into her pocket. 'Let me give you some money.'

Jessica dismissed her with a wave. 'Don't be daft. Let me treat you.'

She went over to the counter and placed her order and then went back and sat at the table. 'A stressful start to the day then?'

Gillian nodded, the ghost of a smile on her face. 'You could say that. I've had to deal with burning toast, wash a sink full of dirty dishes, then just as I was about to make myself a cup of tea before we left for school, I realised that Millie had tried on my red lipstick. Once I'd carried out some damage limitation on Rehab Red — a lipstick I bought years ago and thought I would hold onto *just in case* — and wiped it off her mouth, I discovered that she had used it to draw a heart on our bedroom mirror and then trodden on it, which explained the red marks crisscrossed across the beige carpet floor.'

Jessica gasped. 'All of that before nine o'clock?'

'Tell me about it. I managed to quickly shampoo the carpet and get most of it out. But I am now ready to collapse. And drink lots of very strong coffee.' She smiled gratefully when she saw the waitress bringing it over to their table. 'Thank you so much. Sorry, Jessica, not what you needed to hear. I'm sure it's very different to the usual type of chat you get on a Monday morning in the office.'

'It's fine. Don't apologise. It's much better, in fact,' she said, smiling. 'I'm in awe of you. I'm sure it can't be easy, being a single mum.'

A brief, pained look flashed across her eyes. 'No, it's not one of the easiest things I've ever done and it's not ideal when we're still living with my mum.' She rolled her shoulders and took a sip of coffee. 'That's better.' She sighed and reached across for the croissant. 'Thanks for this.' She broke off a piece and took a bite.

'You're welcome,' said Jessica, just glad that the simple act of buying her a coffee and pastry was making Gillian's day a wee bit better.

'And I got the sense that work isn't that great either?'

Gillian forced a chuckle. 'I'm not usually this doom and gloom. Honestly, I'm usually the life and soul of the party. Enough about my moans and groans. Tell me about you.'

Jessica felt guilty for having lost touch with Gillian over the years, especially when she realised what Gillian had been dealing with. Her mum had told her that Gillian's partner walked out on her when she was pregnant after deciding that she didn't want to become a parent after all. Then Gillian was made redundant from her job during lockdown. Skint and with a small baby to look after, she moved home to live with her mum. 'Not much to say,' she began. 'I'm just back for a break from work. It's fine but all a bit full on this year and I had loads of time to take.' As she spoke, she realised that was all she felt ready to share at the moment.

Gillian broke off another piece of croissant which she chewed thoughtfully. 'Oh, don't let me down. Please give some nugget of information which allows me to believe you are living the dream in London.'

Jessica sighed heavily. 'Sorry to disappoint.' Lifting her cup, she took a sip. 'It's all work, work and more work with demanding, entitled clients who think they're the most important people in the world.' The muffled sounds of other customers chatting occupied her mind for a moment.

'Oh, Jessica. You need to give me something. Have you not got a hot man hidden away there?' She gave a wicked grin. 'Or several?'

Jessica laughed heartily, and then the small stab of pain flickered again at her heart. 'No, not any more. I was seeing someone this time last year. But that all kind of ended suddenly. He, um . . .' She gave a dismissive wave with her hand. 'He wasn't who I thought he was. There hasn't been anyone since . . .' She didn't really want to get into the details of what had happened to Tim. The last thing she needed was for Gillian to feel sorry for her.

'Well, no time like the present for a wee Christmas fling while you're back.' Her eyes crinkled mischievously.

'Anyway, we're not here to chat about my love life or lack of. Tell me about you and *your* love life — and the bakery. What's happening?'

Gillian drained the rest of her coffee. 'Oh gawd. Well, my love life debrief will take exactly two seconds. Nothing is happening there.'

'It must be hard, trying to meet anyone when you don't have a lot of time.'

Gillian shrugged. 'I did go on some online chats and made plans to meet up with someone in Glasgow. But then I had to cancel because Mum couldn't babysit and she quickly lost interest.'

'You know if you want me to look after Millie, I would be more than happy to.'

'Thanks,' she said gratefully. 'But flying up from London to babysit is perhaps a wee bit extreme.'

Jessica laughed suddenly, feeling a bit foolish at her rash offer. She had to keep reminding herself that she lived in London now and was just here for a visit. 'What about work then?'

'Well, for that I will need another coffee.' She stood up. 'Same again?'

Jessica nodded and waited for Gillian to order and come back to the table.

'It's just nice to chat. Thanks, Jessica, for listening.'

As they drank their coffees, she told how the weeks leading up to Christmas were traditionally some of the bakery's busiest and most profitable. But that during these past few months, there had been one drama after another and sales were being impacted. Gillian had been doing as much as she could to help Struan, who owned the business and was the main baker, but he wasn't getting any younger and told her most days that he wasn't sure how much longer he could keep going. He was always complaining about the early starts, the rising cost of ingredients, and all the admin that came with the job. 'I feel for him, I really do, but the thought of no bakery in the village is awful. It has always been such an integral part of Rowan Bay. And now . . .' She choked back a small sob. 'It doesn't bear thinking about.'

'What are the options then?' said Jessica, watching Gillian grip the sides of her coffee cup.

Gillian shook her head sadly. 'Believe it or not, staying in the village was never one of my life ambitions. It was really hard to move back here after living in Glasgow but I was on my own and Millie was just a baby. You know, I think back to those days when I was heartbroken and terrified at the prospect of being a single parent and becoming homeless and jobless. Moving back here was the best thing I could have done at the time. Then lockdown happened and I was stuck. But the job with Struan was a lifeline. It gave me the chance to earn my own money again, knowing that Millie was in safe hands with my mum. I'm so grateful to Struan for all that he's done to help me these past few years and hate to see him so stressed. He told me the other day that he was at breaking point.'

'And could he take anyone else on?' said Jessica, leaning forwards and steepling her fingers together.

She nodded. 'Yes, he did actually. He hired an apprentice baker who did an amazing job but then left to go travelling. Prior to that his head baker, Carl, decided to return to Germany after the implications of Brexit began to cause him visa-related stress.' She closed her eyes briefly and sighed loudly. 'I wish I could do more to help but I'm not sure what the answer is. Struan has been running the business for almost twenty years. I think he's just completely scunnered with it all. And if things don't turn around by the end of the year, then he'll close the bakery, and from a selfish point of view, I will be out of a job and the hub of Rowan Bay will be gone.' She paused. 'That's what bothers me most of all. Some of our older customers come in every day and buy something. They might only want a scone or a sausage roll but going to the bakery each day gets them out and gives them a purpose and the chance to meet up with other villagers. What about the local businesses we supply too?' She lowered her voice. 'This café and the Rowan Bay Inn? What will they do? And we're the only place that does takeaway coffees. They tried it here but it didn't work. They don't have the capacity.'

Jessica listened silently and watched Gillian as her shoulders slumped and her eyes dulled. Her mind was also whirring as she thought about options and ways in which she could help. Being back in the village had reignited her sense of nostalgia and she wanted to help. She wasn't yet sure how or what she could do. She had some work contacts she was going to call, not that she'd tell Gillian any of this quite yet. 'Don't despair. Sometimes things have a way of working out.'

Gillian looked at her with a tight smile as though to say, *aye and pigs might fly*.

'Let's keep our fingers crossed for a Christmas miracle,' said Jessica brightly.

'Don't you worry,' Gillian said drily. 'I've already written to Santa and told him what I'd like for Christmas this year.'

Jessica briefly placed a hand on Gillian's. 'Just don't rule anything out yet. How about I come in and help out?'

'Really?' Gillian's eyes widened in disbelief.

'Yes. I learned how to bake bread a few years ago. And I'm keen to utilise my skills.'

'But you're here for a break.'

Jessica chuckled. 'You know my mum and what she's like ... There's not much chance to sit still in our house. She likes to run a tight ship and delegate tasks. Seriously, I would love to help. You'd be doing me a favour too.'

'How?'

'It will give me something to focus on. Volunteering will be good for me. And get me out of my mum's way.'

Gillian squealed and jumped out of her chair to hug Jessica. 'You're on!'

Jessica grinned. She couldn't wait to get started.

CHAPTER TWENTY-TWO

The countdown was now officially on for the arrival of Murray, Carolyn and Lexi. In five days they would all be back in Rowan Bay and her mum was getting more and more excited by the second. She was like a whirlwind as she worked through her to-do list and crossed off all the tasks. Jessica had watched in awe as she iced several Christmas cakes, baked shortbread and batch-cooked lasagnes and soup, which she then put in the freezer at Primrose Cottage.

Jessica hadn't seen Reuben since the weekend. Her mum told her he was back in Glasgow for a few days. The fact he hadn't told her himself hurt. But then again if he was the same player he had been in high school then he was probably with Belinda. Jessica sighed, frustrated at herself for getting caught up with Reuben. She had fallen for his charm and was kicking herself for being so stupid. But she wasn't about to sit around waiting for an explanation from him and, true to her word, she had started working in the bakery the day after she met with Gillian. When the alarm went off at three in the morning, she did wonder what she had signed herself up to. Especially as it was cold, dark and damp when she walked to the bakery in what felt like the middle of the night. But she reminded herself that she was living a privileged existence and had a choice to do this. Struan had been doing this for years in order to earn a living.

It took a couple of days to find a rhythm with her new routine. But now it was the end of the week she was finding the early starts actually invigorating. She hadn't realised what a delight it would be to work with a real sourdough starter again. She appreciated the tips that Struan taught as he kept a watchful eye over her. She could hardly blame him for being cautious. This business had been his life, especially these past few years in particular. Struan was well into his sixties, with a rotund, ruddy face and thinning hair. He didn't talk about it at all, but his wife had left him eight years ago for her personal instructor. It had caused quite the furore at the time and everyone in the village knew what had happened. Jessica wasn't quite sure what Gillian had told him but he did seem grateful for the extra pair of hands.

'Thanks for doing this,' he said gruffly.

'You are welcome and there's no need to thank me all the time. It's nice to be able to help. I'm really enjoying this. Well, aside from the early starts,' she added. 'But I forgot how therapeutic I found baking.'

He nodded enthusiastically, his eyes lighting up. Then he sighed. 'That's how I felt when I started out.' His shoulders sagged. 'Then I got tired and old. I just don't get the same pleasure from it any more.'

She realised he could be talking about her life too. She felt the same about her career in the law. Yet today she walked home just after one o'clock feeling very fulfilled, glad she had done something meaningful with her day.

'Jessica!' called someone from further up the street.

She turned round and saw Reuben striding towards her looking very smart in dark jeans and a black woollen coat. 'Hi there,' she said, as he reached her. 'How are you?' She kept her voice even, despite having not heard from him since the night of the kiss when Belinda had shown up and he suddenly left for Glasgow. She had told herself to move on and just think of him as Murray's friend but now he was looking at her with such warmth in his eyes, as if he was genuinely pleased to see her. She felt her heart skip a beat and her cheeks flush. Obviously the rest of her body hadn't yet got the memo that he didn't feel the same as her.

He smiled hesitantly at her. 'Better than you,' he said. 'You look utterly knackered.'

'Cheers. Nice to see your chat is as dire as ever.' She smiled in what she hoped was a friendly manner, but Reuben frowned, as if he was confused by her reaction.

'I've just been to yours and your mum filled me in on your latest career move.'

She nodded. 'I know. Who would have thought it?'

'Seriously though, that's a really nice thing you're doing for Gillian and Struan.'

Her cheeks warmed at his compliment. 'They're good people and I just wanted to do something to help. And I've got the time.'

Reuben suddenly looked extremely nervous as he chewed his bottom lip. 'I owe you an apology. For last Saturday. I had no idea that Belinda was going to show up like that.'

She shrugged. 'Don't worry about it.'

'But I do worry about it. I don't want you to get the wrong impression. I was going to call but something came up in Glasgow about a project for next year and, well, I really wanted to talk to you in person.'

She shrugged.

'Look, I wanted to pick your brain about something. I don't suppose you fancy a walk?'

She looked down at her floury trousers. Some fresh air would be good and she could also do with his opinion about her ideas for the bakery before she floated it with Struan and Gillian. 'Do you mean now? Have you time?'

He nodded. 'Yes, I've just come from a meeting in Drymen for a new renovation project and need a break anyway.'

'Okay,' said Jessica. 'Let me get home and change quickly.'

'Me too,' he said, laughing and gesturing at his smart clothes.'

'We could head to Conic Hill or along to Milarrochy Bay?'

He looked at the sky, which was growing heavy. 'I think it might snow so let's stick to the shore just to be safe. I don't fancy tramping up and down those stones. It could get quite slippy.'

'Good thinking,' she said with a nod.

'But I'm definitely up for doing Conic Hill another time. With today, if you're quick we should have time to park at Balmaha and do the loop up to Milarrochy and back.'

That was one of her favourite stretches of beach on the loch. 'Come on then,' she said, nudging him towards his cottage. 'What are you waiting for?' Jessica sped off shouting to Reuben she would be two minutes.

'I'll meet you by the car,' he called after her.

She disappeared through her front door like a whirlwind. Running upstairs, she reminded herself that Reuben just needed her advice, but her heart was racing as she thought about the way he looked at her. Dropping her work clothes on the floor, she then pulled on her jeans, a long-sleeved top and a warm sweater. She ran back downstairs and past her dad who was sitting on the sofa watching his iPad with his earphones in. She grabbed her coat, her boots, hat and gloves. 'Bye, Dad.' He couldn't hear her and she wondered if he would notice if a herd of cows wandered into the house. He was clearly absorbed in the latest Netflix drama.

'Everything okay, love?' said Catriona, emerging from the kitchen holding a tea towel.

'All good, Mum. Just going for a walk with Reuben up to Milarrochy Bay. See you later.' She pulled the door shut with a bang and sprinted towards Reuben's car, but not before catching a knowing smile from her mum.

CHAPTER TWENTY-THREE

It didn't take them long to drive to Balmaha, where Reuben parked the car across the road from the Oak Tree Inn.

'It's been ages since I've been here. I remember we used to go there a lot,' she said, pointing at the hotel. 'They used to do a great Sunday roast.'

Reuben nodded in agreement. 'Yes, and I think they still do. It's a while since I've been there too, but if you're lucky, I might treat you to a hot chocolate when we've finished our walk. The café over there is great.' It was a frosty afternoon and he pulled up the zipper on his coat, glad he had also shoved his hat and gloves in the car.

'You're on.'

They started to walk towards the bay, making their way past the signs for the boatyard and then through the garden with its statue of Tom Weir, a Scottish climber, author and broadcaster. Someone had placed a red bunnet on his head.

'I'd completely forgotten that was there,' said Jessica, nodding at the bronze statue. 'I remember when it was unveiled. How long ago was that?'

'Hmm, over ten years ago now, I think. Apparently, it's very popular with visitors.'

'I can understand why. It's a bit of a talking point.' Jessica shoved her hands deep in her pockets.

Reuben was thoughtful as they made their way along the narrow winding path which led them around the side of the loch. It was quiet and there was something lovely about walking in silence with Jessica by the shoreline. But he couldn't shake the feeling something had changed since the weekend. Had he read the situation wrong and Jessica didn't want to continue whatever had started with the kiss? Or had he not explained the Belinda situation properly? He hoped it was the latter and, given the fact he didn't often open up about these things, he knew he should probably say more about Belinda turning up. And make Jessica see that the more he thought about the kiss the more he wanted to do it again. But before he could speak Jessica broke the silence.

'This is beautiful,' she said softly. 'I forgot how lovely the sound of silence is. It makes me realise how often I am surrounded by noise.'

The path weaved through patches of woodland and on to the white gravelly beach again and Reuben glanced over at her. 'How's it going at the bakery then? Are you enjoying it?'

A smile lit up her face which stirred something in him. 'I love it. It's hard work and I don't *love* the early starts. But I love the simplicity of what it is and the rewards it brings. I can just absorb myself in baking — which I had forgotten how much I enjoy — and then knowing someone will come and buy one of the loaves makes me happy. We've been trialling some festive loaves with cranberries and they've proved a hit.'

'Quite different pace to what you're used to then?' He smiled at her. 'Your mum always said you worked too hard in London.'

'Just a wee bit . . .' she said drily. 'But here I like that I can leave work at the door. When I leave the bakery, that's the end of the shift.' She exhaled loudly. 'I didn't realise what a workaholic I've become.'

'I suppose it's easy though just to get used to your routine and your way of life,' said Reuben. 'Especially when you've

142

got such a demanding job. You're working for one of the top firms, aren't you?'

She nodded. 'That was something I used to be proud of. As though I had made it. Now I realise it doesn't mean a thing.'

'It's difficult to forget that having balance is important,' he said carefully, aware there was more to what she was saying. He wondered what had made her fall out of love with her career.

'I agree. I think that's something I need to work harder at.'

'It must be hard, though, living in London and working in your kind of profession. I assume you need to be available when the clients say jump?'

She nodded. 'Yes. And even the short time that I've been back home has given me a bit of perspective. Work is *all* I do. And I don't even enjoy it much any more. It feels a bit . . . meaningless . . .' Her voice trailed off.

'Which is why you're enjoying working in the bakery?'

'Exactly. It just feels like I'm doing something worthwhile.'

'But I'm sure you must make a difference with your work and helping those out who need it? I thought employment lawyers existed to help those who'd been unfairly treated.'

'Yes, you would think, but not so much in my line of business. It tends to be more about the wealthy clients who are having issues with staff. So it doesn't always feel that rewarding. You did say you wanted to pick my brains though. So, ask away!'

Reuben stopped to admire the view of the water and scuffed his foot on the ground now wishing he had addressed the Belinda situation with Jessica earlier. 'It's Belinda,' he said and immediately could sense Jessica edging away.

'Ah I see.' She kept her voice even.

'But it's not what you think,' Reuben rushed to speak. He was doing this all wrong. Why had he just not called earlier? He was such an idiot.

'Look, we've been separated for more than a year. She had an affair with a man at her place of work in Dubai.'

There was a silence before Jessica eventually spoke. 'I'm sorry, Reuben. I didn't realise. That must have been tough.'

'It was.' He shrugged. 'My male pride took a bit of a bashing, but thinking about it now, we were never suited. I want her to be happy though. When she arrived the other night, she was in a bit of a state. This guy she had the affair with dumped her and her contract was terminated. No coincidence there. But her timing was awful. Especially after what happened between us.' He looked at her, she was standing next to him now, her elbow touching his, smiling. He had never seen someone so beautiful and she had visibly relaxed.' Perhaps he hadn't blown it after all.

Jessica looked thoughtful. 'Let me get this straight. The man she had the affair with has sacked her and she doesn't want to make a fuss because he holds a senior position and could make things tough for her. Especially when she looks for another job in a place where people talk to each other?'

He turned to look at her, stunned. 'How did you know all of that?'

She forced a small laugh. 'It's my job and it's a very common scenario.'

They started to walk again, Jessica clearly deep in thought as she didn't speak for several more minutes. Reuben wondered if Belinda's case was a lost cause. Perhaps she should just try and do her best to move on elsewhere. Yet it didn't feel very fair.

'If you can tell me some details . . . like the name of the firm and the colleague who caused her issues, I will discreetly make some enquiries,' she eventually said. 'I'm not making any promises, but I have a colleague who is well connected and she may well have some helpful advice for Belinda.'

'Thank you. I would appreciate that. It just doesn't seem right that she's been treated this way.' He chuckled. 'And yes, I did just say that out loud. Which is ironic. You definitely can call me a mug because I am one.'

Jessica looked across at him. 'I don't think that at all. I just think you're very kind and have a big heart.'

Her eyes lingered on him and Reuben wanted nothing more than to kiss her. But he needed to know that he hadn't totally blown it. 'And I thought you just saw me as your brother's annoying best friend.' He held his breath as he waited for her to answer.

Jessica grinned. 'I do. You are. But I'm starting to see there is more to you than just pulling my ponytail to annoy me.'

Reuben smirked as he reached over to gently tug at her hair. Relief settled over him as he started to think there was a chance after all.

CHAPTER TWENTY-FOUR

As they continued to walk along, snowflakes began to softly drift from the sky. Jessica laughed playfully as she reached out to try and catch some in her gloved hands. 'You were right about the weather,' she said.

Reuben looked up at the sky. 'It looks like it's getting heavier. I think we should head back or I'll soon be challenging you to a snowball fight.'

'I think you would lose that,' she said teasingly. 'I have a very good aim. But I agree, let's turn back.'

They quickened their pace and Jessica realised that talking to him had definitely cleared the air between them. 'I haven't actually told anyone else this, but I toyed with the idea of buying the bakery.'

'Really?' he said, clearly surprised. 'I wasn't expecting you to say that.'

'Neither was I. It was an idea that came to me and I wanted to help. But then the more I thought about it the more I realised it should be owned as part of the community. It's already like a hub for people and it should stay that way. Wouldn't it be great if it could be owned by the village and we could also offer jobs and apprenticeships to younger people?'

He smiled at her. 'I think it's a great idea. And are Gillian and Struan on board?'

She shook her head. 'Not yet. I haven't spoken to them properly about it. We've got a meeting later in the week and I thought I'd float it past them then to see what they think.'

'If they agree, how long would it take to happen?'

'If we can get things moving then it could take around six months.'

'Well, let me know if I can help in any way.'

'Thanks,' she said now feeling elated at Reuben's encouragement. She hadn't realised how much his opinion mattered to her. The fact she trusted him enough to share her thoughts spoke volumes. She was usually so guarded about what information she shared with anyone. More importantly, she loved how easy it felt again between them. 'Your ears must be bleeding,' she said to Reuben, apologetically. 'You're very easy to talk to.'

'Not at all,' he said with a grin. 'You seem really enthusiastic about it. In fact, it's the most excited I've seen you since you've been back.'

Jessica could feel her smile slip from her face. 'Really? Have I been that miserable?'

He smiled kindly at her. 'Sorry, that maybe wasn't the right thing to say. You've just been a bit distracted. Though not obviously . . .'

'Jeezo, thanks,' said Jessica, now feeling quite deflated. 'I didn't realise I was that bad. I thought I'd done a good job of putting on my happy face.' She forced a smile.

'Hey,' he said lightly, touching her arm. 'You're not at all. I guess I just recognised something in you because it reminded me of . . . well, me. And your mum is always diplomatic but I know she's been worried about you. Your brother too.'

She arched an eyebrow at him. 'I see. So, you've all been talking about me.'

'No, don't be silly. It's just . . . I know they've just been a wee bit concerned. Sorry, Jessie, I've obviously said the wrong thing. How about you let me buy you a hot chocolate over there.' He pointed at the coffee shop, St Mocha, opposite the car park, which did look warm and inviting.

Five minutes later, they were sitting at high stools in the window of the café as two mugs of hot chocolate were placed in front of them along with a piece of lemon-and-coconut slice and millionaire shortbread. 'Thanks,' Jessica said, then lowered her voice. 'This is all good market research.' She tilted her head towards the cakes.

'I am very glad to oblige,' Reuben grinned.

She clasped her hands around the mug, enjoying the warmth. 'To answer your question and Mum and Murray's concerns . . . then yes, it's been a tough year in London for one reason or another.'

Reuben fixed his eyes on hers but didn't say anything.

'I've worked flat out all year and taken no holidays and had issues with some clients . . . and then got burned out . . .'

He gave her an encouraging nod.

'And this time last year I was seeing someone . . . and then he died suddenly.' There, she had said it. She had told him her big secret.

'I'm so sorry to hear that,' he said softly. 'That must have been awful.'

She nodded, and her jaw clenched tightly. 'It was.' As he looked at her, his eyes warm and full of concern, she wanted to tell him the rest of the story. She wanted to tell him *everything*. But then she would be exposing herself and making herself even more vulnerable than she already was at this moment. She didn't want him to judge her or think less of her. She just wanted to stay in this cosy cocoon and be in this moment with him for ever. Then the little niggle of guilt stabbed at her and reminded her of the reality.

'How did you cope?'

She sighed and gave a shrug. 'I worked. And *worked*. But then I realised that wasn't a great coping strategy. I was starting to get irritated with the clients.' She remembered Ivan's conversation with her just a few weeks ago. Things had shifted a lot for her since leaving London. 'I actually don't know if it's something I want to do any more.' Her mouth dropped open. 'There, I have actually said it out loud. I don't want to go back to my old way of life. I don't think I want to be in that corporate world any more.' She lowered her gaze. 'I want to stop hurting,' she added softly. When she glanced up at him, he was looking at her with compassion.

'I know. I understand. And it won't feel like this forever.'

Jessica could feel the tears start to smart in her eyes and decided it was time for a change of subject. 'Anyway, enough of me. Time to try out these cakes.' She lifted up a knife and cut them both in half. 'Dig in,' she said, pointing at the plate.

Reuben paused, still looking at her. Then he reached across and squeezed her hand. It was a small gesture but it made Jessica feel so much better. But would he be so understanding when he found out the truth? It was a risk Jessica wasn't yet ready to take.

CHAPTER TWENTY-FIVE

That night, after her parents had gone to bed and the house was still and quiet, Jessica went into the kitchen. She pulled on her mum's polka-dot apron and washed her hands at the sink. The idea had been percolating in her mind for a while now and she wanted to do something special for Gillian and Struan and to bring some magic to the bakery. She and Gillian had strung some fairy lights and Christmas baubles in the shop window. But it needed something more and Jessica had the perfect plan for a festive window display. She was going to surprise them with a gingerbread house.

She carefully made the dough then rolled it out on a sheet of greaseproof paper she'd placed on the worktop. Following a template she'd found online, she cut out one of the sections then slid it onto a baking tray. Then repeated it until she had everything she needed. As the first batch baked, she leaned against the counter and smiled. The warm scent of cinnamon, ginger and allspice soon filled the kitchen and smelt so comforting. She felt herself begin to unwind. Chatting to Reuben that afternoon had definitely helped her. She was also glad they'd cleared the air between them. As she cut out Christmas trees and stars, using the leftover dough, she sighed. Even the thought of him still made her stomach flip. But despite the chemistry between them, she still hadn't told him the whole truth about Tim.

It was only when all the pieces of gingerbread were cooling on the counter that she realised she had no idea how she was actually going to assemble it all. She stared at the walls and roof pieces, knowing that it would surely collapse if she tried to build the house and then take it to the bakery. She would need to do it there, preferably when nobody else was around. Which meant after Gillian finished her shift tomorrow. But she also knew it could be potentially fiddly and she could do with an extra pair of hands. Someone with the right expertise . . . Dusting her floury hands against her apron, she reached for her phone and sent a message.

Help! I could do with your architectural skills for a secret plan. Can you meet me at the bakery tomorrow evening?

She didn't have to wait long for Reuben's reply.

I am intrigued. I'll be there. What time?

Jessica grinned to herself, already picturing the two of them building a gingerbread house. She quickly typed out a reply.

Does 5 p.m. work? And don't say anything to anyone!

He replied instantly.

I won't say a word. See you there!

* * *

Her dad helped her carefully transport the gingerbread pieces to the bakery the following evening when it was closed. Gillian and Struan had agreed she could use the bakery kitchen, especially when she said she was keen to experiment with a few new festive recipes and that she couldn't use the kitchen at home as her mum was batch cooking. It was a small lie, but one she hoped they would understand.

Now she stood in the bakery surrounded by the carefully baked gingerbread pieces wondering where on earth to start. The bell above the bakery door jingled and she walked through to the front, relieved and glad to see Reuben.

'I hope you're prepared,' she said playfully, before locking the door and leading him through the back.

He shrugged off his coat and hung it over the back of a chair. Jessica couldn't help noticing he was wearing the same checked shirt he wore to the Christmas tree farm that day. The one that made him look extremely hot.

He raised an eyebrow. 'I'm always prepared, Jessie. Though I have no idea what you've got in store.' Then he looked over and saw all the gingerbread pieces. 'Ah, okay. I wasn't expecting this. And I do have to tell you that I've never built a gingerbread house before. Or a real house either. I tend to just be involved in the design process.'

Jessica chuckled, realising it was also the first time she hadn't winced when he had called her Jessie. In fact she was growing to actually quite like it. But there was no way she would tell him that. 'Compared to what you usually do, I'm sure it will be a cinch. I mean how hard can it be?'

He looked at her, his eyes steady and intense, which made her heart race and her cheeks flush with colour. *Why did he always have that effect on her?*

He raised an eyebrow as he rolled up his sleeves and stepped towards the sink to wash his hands. 'So, where do we start?'

'Reuben, that's why you're here. You're supposed to be the expert.'

'Mm,' he said, frowning. 'Well, we need some glue or something to stick it together.'

She gave him a withering look. 'Glue? *Really?* I'm just about to make some icing which will act as the mortar. I'm now wondering if you're up to this challenge at all.'

Reuben laughed. 'I promise I won't let you down.'

Jessica quickly made up the icing, then handed him the piping bag. 'I've got this board to use a base,' she said pointing at a large cake base on the counter. If everything went to plan the house would be the size of a large doll's house which would make an eye-catching showpiece in the window display. 'Should we assemble it here and carry it through? Or just do it in the window?'

Reuben grinned mischievously at her. 'We can do it in the window if you want to. But people might talk.'

Jessica could feel a blush creeping up her cheeks and rolled her eyes in an attempt to lighten the sudden crackling air between them. 'Honestly, you're impossible, Reuben Campbell. Your mind is in the gutter.'

'I was just saying,' he said trying to look straight-faced but failing.

She shook her head and laughed. 'Right. Mr Architect. Let's get to work.'

Within minutes the bakery was filled with the sound of their laughter as they worked side by side. Jessica smeared a thick layer of icing on the board so that it looked like the ground was covered in snow. Then they started to stick the pieces together.

Reuben worked with the focus of a master architect, using cocktail sticks to pin the walls together and piping icing along the top in preparation for the roof. Then he asked Jessica to lift the gingerbread pieces for the roof into place. 'Hold it there. We don't want the roof to slide off. That would be a disaster.'

Jessica giggled. 'You're making me nervous now.'

'This is a very serious business, you know.' As he leaned in to steady the roof in place, his hands brushed against hers and he glanced at her, his eyes lingering on her face.

There was a moment of silence and then Jessica froze. 'Oh no,' she gasped. 'I don't believe it.'

They both watched in horror as half the roof crumbled inwards.'

'There must be a flaw somewhere,' he said, jokingly, with a spark in his eyes. 'I blame the baker.'

Jessica tutted at him and burst out laughing. 'Just as well I came prepared then. I made some extra pieces just in case.' As she walked over to pick up another piece of gingerbread, she took a steadying breath. The moment was gone but she was sure something would have happened if the house hadn't started to fall apart. Perhaps another kiss? She really wanted to kiss him again. She wasn't sure she could just think of him as her brother's best friend any more. Not when she was so attracted to him.

When they finally finished gluing the gingerbread house together, this time without any complications, Jessica sighed. 'All we need to do now is add some icing to the roof, so it looks like snow, and add the sweets and chocolate buttons and these chocolate fingers for the door.'

'That should be the easy part,' he said. 'Now that the heavy construction is done.'

She rolled her eyes and focused on adding the finishing touches with his help. Then she stood back to admire their work. 'It looks amazing. Thanks, Reuben. I couldn't have done it without you.'

'Well, don't speak too soon. We still need to get it into the window. Do you want to carry it or shall I?'

'I'll leave it to you. No pressure at all.'

Reuben grinned as he picked up the cake board and carefully walked to the front of the shop, placing it in the window. 'It is incredible,' he said softly.

She looked at him, expecting him to follow up his comment with a joke. But he was looking at her with sincerity. 'What you've done for Struan and Gillian is wonderful. I think they'll be blown away when they see this. And so will the village. I don't think there's ever been a gingerbread house here before.'

For a moment they stood together quietly admiring their work. She looked up at him, his gaze dropping to her mouth just as he leaned towards her. Suddenly there was a knock at the door, interrupting the moment.

'It's Struan,' said Jessica when she saw his face pressed up against the glass. 'I told him to pop in if he was passing.'

Reuben cleared his throat and moved away from Jessica. 'We make a good team,' he said softly.

Jessica smiled wistfully. 'We'd better let him in and show him what we've done.'

CHAPTER TWENTY-SIX

The next couple of days passed quickly for Reuben as he put the finishing touches to Primrose Cottage. Brodie had been round to work on the window seat in the room upstairs which looked great. It was the perfect nook to curl up in and look out at the garden. As Reuben finally packed away his tools, he shook his head, thinking about someone telling his younger self that, one day, he would find himself falling for the girl up the road. He stopped himself in his tracks when he realised what he had just admitted to himself. There was no doubt he felt a sense of connection to Jessica, but he was also plagued with self-doubt. Did she feel the same? Or did the fact his ex-wife was still on the scene muddy things for her? The last thing he wanted to do was complicate her life any further. On the drive back to Rowan Bay the other afternoon, after their walk, they had chatted generally about the latest box sets they'd been watching on television and music they liked. She hadn't said anything else about her ex and he hadn't mentioned Belinda again. The curious part of him did wonder what she was holding back. Things had definitely shifted between them and the more time he spent with her, the more captivated he was becoming. Especially after that night at the bakery. There had definitely been another moment between them. When they walked back to Rowan Lane together later on, they had joked and laughed together and he had even found himself offering to take her paddleboarding in the loch when the weather got a bit warmer. Then he had realised he was getting ahead of himself and quickly changed the conversation.

Perhaps having some space away from each other would be for the best right now. It wasn't that he didn't want to be near her. He absolutely did and it scared him. Murray and family were due to arrive later that afternoon and he had promised Catriona and Angus he would drop the keys round to them. He didn't want to intrude on their family reunion. He gave the cottage one last glance and pulled the door shut. He would miss it. The thought of returning to Glasgow didn't appeal at all. He walked the few metres up the road to Thistle Cottage. As he approached, Catriona swung the door open, holding a wreath.

'Reuben, there you are. I was just coming to see you,' she said. 'I had some bits and bobs left over from the wreath-making workshop and I thought I'd just rustle this up for you.'

'Catriona, what would I do without you,' he said fondly.

'Probably have a much quieter life,' she said chuckling. 'Shall I just come down and put it on the door now.'

'Sure.' He followed Catriona back to his cottage and watched as she pulled a hammer and nail from her jacket pocket. 'Oh, I suppose I should ask if you mind me defacing your newly painted front door?'

'Hammer away.'

It took just a few moments for Catriona to arrange it to her liking and she stood back, folding her arms in satisfaction. 'What do you think?'

'Great,' he said, wondering if he should say anything else. It was fair to say it wasn't the most traditional of wreaths with its random assortment of baubles and tinsel. 'It's quite, um, different.'

'It's upcycled,' she said firmly, eyeing him suspiciously. 'Funnily enough, Angus said exactly the same as you. Well, not quite — he described it as *unusual*.'

He inwardly groaned. 'I'm sure Lexi will love it,' he said quickly. 'It's bright and shiny and very Christmassy. You must be excited about seeing them? In fact, I was just coming up to give you the keys.'

She clapped her hands together, her eyes dancing. 'I can't wait.' Then she glanced at her watch. 'Only a day to go.'

He narrowed his eyes and looked at her confused. 'What do you mean? I thought they were due in very soon?'

She shook her head. 'They were. But the blooming airline bumped them off their connecting flight and so they've been put up in a hotel at Heathrow. Which is not ideal at all with the wee one. She will be exhausted. It's such a long way to fly. But at least we don't have to wait too much longer.'

'Ah, that's a pain,' he said. He knew she had been ticking the days off on the calendar since Murray announced they were coming back.

'What can you do? I can sit about and mope or just get on with things. Which is why I made the wreath. Now tell me, do you have time for a cuppa?'

It was an appealing thought and he was torn over whether to go and sit in the cosy kitchen at Thistle Cottage or return to his cold, empty flat in the city. He hesitated only for a moment. There was no immediate rush for him to leave Rowan Bay.

'Go on. I've got some banana bread that I've just taken out the oven,' she said.

'You're on.' He followed her as she strode back towards the house, and he kicked off his shoes at the door. She led them through to the kitchen.

'Jess is out just now,' said Catriona as though she was reading his mind. 'She was having a brainstorming session with Gillian and Struan at the inn.'

'I see. It sounds like she's got a lot of great ideas when it comes to the bakery. That gingerbread house was genius.

It's been the talk of the village.' It did look great though, sitting proudly in the window, dusted with icing sugar and surrounded by twinkling fairly lights.

Catriona filled the kettle, flicked the switch on and then busied herself with pouring milk into a jug and bringing the cake and some plates over to the table. 'Between you and me, Reuben, it's been a bit of a lifesaver for her. I can't believe how much she's changed since she arrived here. For the better.'

He nodded sympathetically.

'She's had a hard time of it this past year. Anyway,' she said, 'it's great seeing her so enthused again and to have the sparkle back in her eyes.'

He was certain that she was giving him a bit of a meaningful look and he wondered if she also sensed the connection he and Jessica had developed. She poured him some tea and told him to help himself to the banana bread.

'It's delicious,' he said between mouthfuls.

'Thank you,' she said, clearly pleased. 'It's been nice having Jessica home to cook for, and with Murray and the family arriving too, it's given me a bit of focus.' She lifted her mug to her lips and sipped. 'You've done an amazing job with that house of yours. Are you pleased with it?'

'I am. I guess it will always feel like home to me in a way, but it's so different now, the way things are . . .' He gripped the mug tightly.

Catriona pulled a chair out and sat next to him at the table. 'You did the right thing by your dad, Reuben. I know it's not easy, but at least he is safe and being looked after where he is.'

Reuben nodded, grateful that she always said something reassuring to him when it came to his dad. Plenty of people had made sweeping and insensitive comments about how they could never put their parents in a care home.

Catriona regarded him for a moment. 'You know you're very welcome to spend Christmas here with us if you'd like? I don't know if you have plans or not . . . I know Belinda is back. She's welcome to come too.'

He almost choked on his tea and had to cough to clear his throat. 'She was back very briefly,' he said dismissively. 'She just wanted some advice about a work situation which I am hoping Jessica may be able to help with. But as far as I know, she was due to fly back out yesterday.' He paused. 'We are finally getting a divorce.' He exhaled loudly. 'To be honest, I am so relieved.'

Catriona nodded kindly. 'I'm sure you must be. You've been under so much strain. And I'm glad Jessica may be able to help with some legal advice. That's very noble of you . . . and that would explain why Jessica has been on her phone a lot. There seem to have been quite a few hushed conversations and her phone has been beeping constantly with texts. Maybe she can give you an update when you see her.'

Reuben wondered when that might be. He wanted to make sure he gave them all a bit of space and didn't want to be hanging around like a spare part. He really appreciated Catriona's kindness and her offer to have him at Christmas, but he didn't want her to feel responsible for him. He knew how much she was looking forward to having her family together again and the last thing she needed was an extra mouth to feed. He finished the rest of his tea and then glanced at his watch. 'I think I might try and see her before I head back to Glasgow. I'll go to the inn now and then head back to my flat from there.'

Catriona nodded. 'Don't be a stranger, Reuben. I know you want to give Murray some space but he'll be excited to see you. You're always welcome here.'

'I know. I'll give them a few days to settle in and recover from the jet lag and I'll be in touch,' he said, standing up. 'Thanks for the cuppa and cake.'

'Any time, dear,' she said, showing him out.

It didn't take him long to drive to the inn, and as he pulled the car into a parking bay, he was lost in thought. He was thinking about Jessica again. She was smart and funny and beautiful. But plenty of women he had previously dated ticked all those boxes. Was it that familiar connection? Or that there was something else? Something that made him feel as though he wanted to protect her? Thinking back, perhaps he had always felt it, even when they were younger. Even though he'd teased her, he had always kept an eye on her to make sure she was okay.

As he walked through the door and into the hotel's entrance, he looked towards the reception, which was unmanned. But he was aware of someone sitting with their back to him in one of the chairs by the fire, talking into their phone. Then he realised it was Jessica. He was about to let her know he was there and would wait in the bar, but he paused at the tone of her voice. It didn't sound like she was having a friendly conversation. In fact, the tone of her voice sounded quite serious. He started to back away before he became privy to what was clearly a private conversation and found himself partly hidden by the hotel's large Christmas tree, though he could still see her. As her voice rose, he could hear every single word she was saying.

'We have already been through this. What is it you want from me?' She leaned forward in her seat and pressed her forehead into her hand. 'If I could go back in time, I would. But I can't and I'm sorry. I have tried to be understanding.' She sighed. 'The last thing I would do is get involved with someone who is married.' She shook her head as she listened. 'Or *separated*. There are clearly a lot of unresolved issues here and there's not much I can do about that for obvious reasons. Married men are not my thing.'

Reuben's eyes widened. It was as though she was talking about him. For a moment, he wondered if she could even be talking to Belinda. Surely not. But what did it matter? He had just heard how she really felt. She didn't believe in getting together with someone who was married or separated, which he was. Hadn't he made it clear enough to her though that he and Belinda were over? He racked his brains trying to remember. But he couldn't recall any specific conversation with her in which he'd told her they were getting divorced.

As the thoughts and questions crowded his mind, he decided it would be better if he left her to it. He certainly didn't want to get caught eavesdropping this way. He had no idea what was going on and wasn't quite sure he wanted to. Surely life shouldn't be this complicated. And whatever she was talking about was none of his business. Except it was, he told himself. She *had* to be referring to him. It sounded exactly like his own situation. It was too much of a coincidence. He had clearly misread the signals from her. When would he learn that his own judgement with women was not to be trusted? He quietly backed away so she wouldn't see him and went back out to his car.

CHAPTER TWENTY-SEVEN

When Jessica arrived home later, her mum was folding laundry at the kitchen table.

'Hi, dear, how was your meeting?'

'All fine thanks.' She picked up an apple from the fruit basket and bit into it, chewing absent-mindedly and thinking about the earlier phone call at the inn.

'Everything okay, dear? You're miles away.' Her mum looked at her curiously.

'Sorry, Mum, yes fine. I had to deal with a call earlier which is on my mind.'

She tutted. 'You're supposed to be off work though?'

Jessica shrugged. 'It wasn't really work.'

'Oh, did Reuben catch you?'

'What do you mean?' She was now over at the sink, her back to her mum.

'He said he was going to pop by the inn to see you.'

'When was that?' she said in surprise.

'Just a wee while ago.'

'And he definitely said he was going to come by the inn?'

Her mum nodded. 'Yes, he said he was keen to see you.'

The apple turned to cotton wool in her mouth and she spat it out. Her heart plummeted as she anxiously wondered if he had walked in and heard her on the phone. Surely she would have noticed? Then she remembered the chair had been positioned away from the door and her voice had been raised as the blood had rushed through her head. She wouldn't have noticed a herd of elephants rushing past. 'No,' she said quietly. 'I didn't see him. Maybe he decided against it,' she said hopefully.

Her mum frowned. 'Nope. He was definite he was going to come past and see you before he headed back to Glasgow. He seemed quite cheery at the thought.'

'I didn't see him,' she said, pursing her lips and shaking her head. 'He must just have missed me.'

'Never mind. I'm sure he'll be back very soon to see Murray. This time tomorrow they'll be here, Jess,' she said excitedly. The front door slammed shut and she jumped. 'Angus, what have I said to you about that door?'

He grinned as he walked into the kitchen. 'That coming from you.' He shook his head. 'Do you want to see my outfit?' he said, holding up a Santa suit?

'Did you get the milk I asked you for?' said Catriona, ignoring it completely.

He clasped his hand over his mouth. 'Sorry. I forgot. I'll head back out. I got caught up with this.' He beamed and pointed to the red-and-white costume.

Catriona shook her head in disbelief. 'Seriously?'

'I thought the wee one might like it.'

'What do you mean? Are you telling me you're going to try and get down the chimney dressed as Santa?'

'I'm not that daft,' he said with a chuckle. 'I thought I could go and meet them at the airport wearing it?'

'Tell me you're joking?' said Catriona looking aghast. 'Surely it would be better to leave *that* surprise until Christmas Eve? Or never,' she said, muttering under her breath.

Catriona folded the last piece of laundry and placed it in the basket. 'The last thing you want to do is frighten the wee one. Especially when she hasn't seen you for so long. Anyway, have you forgotten they've got a hire car arranged? There's no need for us to go and collect them. Sometimes I wonder if you listen to a word I say.' Then with a shake of her head she disappeared out of the room.

Jessica had to push aside any thoughts of Reuben and what he may or may not have heard her saying and step in to mediate. 'I think buying a Santa suit is a lovely idea, Dad. But perhaps arriving at the airport might be a tad much? Especially as Lexi hasn't seen you since last Christmas. You don't want to overwhelm her. And Mum's right. They've sorted a hire car.'

Her dad placed the suit on the table and sat down, deflated. 'We're not saying you can't wear it, Dad. We just need to be mindful of the timing of it all.'

'Okey dokey,' he said, his shoulders slumping. 'Why has your mum flounced off?'

'I think she's just a bit over-excited and on edge about their arrival tomorrow. You know how much of a perfectionist she is. She wants everything to be just right for them.' She placed a reassuring hand on his shoulder.

'Thanks, love. You're right.' He jumped up and grabbed the suit. 'Doesn't mean I can't go try it on though, does it?'

'I suppose not,' said Jessica. 'And, Dad, I'll go and get the milk.'

'Oh right, I forgot about that. Thanks, dear. I'll go and try to make your mum laugh.' He ran out the room and up the stairs, taking them two at a time.

Jessica sighed loudly. This in-house mediating could be exhausting. She needed to get out and give her parents some space. Taking a walk would give her a chance to process what had happened earlier. As she walked down to the Co-op, she thought about Reuben. She had pretty much convinced herself that he had walked in and heard her conversation. She racked her brain, trying to think what she could have said that meant he didn't stay. After their meeting about the options and possibilities for the bakery, Gillian and Struan, both buoyed with excitement, headed home, and Freda called to give her an update on Belinda's predicament. She had made some discreet inquiries and confirmed that yes, the man she had the affair with was an utter tool and known for his womanising ways. He made passive aggressive threats should any of the women he had used, dumped then fired try to take action against him. One of Freda's contacts — Jessica never probed for too many details as Freda had contacts *everywhere* — said that he had a reputation for it, and though he thought he was getting away with it, had in fact made a lot of enemies. It sounded like, as well as being a serial womaniser, he was also a serious drug abuser and was known for his fondness of a certain white substance.

'From what I am told, Jessica, it sounds like he is now walking a very thin line. There is a zero-tolerance approach to drugs out there. I think it will only be a matter of time before he's back in London for good. By all accounts, there is more going on and more complaints being made against him. It looks like things are moving in the right direction if Belinda can just hold on a bit longer.'

It did sound like, if Belinda bided her time, he would soon get his comeuppance. 'Thanks for checking it out, Freda. I appreciate it. How are things at work?'

'The usual,' she'd said, her voice clipped. 'Ivan is becoming more of a control freak by the day and the newbies are all falling over each other to impress. I miss you.'

Jessica appreciated her words but knew that Freda wouldn't have very much time to miss her. She absolutely relished every second of work and was brilliant — she was passionate about it and loved what she did. 'That's sweet, but I'm sure you don't have time to miss me. Um, one other thing . . . the text messages have started again.'

'Seriously?' Freda had said with a snort.

'Yes. I'm not quite sure what to do. I've ignored the messages but they are getting more frequent.'

'Report it to Ivan.'

Jessica had felt her face colouring. 'Isn't that a bit extreme?'

'This is now stalking and harassment, Jessica.'

'They're upset.'

'So are you,' she'd said sharply.

'Leave it with me and I'll try and get some closure.'

Freda had hesitated. 'Do you really think that's a good idea?' Then in a gentler voice she'd said, 'You are supposed to be on leave from work and this is not helping you move forward with your life. Remember, you're dealing with someone who can't be reasoned with. And, Jessica, think back to the state you were in at the start of the month . . . I am more than happy to take care of it.'

Jessica had paused, tempted by Freda's offer.

'If the roles were reversed, what would you advise me to do?' she'd asked.

Now, as she walked into the Co-op and reflected on Freda's words, she wished she *had* taken her up on her offer to deal with it. She thought she was doing the right thing by making the call herself — even if it was extremely uncomfortable. She knew it was her responsibility and she had to face it herself. But doing the right thing might have come at a cost, especially if Reuben had overheard her on the phone and jumped to the wrong conclusion.

CHAPTER TWENTY-EIGHT

'Hey, sis!' said Murray as he got out the hire car the next day.

Jessica flung herself at her brother. 'I can't believe you're finally here!' she squealed. She looked over at Carolyn, who beamed at her. Catriona and Angus rushed out the front door and hugged her and then their son, before anxiously hopping around waiting for the star guest to appear. Carolyn leaned into the back seat and unclipped Lexi who was clutching a pale blue rabbit.

'Hello, sweetheart,' said Catriona, gently patting Lexi's strawberry-blonde curls. 'We are so excited to see you.'

Lexi buried her face in her mum's neck. Jessica watched cautiously, not wanting to overwhelm her niece any more than she already was.

'Come on, toots,' said Catriona. 'Shall we show you Primrose Cottage where you are going to be staying while you're here? And your very special bedroom.'

Lexi looked up, seemingly intrigued.

'That sounds exciting, doesn't it?' said Carolyn encouragingly.

'Wait until you see what Reuben has done with this place. He has transformed it,' said Catriona, grinning.

Murray walked over to his parents and gave them another hug. 'It's good to be home,' he said. 'But where's Reuben? I thought he'd be part of the welcome party and giving us the official tour.'

'He wanted to give you all some space to settle in. He knew you'd be tired,' said Angus. 'He's a thoughtful lad. But I'm sure he'll be over to see you soon.'

Jessica felt a strange pang of longing for Reuben and wished he was there too. It felt really strange without him and she resolved to text him to check he was okay. 'Let me help you with your bags,' she said, giving her brother a hand with the cases from the boot. 'How're you feeling?'

He yawned. 'A bit weary, you know, but I'm sure I'll be fine after a couple of days. Brr,' he said with a shiver. 'I forgot how cold and damp it gets here in the winter.'

'The weather was one of the reasons you moved to the other side of the world,' said Jessica with a smile. 'I'm sure this will feel like a total culture shock.'

She and Murray followed their parents, who led the way towards Primrose Cottage, Lexi still holding tightly on to her mum but watching curiously.

'Interesting wreath. Did Reuben make that?' Murray said with a smirk.

Jessica threw him a look and tilted her head towards their mum.

'No, I did. So watch what you're saying,' said Catriona firmly, her eyes amused.

'Erm, it looks wonderful, Mum. Very *artistic*,' said Murray smoothly.

Jessica waited until her mum had unlocked the front door and then followed the party in and put the cases in the front room. She pulled a funny face at Lexi, who was peeking at her over Carolyn's shoulder. The little girl started to giggle. 'I'm going to give you some space, too,' Jessica continued, 'and let Mum and Dad get you settled.'

'There's no need to rush off,' said Carolyn.

'It's fine, honestly. I'll catch up with you later. It's a lot for the wee one to take in. I'll see you later but shout if you need anything. I'm only two doors along.'

'Okay, Jess, see you later on,' called Murray as he disappeared into the kitchen after their parents.

She blew Lexi a kiss and then pulled the door closed behind her and trudged back up to Thistle Cottage. Slumping on the sofa, she sent Reuben a message.

Hey Reuben, how are you? Murray and fam have arrived and are asking after you. We would love to see you.

She chewed her lip for a minute and deleted the last line and instead added, *It would be great to see you* ☺ Then she pressed send.

He didn't respond immediately and Jessica went through to the kitchen to make a cup of tea. It was definitely the cosiest room in the house. She loved the way her mum always decorated it with festive lights, which she hung around the windowsill, also making sure she had festive tea towels and oven gloves slung over the oven door. Her phone buzzed. She walked over to the table and picked it up.

Glad they've arrived. Tell Murray I'll be in touch.

That was it. Short and perfunctory. No, how are they? Or how are you? They were nothing like his previous messages and she wondered why he was being so cold. Especially as he had apparently been all set to drop by and see her at the inn yesterday. It just fuelled her suspicions that she had done something to upset him. She tried to think about her phone conversation again and what he might have overheard. Or could it be that he was embarrassed to see her now that Murray was home? After everything that had happened the last few days, things now felt a bit strange. Jessica still liked him. That hadn't changed. But she was confused and now wondering whether he regretted it. Shaking her head, she decided she had to stop thinking about it. She couldn't control what he did or thought and the last thing she needed at the moment was any extra hassle. She was meant to be at home to escape.

CHAPTER TWENTY-NINE

The next afternoon, Jessica was sitting on the floor playing cars with Lexi. Catriona had dug out the old play rug, complete with printed roads and roundabouts, that she and Murray played with as kids.

'You've still got it, Mum?' said Murray in delight as Catriona unrolled it on the lounge floor at Primrose Cottage.

'I thought it might come in handy one of these days,' she said, setting down a plastic box of cars beside it.

'Come on, Lexi, let's play cars,' said Jessica in delight. She helped Lexi prise the lid off the box and Lexi pulled out a small blue car and an orange van. Lexi had been very shy with Jessica until now and she hoped that this would help them to bond.

'Okay,' she said, dipping her hand in and pulling out a motorbike and a small sports car. 'Where are we driving to, Lexi?'

'Hmm. Beach.'

'Okay, let's go to the beach.' There was no beach on the mat but Jessica quickly improvised and pulled off her yellow scarf and crumpled it up at the end of the mat. 'That's the sand, okay?'

Lexi giggled. 'Otay.'

Catriona disappeared into the kitchen to check again that they had enough supplies — despite them having enough to last them until Easter — and Jessica and Lexi became absorbed in the game. They were so engrossed that they didn't notice Murray stepping past them to open the front door.

'Hey, stranger,' he said.

Jessica looked up and blinked. She hadn't even heard a knock at the door and was surprised to see Reuben walk in, looking as gorgeous as ever. She was really trying not to look at him in that way, but it was extremely difficult when he looked the way he did.

'Hey, Muz,' he said grabbing Murray for a hug.

Jessica smiled at the sight of them being reunited. 'It's like a proper bromance,' she said sarcastically.

'Hi, Jessica,' he said crisply, before looking away.

Ouch. What was with his tone? He definitely was being offhand and weird, and she felt slightly hurt. 'Hi, Reuben.' She could play it cool too. Lexi climbed on her lap and snuggled in and Jessica put her arms around her protectively.

'Hello, Lexi,' said Reuben, crouching down. 'I'm your daddy's friend, Reuben.'

Lexi, clearly overwhelmed with shyness, shoved her thumb in her mouth and buried her head in Jessica's shoulder. At that moment, she felt a wave of utter love for her little niece. She glanced up at Reuben, who looked at her briefly. But she could see confusion and hurt in his eyes. Then he stood up.

Murray grinned. 'It's so good to see you, mate. Carolyn is having a nap. The jet lag has caught up with her. She'll be down soon, though. You know Jess, obviously. And Mum is in the kitchen. She'll be through in a second, I'm sure, to take your tea order.'

Reuben laughed. Just at that moment, Catriona stuck her head around the door. 'Oh, Reuben, I'm glad you're here. We missed you yesterday. Great timing. I'm just boiling the kettle.'

'Thanks,' he said and took a seat on the sofa.

While he and Murray chatted, Lexi climbed back onto the floor and started playing with the cars again. Jessica followed her lead as she went to and from the pretend beach making 'beep beep' and 'toot toot' noises. Then she stood up and tugged at her trousers. 'Daddy.'

Murray jumped up. 'Do you need to go to the loo?'

She nodded.

'Come on then,' he said, holding out his hand and leading her to the cloakroom off the hallway.

There was an awkward silence as Jessica and Reuben were left alone.

'How are you?' she said evenly.

'Fine thanks. You?'

She sighed in exasperation. Why was he being so weird? 'Yup. Fine thanks. By the way, I spoke to my lawyer contact about Belinda's situation.'

He nodded. 'Thanks.'

'She said he's got a reputation for it. But if Belinda can hang on and wait, then it looks like there might be something in the offing.'

'Right. I'll let her know when I speak to her. Not that she was keen to do anything about it. It was just me trying to be helpful.'

At that moment, Jessica wished she hadn't bothered trying to help. He clearly didn't appreciate it and, for whatever reason, was now behaving like a dick and barely looking at her.

'Here you go,' said Catriona, arriving with a tray of tea and a plate of Stollen bites.

Jessica caught the puzzled look on her mum's face, almost as though she detected some kind of tension between them.

'Tell me,' said Catriona to Reuben. 'Does this feel weird now, us all being in your house?'

He shook his head. 'It makes a nice change from me always sitting in your house, Catriona. Although shouldn't I be making the tea rather than you?'

'Not at all,' she said gaily.

Murray and Lexi appeared and he walked over to the Christmas tree, looking up at the twinkling lights in wonder. 'Did you do this, Reuben, or was it Mum?'

Catriona chuckled. 'Both Reuben and your sister went to choose it at the tree farm.'

Murray raised his eyebrows at them. 'How did you manage that, Reuben?' he joked. 'You two couldn't even be left in the same room when we were kids.'

'That's because he annoyed me,' said Jessica. 'And still does,' she muttered under her breath. She was aware that her brother was now looking at her quizzically. She knew he would interrogate her later.

'Look, Daddy,' said Lexi, pulling at his trouser leg. 'See angel.' She pointed to the top of the tree.

Murray bent down to pick her up so she could get a better view of it and Jessica couldn't help but smile at them. She really hoped Lexi would have a magical Christmas here. She could feel Reuben's eyes on her but she stubbornly refused to look at him.

'Isn't this great?' said Catriona. 'It's wonderful to have you all back together. Which reminds me, Reuben . . . please remember you are very welcome to join us for Christmas dinner. I don't want you to feel you have to stay out the way because Murray is here in your house. You are always welcome to stay with us any time. There's a sofa bed in the love room.'

Murray caught Jessica's glance and she had to stifle a giggle.

'Mum, I wish you wouldn't call it that. It sounds so dodgy,' said Murray.

'Oh, don't be ridiculous. You know what I mean,' said Catriona, matter-of-factly. 'Anyway, Reuben, the offer is there. You are very welcome. Any time.'

'Thanks. That's very kind,' he said. 'I'm still unsure of my plans but I will, of course, let you know.'

Despite everything, Jessica felt a flicker of disappointment that he was being vague. In her mind it sounded like he had better things to do. Murray must have sensed the disappointed expression on her face as he looked at her and gave her a kind, understanding smile.

CHAPTER THIRTY

Later that night, Reuben drove back to Glasgow, keen to get a bit of space and some perspective on his thoughts. Especially as his head was in a spin over Jessica and the effect she had on him. He was annoyed at himself for being offhand and cold with her. Especially when he saw the confusion and hurt in her eyes. It hadn't been intentional, it was just his clumsy attempt to protect himself from the feelings he had towards her. Now Murray was back and, after hearing her on the phone at the inn the other day, he wasn't quite sure how to behave. He knew it was stupid to jump to conclusions but the doubt had crept in anyway and Reuben had started to wonder if she felt the same way. Maybe that kiss had meant more to him than it had to her. Maybe he had imagined the almost kiss at the bakery the other night. Now everything just felt a mess and he had no idea how to fix it.

As he reached the outskirts of the city, he thought back to this time last year when he'd settled his dad into the home just before Christmas and how guilty he felt. He had tried really hard to make the room as homely and comfortable as possible and made sure there were some reminders from home including his father's favourite chair, some photographs of his mum and the print of Elvis Presley that he had always cherished. He had tried to visit his dad as much as possible, but he was also in the midst of his marriage breakdown and juggling a challenging work project. On Christmas Day, he had visited his dad, who had become quiet and withdrawn. In fact, he would barely talk to him, which then just compounded all the feelings of guilt Reuben had. Eventually, after sitting with him for a couple of hours, and trying his best to make some jolly conversation, he had driven back to Glasgow where he heated up a frozen pizza and ate it in front of the television. Then the next day, when it was all over, he was left feeling sad and exhausted. It was fair to say that the thought of doing the same again was leaving him completely subdued.

He let himself into his flat and wandered from room to room restlessly. Picking up his phone, he scrolled through the pictures of Primrose Cottage, pleased that he had finished it on time for Murray. He felt a flicker of envy at how welcoming and kind the Stewart family were. He wished he was part of it — he always had been, growing up with Murray. But something had changed — his feelings towards Jessica had changed, but she was obviously dealing with something or someone else. Much as he tried to push her out of his mind, she had a way of dominating all his thoughts. He told himself that was also why he was trying to distance himself.

Reuben knew that Christmas was a time of joyful anticipation for many people, that they looked forward to the festivities all year. Since his mum died, when he was twenty-two, his dad had always tried to keep Christmas as upbeat as possible, knowing that's what she would have wanted. But her death had left a massive hole in both their lives that no amount of forced festivities could cover over. He missed his mum even more this past year and felt her absence more keenly around Christmas. He wished he could talk to her about Jessica. She would have known what to say. *You always did like her, Mum*, he said to himself, smiling as he remembered his mum telling him off for pulling Jessica's ponytail when she was younger.

What should I do now though? He could picture his mum smiling as she sat at the kitchen table, holding her favourite mug. She always used to tell him that everything would be okay. Whether it was studying for and worrying about exams or nerves before his driving test, she always had the same advice. And even now all these years later, he could still hear her voice softly in his mind. It was a reminder that he had to trust that things would work out. *Everything will be okay. You'll always find a way.*

He raked his hands through his hair, reminding himself that he was at risk of sounding like a maudlin idiot. He had lots to be grateful for, and he was truly appreciative of Catriona's invite to join them at Christmas. But he didn't want to intrude any more than he had or have anyone feeling sorry for him. Giving himself a shake, he grabbed his gym bag. He would go for a swim and use the steam room at the gym. He shivered as he walked outside and to his car. It was freezing, raining and almost dark. He could now appreciate why Belinda was in such a rush to get back to the sunshine in Dubai. The thought of azure skies and warm sunshine was a welcome one. His brows furrowed. Maybe a huge dose of vitamin D was what he needed? Perhaps he should just book himself a week away in the sun over Christmas. Definitely *not* Dubai, but maybe somewhere else. Then he remembered Brodie and his planned trip to Costa Rica. Okay, flying to the Caribbean coast was perhaps a bit extreme, though tempting, and he was sure Brodie was heading there for two weeks. But maybe he could go to one of the Canary Islands like Lanzarote or Gran Canaria. It would definitely be warm this time of year and that way he could just remove himself from the whole festive situation and escape.

He allowed himself a smile before the small voice in his head reminded him he would need to visit his dad. The guilt rippled through him again, and he took a breath, reasoning with himself that he could visit his dad before he flew off anywhere — it would only be for a week. Would his dad mind?

Would he even realise he hadn't been to visit? He sighed. There was a constant loop of swirling thoughts in his head around his dad and whether he was doing enough or could do more. His dad had always told him to make the best of life and enjoy himself while he was young and he could. He once again wished he had a sibling he could share the emotional load with. Sometimes it just felt too much. *Which is a sign you need a break, Reuben*, he told himself. It had been a long time since he'd had a proper holiday. In fact, the last time he'd been away anywhere hot was to Dubai when he visited Belinda eighteen months ago. Then shortly after, she cheated on him and broke the news that she'd been having an affair.

With a sigh, he started the engine and thought about at least exploring his options. Perhaps a week's holiday away from the *joy of Christmas* might well offer him some kind of solution.

CHAPTER THIRTY-ONE

'Do you fancy coming to the pub tonight with me and Lily?'
Gillian had started scrubbing the worktops in the back kitchen
at the bakery and she looked over at Jessica.

Jessica considered her question for a moment, automatically thinking about an excuse she could make as that's what she'd spent the past year doing. Then she remembered she had none. Murray, Carolyn and Lexi were settling into the cottage, and she had seen them every day since they'd arrived back in Rowan Bay last week. She had even managed another visit to the sauna, this time with Carolyn. It had been so nice to spend time with them and enjoy being part of a family again. But tonight, she had nowhere else she needed to be. She could go out and spend time with friends. 'Sure,' she said. 'That sounds nice. Thanks for asking me.'

Gillian gave her a thumbs-up. 'Great. Mum said she would babysit and it's been ages since I've been out. We could even grab a bite to eat there too.'

Jessica nodded vaguely, then a fleeting thought of Reuben floated through her mind. She hadn't seen him since that day last week at Primrose Cottage. She wondered for the umpteenth time why he'd suddenly backed off when they were getting on so well. It had to have been that phone call and his either jumping to the wrong conclusion or judging her. And if she was honest, she was annoyed. She was annoyed that he had been offhand with her and had clearly jumped to the wrong conclusion without giving her the chance to explain. She had every intention of asking him if he had overheard her at the inn. But given he was now avoiding her that was proving tricky. She needed to stop ruminating over it and thinking about him. There was no point. But that didn't make it any easier, especially when she was so attracted to him and he'd kissed her the way that he did.

She turned her focus back to the task at hand. She had just finished making the last batch of cinnamon buns which were now in the oven. There was a wonderful scent of cinnamon and nutmeg in the air. It was a smell she didn't think she would ever tire of. The bakery was as busy as ever and she knew she would miss this strange routine she had quickly settled into. Volunteering in this way had given her trip back home a bit of structure and purpose, and she was hopeful that Struan was now feeling more enthused about the possibility of a community buyout. Just yesterday he indicated to both her and Gillian that the thought was keeping him going.

'If I could put the flat upstairs on the market in the new year and get some money for it that would be something,' he had said. 'It would make me feel more in control and definitely help with the cash flow. That way I could be more focused on trying to get the community bid underway.'

It was the most enthused she had seen Struan since she had met him, and even Gillian had commented on how much happier and less stressed he seemed now there was a bit of a plan in place. It felt good to be able to help them out. Jessica started to whistle as she drizzled the icing on the buns and stepped back to admire them.

'I tell you what, doll,' said Struan, who had just walked in. 'You are giving me a run for your money with your buns. I'm not sure what we'll do when you go. I'm sure yours are even more popular than mine. They sold out even quicker than usual yesterday. I think they're the talk of the town.'

Jessica smiled, pleased at the compliment. 'Yours are delicious and I'm sure they will still fly out the door when you take over again.' The thought of not being here felt odd and her mood deflated slightly. Gillian, Struan and the bakery had given her a sense of comfort and friendship when she had needed it most. She was relieved she didn't need to think about leaving quite yet. Christmas was less than a week away and she wasn't due back in London until the fifth of January. So, she had just over two weeks to make the most of being here. She was sure the novelty would have worn off by then.

* * *

Later that afternoon, Jessica had an appointment with Agata to have her hair done. It had taken her ages to get an appointment with her as December was always Agata's busiest month. She had timed it nicely, especially as she was meeting Gillian and Lily at the Rowan Bar later. Her hair was long overdue a cut and she was looking forward to having it done. Agata always did her mum's hair, and when she sat in the chair at the salon, Jessica felt immediately at ease. She didn't have to say much as Agata was happy to do all the talking while she applied honeyed highlights through her hair and then snipped and cut Jessica's hair into a choppy bob.

'Wow, that looks and feels so much better,' Jessica said when she saw her reflection in the mirror. 'It was badly needing to be done. You have transformed me, Agata. Thank you.'

Agata beamed at her as she brushed away some stray bits of hair from Jessica's shoulders. 'You look beautiful and all ready for a night out.'

Jessica laughed. 'It's lucky that I am doing the very thing tonight.'

Agata squealed. 'A hot date?'

She shook her head. 'Well, a hot date with two friends at the pub. That's about as exciting as it gets.'

'No man then?'

'Too much like hard work,' said Jessica.

Agata giggled. 'I have a brother who is single and always looking for love.'

Jessica nodded awkwardly. *Oh please, no.* She always hated it when well-meaning people tried to set her up.

'He's a butcher in Glasgow and very nice.'

The image of a man covered in blood immediately formed in her mind. She knew she was being completely judgemental and making all sorts of wrong assumptions, but the thought of dating a butcher did not appeal in the slightest. Especially as she wasn't a huge meat eater. In fact, the thought of going out with anyone didn't appeal at all. *Unless it's Reuben,* said the voice in her head. She pulled out her phone to pay. It was time for her to exit before Agata had a date all organised. 'I'm sure he is,' she said politely. 'But I head back to London soon and I have no time for men.'

'Fair enough,' she said, walking over to the till. 'It was worth a try. You enjoy your night with your friends. And let me know if you change your mind.'

Jessica tapped her phone against Agata's machine. 'I will do. See you later. And thank you for doing such a great job with my hair.'

'You are welcome. It certainly needed it.'

Jessica couldn't help but laugh. Agata had a way with words.

Jessica had agreed to meet Gillian and Lily in the pub at six, and although she was a bit early, Jessica decided to walk directly there and wait rather than go home.

The Rowan Bar was a small pub tucked in a corner of the high street and very easy to miss unless you knew what you were looking for. From the outside it didn't look at all fancy with its plain white facade and red lettering. But as soon as you opened the door and entered, it was a sprawling and warm welcoming place with lots of tables and chairs tucked in nooks and crannies. There was a log fire roaring in the centre which filled the room with the scent of woodsmoke and made it feel like a cosy hideaway. She found herself a quiet, cosy corner and sat down and started to scroll through her phone.

Jessica was lost in thought when Gillian and Lily arrived together, bundled up in their winter coats with hats and scarves.

The woman with brown hair and sparkling eyes grinned at her. 'Hiya, you must be Jessica. I'm Lily,' she said in a soft Yorkshire lilt. She smiled warmly at Jessica as she pulled off her hat and looked towards the bar.

'And you know me,' said Gillian, laughing.

'It's lovely to meet you, Lily. Here, you two sit down and I'll go to the bar. What would you like?'

'A glass of red wine would be lovely, thank you,' said Lily.

'Same here.'

'I'll be right back.' Jessica walked over to the bar and ordered a bottle of wine with three glasses and took it back to the table. 'There you go,' she said, filling each glass up. 'Well, cheers.' The women clinked the glasses together and took a sip.

'It's good to finally meet you, Lily. Gillian told me that you're working at the inn. Have you been there long?'

'I've been there for a couple of years.'

'Where did you move from?' asked Jessica.

Lily waved her hand. 'I've lived all over. Up in the Highlands, in Yorkshire, over in Spain and down south.'

Jessica noted Lily's vague answer but knew it wasn't her place to pry. 'And what do you make of Rowan Bay then? It must be very different to the other places you've stayed?'

Lily paused for a moment. 'I love it here,' she said thoughtfully. 'It's the only place I have ever really settled and felt at home.'

Jessica understood what she meant, and once again she felt a pang of sadness at the thought of leaving Rowan Bay behind. 'It's certainly a special place. I forgot how much I miss the loch.'

'You work in London?'

'I do. Although the thought of going back doesn't appeal.'

'I wish you could stay,' said Gillian. 'It's been so good having you here.'

Jessica smiled at her friend. 'I've really enjoyed being back.'

'You must come to the Hogmanay party at the inn, if you're still here?' said Lily. 'Practically the whole village comes along these days.'

The thought cheered Jessica up. 'That sounds fun. I'm sure my parents mentioned something about it.'

Lily's eyes lit up. 'Of course, you're Catriona and Angus's daughter? They're some of our best customers.'

Jessica smiled. 'Yes, they're always raving about how good the food is and how much it's improved.'

'I put that down to the new management,' said Gillian with a wink, and then she waved at someone at the bar. 'Hey, Brodie,' she called.

Jessica looked over to see a tall, broad man with dark hair walking over to their table.

'Evening,' he said with a grin. 'How're you doing?'

'Good thanks,' said Lily with a smile. 'Do you want to join us?'

He shook his head. 'No, thanks, I'm not stopping. I've got loads to do before I go away.'

'Brodie, this is Jessica,' said Gillian. 'Her parents live at Thistle Cottage.'

There was a flicker of recognition on his face. 'Ah, yes, I've heard about you. Your brother is home soon to stay in Primrose Cottage? I've been helping Reuben with some stuff there.'

Jessica smiled. 'Well, you've done a brilliant job.' She noticed that he had flecks of paint on his sleeves.

He shrugged. 'It's just been good to help him out, you know? The place looks great. It's all down to Reuben.'

'You're so modest, Brodie,' teased Gillian.

He blushed. 'Well, I will leave you to your drinks, ladies. If I don't see you, have a good Christmas when it comes.'

'Thanks, Brodie. Same to you and good to meet you,' said Jessica. He turned and walked away and Lily looked at Jessica suggestively. 'He's cute, isn't he?'

Jessica nodded. 'He's a good-looking guy.'

'And he's single,' said Lily. 'If you want me to put in a good word. Although it will have to wait until next year as he's off to Costa Rica over Christmas and New Year.'

Jessica's drink suddenly proved difficult to swallow. 'Uh no. But thank you. He seems a nice guy but he's not really my type.' She wasn't sure if she was being paranoid or whether Gillian was giving her a bit of a look.

'What about you?' asked Jessica quickly.

Lily shook her head dismissively. 'Gawd no. He's like my brother.'

'Ah, not your type then?'

'Definitely not. He's the loveliest of guys but we are definitely just friends.'

'Which is a shame,' said Gillian, 'as he's very easy on the eye.'

'I am very happily single,' said Lily with a laugh. 'Men are way too much hassle.'

'Anyway, what were we talking about before Brodie arrived? Ah, yes, the Hogmanay party,' said Jessica smoothly.

Gillian smirked. 'I agree with Lily. You should come to the party. It's brilliant. There's a ceilidh band and dancing. It's nothing like the sort of thing we used to do when we were younger.'

Jessica chuckled. 'Remember the times we used to trail into George Square in Glasgow to bring in the bells?'

'And try and persuade someone's parents to pick us up? Or those stay up all night parties,' said Gillian wistfully.

Jessica smiled and took a sip of wine. It had to beat last year when she was in bed by nine o'clock and had cried herself to sleep. The party at the inn sounded like a perfect and uplifting way to end what had been a horrible year. 'You're on. It's a date. I'll be there.'

CHAPTER THIRTY-TWO

Christmas was just four days away, and although it was Sunday, and the bakery was closed, Jessica had got used to rising early so this morning was dressed and downstairs before her parents. It looked like the perfect day for a walk — the sky was blue and the sun was shining — and she picked up her phone to text her brother.

Hey, M. Are you up? Do you fancy a walk up Conic Hill?

It took less than a minute for him to respond.

You're on. Leave in 10? I'll drive.

She quickly scribbled a note to her parents to let them know where she was. There hadn't been much opportunity to catch up with Murray on his own since he'd arrived back. She was excited and looking forward to a proper chat with her brother, and this could be the only chance they had. She stood at the window of Thistle Cottage and waited and watched, waving at him when she saw him at his car.

'It's good you were up,' she said.

'I'm always up early,' he said drily. 'Having a toddler means saying goodbye to lie-ins.'

'When did Lexi get up?'

He stifled a yawn. 'At five o'clock. But I've just tucked her in beside Carolyn and she's gone off again.'

'That's tough for you. You sure you don't want me to drive?'

He winked. 'Thanks, but it's fine. I'd like to get there in one piece.'

'Ha ha,' she said. 'Cheeky. Okay, let's go.'

It didn't take them long to get to Balmaha and she thought about the last time she had been here with Reuben then pushed the thought aside.

'It's been years since I've been here,' said Murray. 'Yet it still all looks the same.' He glanced around. 'It always feels like home.'

'I know what you mean. I've missed this walk. And remember when we were kids and Mum would take us on the ferry over to the island for picnics.' She pointed at Inchcailloch Island just across the water. It was an uninhabited island which used to be home to a nunnery and then was a burial ground. Now walkers and birdwatchers would go across to explore it. Jessica had so many happy memories of exploring the woodland paths and having picnics on the beach.

'I know. When you think about it, we really did have quite a magical upbringing,' said Murray.

Jessica nodded in agreement. 'We did. Come on then,' she said, 'let's get going before I change my mind. Oh, and there's a great café there,' she said pointing across the road. 'We should go if there's time. Reuben and I went the other week.' The words were out before she realised what she'd said and she clocked her brother giving her a look.

They made their way along the slushy path, which led them up through a wooded area and then through a small gate.

'I forgot how steep this path was,' said Murray.

'And how many steps there are.' Jessica looked up towards Conic Hill. She didn't like to think how many steps there were still to climb.

'It will be worth it when we get to the top though. It's a view I love. And look how beautiful it all looks with that blanket of snow,' said Murray, gesturing across the land. 'Just watch your footing in case any of it is slippery.'

They both focused on climbing and then slowed their pace so they could hold a conversation. 'So, how are things in Melbourne then? How does it feel to be home?'

Murray was an accountant in Melbourne. He and Carolyn had moved over there five years ago after he was offered an incredible promotion. 'It's still great. We love the weather and the lifestyle. But . . . since having Lexi, it's made us realise how much we miss family.' Carolyn's parents had both died before they moved to Australia but she was still close to her brothers who both lived in Edinburgh. They were planning to go and visit them after Christmas.

'I can understand that. We miss you too. And Lexi is growing up so fast.'

'I know. Anyway, we shall see what happens. No plans to do anything major yet,' he said quickly.

Jessica knew he didn't want to talk more about what their future plans might entail. Murray had always played his cards close to his chest, too.

'What about you? I get the sense it's not been an easy year for you.'

She shrugged and dipped her head. 'Nope. But I feel much better having been home for a few weeks. I'm glad I took some time away from work.'

He watched her curiously and waited for her to expand.

'Work has been stressful. And . . .' Her voice trailed away.

'Mum told me about the guy you were seeing. I am sorry, Jess.'

She looked across at Murray and grimaced. 'Yes. It wasn't ideal.'

'I wish you'd told me, you know.'

'I didn't really tell anyone. It was too difficult to talk about.'

He nodded, his expression full of compassion. 'I can understand that.'

Jessica felt a tear form in the corner of her eye and she wiped it away. How she had missed seeing her brother and talking to him in person. She always opened up to him when they were physically together in the same place.

'And it sounds like you've been spending time with Reuben?' he said.

Her cheeks flushed. 'Yes, but just as friends, Murray.'

Murray raised an eyebrow and gave her a knowing look.

'Stop it,' she said, growing flustered. 'Stop looking at me like that. I know you're jumping to conclusions. But we are just friends.'

He raised his hands defensively and laughed. 'You are protesting a wee bit too much.'

Jessica stopped to catch her breath just as they reached the summit of the hill. 'Will you be quiet and look at that view.'

They stood and admired the sight below of the string of islands in the loch which were in the exact line of the Highland Boundary Fault. She took a few gulps of fresh air and exhaled.

'It's obvious you both like each other,' said Murray, looking at her curiously.

His words caught her off guard and she felt her heart start to race. 'How so?' she said trying to sound super casual.

'Because I know my friend. He's a pretty laid-back guy. But when we were all together the other day there was a definite tension between you both.'

Jessica looked at him and frowned in disbelief. 'Really?'

He gave a small shrug, his lips curving into a smile. 'Yup. What's the story? Come on, Jess, spill the beans!'

She brushed her hands down over her jacket and tried to keep a neutral smile on her face. 'Nothing's going on. Except . . . Well, he's been a bit off with me since last week.' She paused, thinking back to the fun she thought they'd had, until

Reuben suddenly started acting strangely. 'But that's all on him,' said Jessica briskly. 'I don't know what I've done wrong.'

Murray rolled his eyes as if she was completely clueless. 'It's maybe about self-preservation, Jess.'

'What do you mean?'

'Look at you. You're a successful lawyer living in London and you're only here temporarily. If there is something between you and believe me there is,' Murray said teasingly, 'perhaps he's backed off because he's afraid of getting hurt or making a mistake again.'

Jessica sighed. 'Anyway, it doesn't matter. I swore I would never again get involved with a married or separated man, and the baggage that brings—' Jessica froze. What had she said?

'What do you mean, again?'

She paused while she plucked up the courage to say the words out loud.

'Because Tim was married,' she said, her tone flat as she spoke. 'But I didn't find out until after he'd died. I had no idea.'

CHAPTER THIRTY-THREE

Jessica blinked back tears as they made their way down the hill. But this time the tears were caused by the cold wind nipping at her eyes rather than sadness or frustration. She felt as though she had now done all of her crying for Tim. She rubbed her hands together, glad she had worn gloves.

'How did you find out?' asked Murray gently, his face full of concern.

'When I found out he was dead, I was in a state of shock and didn't know what to do. I didn't know if I should go to his funeral or if there even was a funeral. I hadn't ever met any of his family or friends and all I knew was that he lived in Boston and travelled a lot with work.' She paused so she could navigate a tricky bit of the steep descent. 'Then I realised that all I knew was his name and the company he'd worked for. I started obsessively checking online funeral sites for details of a service or an obituary. I was all set to book myself a flight to Boston and go. I was in love with him. At least, I thought I was.'

Murray shook his head in sorrow. 'Oh, Jess, you poor thing. What an awful thing to go through.'

She thought about the days where she was online from early in the morning until last thing at night, constantly refreshing pages she had checked and checked again in the hope she could find out something about his funeral. She was worried that, because of the delay, she might have missed it. But she knew because of the time of year that things might have slowed down. 'Eventually, I did find an obituary. The funeral had been a private service so I *had* missed it. And when I read the tribute to him, I realised I didn't know him at all. That was when I learned he was survived by his *loving* wife.'

Murray groaned. 'That's awful. What a way to find out.'

'I know. I felt terrible. I had absolutely no idea.' They had now reached the bottom of the hill and were making their way down the path back towards the car park. 'I can't believe we're back already. And I haven't even finished telling you the rest of the story.'

Murray's eyes widened. 'There's *more* — what else could possibly have happened?'

'You can buy the coffees and scones and I will tell you more.'

'You're on.' He slung his arm around her and pulled her in close for a hug before they headed to the café.

As she pulled out one of the chairs she had sat on with Reuben, she felt a sudden pang of longing for him. Especially as that afternoon with him had felt quite intimate. It was when she had opened up properly for the first time.

'Are you okay, sis?' said Murray. 'You seem miles away.'

'Sorry,' she said. 'I'm fine.' She pulled her thoughts away from Reuben and looked at her brother. She wondered what he would think if he knew she was thinking of his best friend in that way.

'You were about to tell me about Tim,' he said gently.

'Yes,' she said, inwardly groaning. 'By the way, I haven't told Mum any of this about him being married.'

'How come? I don't think she would be bothered.'

'I just felt as though I'd offloaded enough and really what difference would it make? I can't change any of it. I just need to try and move on.'

'Go on then,' he said, nodding his thanks to the waitress, who had just set down their coffees and fruit scones.

Jessica looked at her brother. 'Two months after he died, I had to fly back to New York on client business. I had tried to put it off for as long as possible but there was no way I could avoid it unless I wanted to draw attention to the reason I didn't want to return. Nobody really knew the details of what had happened, you see.' She remembered how glad she was that Freda was also flying out with her, how Freda had noticed she was quiet. That was when she told her about Tim. 'I know this is hard for you,' she had said. 'But we are here to work and it will all be done and dusted soon and then we will be back in London.' She remembered how grateful she was for Freda's moral support. Somehow it felt easier to have a colleague there with her rather than be completely on her own. Especially at night when they were back in the hotel.

Murray waited for her to continue.

'At the first meeting, one of the clients was being quite offhand and rude to me and I couldn't work out what was going on. Had I done something wrong? Had I messed up somewhere? Which was possible as I had been so sad and tired. Anyway, it left me feeling totally flustered and I started to second-guess myself.'

Murray opened the pat of butter and started to spread it on the scone. 'Just what you needed,' he said sympathetically.

'Turns out that she was Tim's wife.'

'No!' gasped Murray, clearly shocked. He placed the knife down with a clatter. 'And did she know who *you* were?'

Her lips were pressed tightly together as she nodded. 'She did.'

'What happened next? Did she confront you?'

'Yes, later on, after the meeting, she asked if she could have a quick word. She was actually apologetic for being horrible in the meeting. And said she had been under a lot of stress as she had recently lost her husband. The penny still didn't drop . . . then she announced she was Tim's wife. She said she had worked out who I was from the messages on Tim's phone and couldn't believe that we both worked for the same company. She worked for the Boston firm. This was her way of letting me know she knew all about me and that she was the grieving widow.'

'And were they still together when he died?'

Jessica's gaze fell on the window as she remembered the sense of helplessness she felt when Dana had told her they were still together and that she'd thought that they were happily married. 'I felt awful. I would never ever have become involved if I'd known. I never ever wanted to be the other woman.'

Murray puffed his cheeks out and sighed. 'I guess there are always two sides to every story.'

'And I will never know the truth,' she said, breaking a piece of scone and popping it into her mouth. It made her realise that everything she and Tim had shared was a lie. How could she possibly mourn the death of a man who wasn't hers to love in the first place?

'You didn't suspect a thing about him being married then?' said Murray. He pushed his plate away and wiped his mouth with a napkin.

'Not at all. Though now when I think about it, perhaps the signs had always been there that we didn't have a future together. He was always quite vague about his whereabouts and when he would next be in town. But I just thought that was because he was so busy with work. And I missed him. I missed what I thought we had. Then I reminded myself it was all a lie. It's really made me doubt my ability to trust anyone again.'

'No wonder,' said Murray. 'I can't even begin to imagine the shock.'

'Anyway, his wife has spent much of the past year texting and asking for details of what happened. I know she's hurting and wants closure. Initially, I did try to help, but it's too much. It all came to a head the other night when I was at the inn and I called her to tell her to stop. I just want her to leave me alone and she wasn't getting the message.' Jessica hoped that after their conversation the other night she *would* move on. She felt sorry for her and she wished things were different. But there was nothing else to say. There was no going back. They had both loved Tim in different ways and she knew that hers was a passionate type of love that may not have lasted. But for a while it had consumed her. But now Tim was gone, they both had to move on with their lives. 'Thanks for listening, bruv. It's actually really helped.'

Murray hesitated for a moment before speaking. 'You weren't to know this would happen.' He clenched his jaw and Jessica knew he was angry but was trying his best to refrain from saying what he really wanted to. 'Can I make a suggestion?'

'Sure. Of course you can.'

'You aren't that person, Jessica. You didn't know he was married. It's not your fault so don't let it define you. Move on with your life and find someone who deserves you.' He paused before giving her a sly smile. 'Like Reuben?'

She tried to casually sip her coffee and not react. Reuben aside, Jessica knew his words about Tim made sense, and as she let his advice sink in, she felt a sense of stillness and light-ness move through her. Murray was right. She needed to let Tim go and move on.

CHAPTER THIRTY-FOUR

Reuben sat perched on a stool at the breakfast bar in the kitchen of his flat. For the past hour or so he had been scrolling through various holiday sites and had now lost track of where he wanted to go. He had about fifteen different tabs open on his laptop after clicking on various resorts in the Canary Islands which had looked okay in the pictures. When he glanced out the window, all he could see was a thick bank of dense grey cloud and stark, bare trees. Staring at pictures of bright blue skies, sandy beaches, lush palm trees and magenta flowers was far preferable. But then when he had opened up reviews on Tripadvisor to get the realistic detail of the places he was looking at, he had quickly become overwhelmed and forgotten whether it was Lanzarote that held most appeal or Gran Canaria. He closed the lid of his computer and stretched his hands above his head. The reality was that he still wasn't quite sure what to do. There were only three days until Christmas. He had to make a decision soon. Because if he was going, he would need to fly out either tomorrow or Christmas Eve. And he had to go and see his dad and let Catriona know what his plans were. He already felt bad that he hadn't yet told her if he would be there or not, even though she said to leave it until the last minute.

He slipped off the stool and walked over to the window, looking out as he contemplated his options. He could visit his dad in the care home and then come back to the flat for a dinner for one. He could visit his dad and then go and spend the rest of Christmas Day with Murray's family in Rowan Bay. Which would mean seeing Jessica, who he wanted to avoid, given that he had now created an atmosphere between them. Or he could escape to the sun. Which seemed the obvious and easiest choice. But something in his gut told him it wasn't necessarily the right choice.

His phone buzzed and he saw it was Belinda. 'Hello.'

'Hey, Reubs. It's just me. How are you?'

'Good,' he said guardedly. 'And you? What's up?'

'I was calling to say thanks for the employment advice.'

'That's okay.'

'I've got myself a new job with another marketing company out here and I start after Christmas.'

'That's great news,' he said, genuinely pleased for her.

'And I've heard that the guy who sacked me has just been made redundant from his firm and is moving back to London.'

'Right. How do you feel about that?'

She laughed bitterly. 'Glad. Hopefully it's karma.'

He nodded. 'I hope it means you can move on with your life out there.'

'It does. I'm just very relieved that I've got another job. I wanted to thank you for your help.'

'I didn't do anything,' he said dismissively.

'You did. You gave me some good advice.'

It was Jessica's advice, not mine, he thought sadly. 'I'm glad it helped.'

'I just wanted to wish you a Merry Christmas and a Happy New Year.'

'Same to you.'

'And Reuben . . .'

Reuben felt his stomach sink at what she might say next.

'You deserve to be happy. I really do hope you have a good life.'

'Thanks,' he said softly. 'And the same goes for you.'

'Okay, I'd better go before the girls think I've gone missing in action. We're going out for dinner. After cocktails, of course.' She giggled.

He shook his head, thinking how apt that was. He knew as soon as she had ended the call, she would be toasting the end of her marriage and making plans for a divorce party or some kind of celebration. Which he supposed was fair enough. It just wasn't his style. 'Bye, Belinda.'

'Thanks, Reuben.'

He placed the phone on his worktop, feeling a bit restless. He was relieved they were both in a place where they could move on and get the paperwork finalised. But the last thing he wanted to do was go out and celebrate the end of his marriage. He stood for a moment, wondering what to do. Another workout at the gym didn't appeal in the slightest and neither did going for an afternoon pint at the pub. He was still in two minds as to which holiday he should book. He thought about the case sitting in the hallway. He had pulled it out from the cupboard although hadn't yet started to pack. If he *was* going to be heading to the airport in the next day or two then he had better get himself organised. He still had a couple of presents to buy and would need to take his gifts out to his dad at the care home and then pop past Primrose Cottage with his presents for them. Reuben grabbed his coat and wallet, and before he could change his mind, he was walking briskly to the nearby station to catch the next train into town.

CHAPTER THIRTY-FIVE

Jessica decided to make the most of her day off and go into town. It had been years since she had been into Glasgow's city centre, and she couldn't believe how much it had changed. It was also mobbed, which made sense given the limited number of shopping days until Christmas Day. She was glad she had decided to come in by train rather than try and get parked in one of the multi-storey car parks in the centre. Fortunately, her parents had been doing their final big supermarket shop before Christmas at the big Tesco in Milngavie and they had dropped her at the train station there.

She walked upstairs to the main concourse at the new and revamped Queen Street station and on to George Square which was home to a Christmas market. It had a huge gold-and-blue tree and an ice rink and was bustling with shoppers and people soaking up the festive atmosphere. She could smell the scent of vanilla, ginger and frankincense in the air. Jessica had always enjoyed people watching and she stood for a few minutes doing just that before the damp air made her shiver and move on to keep warm. She made her way towards Buchanan Street, which was a long pedestrianised thoroughfare, and weaved her way in and out of the crowds, feeling slightly alarmed at the number of people who, like her, had left their shopping until the last minute. Jessica wasn't sure she liked being back in a city having now been used to a quieter village life where there was plenty of space and she could see Loch Lomond every day. She chuckled to herself. Who would have thought that she could become a country bumpkin?

She headed to the fancy chocolate shop at the entrance to Princes Square to pick up some whisky truffles for Murray and her dad and also some chocolates for her mum. She just hoped that Lexi would like the fairy costume she had bought for her. As she glanced at the rows of different types of chocolate, the millionaire shortbread chocolates made her think of Reuben and their afternoon at the coffee shop at Balmaha. Impulsively, she picked up a box. She wasn't sure if she would see him at Christmas or even before she returned to London, but surely it would be better to be prepared and have a small festive gesture for him. Her mum hadn't said one way or the other if he was joining them, instead saying it was an open invitation. Murray was equally non-committal and said he didn't know what Reuben's plans were and that he had mentioned he may take himself off to the sun. She couldn't blame him.

Joining the queue to pay, she listened in to the shoppers in front chatting excitedly with each other. After navigating the tills she went out the back of the shop and strolled into Princes Square shopping mall. As she looked around, she couldn't believe how much it had changed. The interior hadn't changed, but the shops all seemed different to when she was last there and there was a small café to the left which she couldn't remember having seen before. Unsure where to go next, she paused for a moment by the escalator and, seeing that someone had just stood up and left their table, she quickly decided to grab it. She would stop and have a quick coffee before deciding where to go next.

She smiled as she sat looking over at the carol singers who were gathered in the courtyard below singing "Hark! The

Herald Angels Sing" and soon found herself humming along in time to the music. This was what she used to love about Christmas. The traditions she used to embrace when she was younger and coming in here to listen to the carol singers had been such a part of that. She pulled out her phone to check her messages then saw her email notifications. She hesitated when she saw two from Dana Matthews. She'd really hoped that the conversation the other day had drawn a line under things and that she wouldn't be back in touch. She opened the first email.

> *Greetings,*
>
> *I hope you have a peaceful holiday season and happy new year.*
>
> *Thanks for your business this past year. I am moving on to pastures new and will no longer be at this email address as of December 20. If you would like to stay in touch do email me for my new contact details.*
>
> *Season's Greetings,*
>
> *Dana*

Jessica frowned. It looked as though she had sent it to all her contacts. Maybe she had actually listened to Jessica on the phone the other night. Maybe she was actually going to move on. Then she clicked on the next email.

> *Dear Jessica,*
>
> *I wanted to reach out and thank you for taking the time to talk to me the other night. I know Tim's death hasn't been easy for you either.*
>
> *I've had some time to process our conversation and wanted to let you know I'm sorry. I'm sorry for taking my anger and grief out on you this past year.*
>
> *I now finally accept that you didn't know my husband was married.*

*I'm moving on to a different chapter in my life, and I
hope we can both find peace with what's happened.
Wishing you all the best,
Dana Matthews*

She read the email again and again before deleting it.
There was no need for them to keep in touch. Jessica had
said all she wanted to and more to the woman this past year.
She truly hoped that she found some peace with whatever she
chose to do next.

Jessica felt the knot of tension in her chest loosen and
as she sipped her latte, she actually felt not just relief but . . .
content. Sighing deeply, she had a feeling that everything was
going to be okay. Coming home for Christmas had been the
best thing she could have done. And telling her brother the
whole story about Tim had lifted a huge burden from her
shoulders. She just wished she had done it sooner.

'Well, well, well,' said a nasally voice behind her. 'Look
who it is. If it isn't Ms Stewart.'

Jessica didn't need to turn around to know who it was. It
was bloody *Zander Harrison*. The patronising client from work
who Ivan had talked to her about just before she went off on
leave. But what on earth was he doing here? In Glasgow? This
was the very last place she would have expected to see him. He
took a seat across from her.

'Fancy seeing you here. Mind if I join you?' he said with
a smirk, not letting her answer. 'I had heard you were on some
kind of extended leave of absence.'

'Hello, Zander,' she said, through gritted teeth. The man
was a complete prick, but she had to remind herself that he
was still a work client. 'What brings you to Glasgow?' She
forced a smile.

'Business,' he said with a shudder. 'Glad to say I'm off to
catch the train back to London soon. And it can't come fast
enough. This is a ghastly place.'

She bristled at how rude he was being. 'Right. Well, don't let me keep you.'

He glanced at his watch. 'I'm not in a rush. I've time to join you for a drink. Though do you fancy something stronger? A *wee* nip of whisky perhaps?'

She shook her head. 'No thanks. I'm fine with my coffee.' She wanted to throw the rest of it in his lap and now felt herself growing edgy as he continued to leer at her.

'Well, that's not very social of you. But I suppose I could have a coffee too.' He clicked his fingers into the air.

'It's self-service,' she said witheringly. *Eejit.*

He rolled his eyes in despair and strode over to bark his order at the waitress behind the counter. All too soon he had sat down again. 'Back at work soon, I hope. I did say to Ivan I'd been missing your company.'

'I'm sure that you've been well looked after by my colleagues,' she said curtly.

He leaned in towards her. 'Yes, but they're not quite like you, are they? You're a feisty *wee* thing.'

She wished he would stop saying the word *wee*. She had never before heard him use it. Did he think he had to keep slipping it into the conversation because he was north of the border? He really was an utter knob.

He sat back. 'Though your colleagues do seem to be more experienced. At least I don't have to keep explaining myself to them.'

Jessica was starting to lose her patience. 'Is that so?'

'I'm only winding you up, of course. But you do always, without fail, take the bait. I rather like that about you, Jessica. You've got a real fire in your belly. It's just a shame that I don't have longer until my train leaves for the big smoke. Otherwise we could have made an evening of it.' He raised an eyebrow suggestively.

Jessica couldn't quite believe what he was saying. He had always been a patronising prick but the fact he was now trying to flirt with her and actually suggest they spend the evening together made her want to vomit. She felt bile rise to the back of her throat and her cheeks flamed in indignation.

'But you do know that I can change my plans? I can get a train in the morning if you catch my drift. I think you'd like that, wouldn't you?'

How dare he. Jessica knew she needed to get out of here now before she punched him. She took a final sip of coffee and put her cup back on its saucer and stood up. 'Actually, do you know what I want, Zander? I want you to piss off. You have crossed a line for the final time.' She pulled on her coat and gathered her bags. 'Make sure you don't miss your train.'

But just as Jessica turned to go, Zander leaned forward and gripped her wrist hard. 'Not so fast. Remember I am the client and the client always gets what they want.'

Jessica flinched and tried to pull away.

'It would be extremely rude of you to leave like this and I'm sure Ivan wouldn't want me to complain again now, would he?'

'Get your hands off me,' she said calmly and firmly, trying to pull her arm away, but he dug his nails into her. He licked his lips and she shivered in disgust. 'Get off me, Zander. *Now*.'

CHAPTER THIRTY-SIX

Reuben had spent the last hour in the Buchanan Galleries shopping centre picking up the gifts he needed. Shopping was not one of his favourite pastimes and he was quite horrified by the frenzied energy that the hordes of shoppers brought to the city centre. He made his way down Buchanan Street, toying with the idea of just catching the next train home. But it had been ages since he'd been to Princes Square and as he made his way into the mall he heard the carol singers. He headed across to the balcony so he could look over at them in the courtyard below. Then he did a double take when he spotted Jessica sitting in the small café next to the escalators. That familiar fluttering in his stomach appeared whenever she was in his line of vision. He knew he should go over and speak to her but felt embarrassed at how aloof he was with her last week. She might not be all that pleased to see him and he wasn't sure he could handle the rejection. He stood for a moment, dithering, and then walked towards her.

As he neared, he realised she had company. It was an older man. He wondered who it was and felt a flicker of jealousy. He wanted to be the one sitting opposite her while they listened to Christmas carols and did their last-minute shopping together.

But he only had himself to blame for being so cool towards her. She probably wouldn't ever want to talk to him again. Then he looked more closely at her face. She was frowning and didn't look very happy with the man. She looked entirely pissed off. He watched as she pulled her coat on and gathered her bags, clearly getting ready to leave. But then the man reached over and grabbed at her wrist, pulling her back. Feeling a surge of anger, Reuben strode towards the table as Jessica tried to pull away. Just as he got to the table, Jessica glanced up and looked at him in relief. He placed a firm hand on the man's shoulder. 'Even from a distance I can see the lady has made herself perfectly clear. Take your hands off her.'

Zander looked round at him in surprise, which caused him to pull his hand away and off Jessica's. 'Mind your own business,' he said, his slimy smile suddenly vanishing.

'This *is* my business.' Reuben glowered down at him and the man shrank under his gaze. 'You're making the lady feel uncomfortable.'

A shaken Jessica took a step back, clutching her bags close.

'And who are you to tell me what to do?' said Zander, standing up suddenly and taking a step towards him.

'Don't make a scene,' said Reuben. 'They don't like fuss in here. The security guards will have you out of here in a second.' He glanced over towards the doors, hoping that a security guard would be there if he *did* start to argue. He glanced over at Jessica. 'Are you okay?'

Jessica looked at him and managed a small nod.

'I don't know who you are or what you think you're doing, but Ms Stewart and I were having a chat about work,' he said with a sneer. 'I'm one of her clients.'

Jessica cleared her throat. 'Actually, that's wrong. You are a bullying misogynist who has no respect for women. I will not represent you ever again, and I am sure Ivan will have plenty to say when he hears what you just tried to do. Now, do as I asked and piss off.'

Zander's face paled.

'Not such a big man now, are you? In fact, you're lucky she didn't give you a Glasgow kiss,' said Reuben firmly. The man looked back at him with a vacant expression, clearly unsure what he meant. 'Google it, you twat.'

And with that, Reuben clasped Jessica's hand and hurried her away from the café and out onto Buchanan Street.

CHAPTER THIRTY-SEVEN

Jessica was grateful for the warmth of Reuben's hand around hers and she didn't want to let go. She gripped it more tightly as he led her through the crowds and out of the way of the main throng of shoppers. Neither of them spoke as they walked up Buchanan Street and away from Zander and Princes Square. Reuben only stopped when they reached the inside of Queen Street station.

He turned to look at her. 'Are you okay?' he said, his voice etched with concern. He reached out and touched her face tenderly.

Jessica put her hand over his. 'Thank you.' She was so glad that he had turned up when he did. Although she had never been the type who needed the cavalry to step in and fight her corner, she wasn't quite sure what she would have done if Reuben hadn't arrived.

'You don't need to thank me,' he said softly. 'I'm just glad that I arrived when I did.'

'Me too.'

'Your face is white. You're in shock.'

Jessica's teeth were now chattering. 'I should probably go home.'

He shook his head and took a long, ragged breath. 'Come back to mine. Let me get you warmed up properly, Jess. And then I'll take you back home to Rowan Bay.'

Jessica was shivering and her mouth felt dry. She nodded at Reuben and he took her shopping bags from her, then reached for her hand, wrapping his fingers tightly around hers.

'Much as I'd like to grab a taxi, I think we'll be quicker getting the train.'

She nodded slowly and followed him in a daze as he led her to the platform downstairs. There were only a few stops to where Reuben's flat was in Hyndland and a train was about to leave. He led her on, his hand at the small of her back, which was reassuring and made her feel better. It made her feel *safe*. She was also too aware of the fact that the nerves in her body were tingling at his touch. It didn't matter how hard she tried not to be, she was so attracted to him, and even more so after he had come to her rescue. The journey was brief and they didn't talk at all. As they left the station, the snow started to fall, and Reuben pulled her close. He kept his arm round her until they got back to his flat, which was a main door apartment in a Victorian building five minutes' walk from the station.

Opening the door, he put down her shopping bags then took her snow-covered jacket from her and she slipped off her shoes.

'Come and sit down,' he said, leading her to the sofa. 'I'll make you some tea.'

'Thank you.' She sank onto the sofa gratefully, shivering.

'Here,' he said, placing a blanket over her shoulders. 'Hopefully you'll start to warm up soon.'

While she waited for him to make the tea, she curled her feet up underneath her and burrowed into the seat. It was dark outside now and she stared at the glow of the street lamps and watched the snow as it fell more heavily and started to blanket the road. She listened to the sounds of horns honking and sirens outside. It was so noisy compared to home. Looking around, she realised that there were no photographs on the walls and no personal touches. Although it was stylishly decorated, with its polished wooden flooring and period touches like the cast iron fireplace with its tiled hearth, she couldn't help noticing how sparsely decorated it was in comparison to Primrose Cottage. It felt like a functional living space rather than a home.

'It's a bit different to Primrose Cottage,' he said, walking back into the room with two mugs.

'You must have read my mind.' She smiled as he handed her a mug. 'It's just very . . . different. A bachelor's pad.'

The air felt charged as though something was about to happen. She leaned forward and put her mug on the floor, her hands growing clammy. She knew she wanted to kiss him. But all of a sudden she was overcome with nerves.

CHAPTER THIRTY-EIGHT

Reuben stood up to close the shutters and took a steadying breath as he stared at the snow outside. He was conscious that it was dark and people walking past could see into his lounge. He couldn't quite believe that Jessica was here with him in his flat and the circumstances that had brought her here. Reuben was furious at the way she'd been treated in town and hated to think what would have happened if he hadn't been there. He had been so worried about her and his priority was to get her away and make sure she was okay. Even though he longed to wrap his arms around her, he didn't want to overstep the mark especially when she'd had such a shock. But he knew he hadn't imagined the look in her eyes today. He had to stop himself from kissing her at the train station even though he desperately wanted to. But first he knew he owed her an apology.

He turned round and went to sit down beside her on the sofa. 'I just wanted to say that I'm sorry I've been offhand with you.' His eyes searched hers. 'I didn't mean to be. I just didn't know what to do with my feelings and that wasn't fair on you.'

'I thought I'd done something wrong,' said Jessica quietly.

He shook his head. 'It was me. I thought there was something between us especially after that kiss at the cottage. But then Belinda turned up and then I heard you on the phone at the inn. And I got the impression you weren't interested because I had been married.'

She nodded. 'Mum told me you'd come by to see me at the inn.'

'I know. I did. It's my own stupid fault. And I'm sorry. I should have spoken to you rather than jumping to conclusions.' He waited, anxious that he hadn't overstepped the mark.

'I'm sorry. I think we've both been confused. I wasn't talking about you on the phone, Reuben. I was talking about Tim.' She glanced away. 'After he died, I found out he'd been married.'

He gently tilted her chin up so she was looking at him. 'And you thought I would judge you for it?'

She nodded. 'I had no idea and if I had . . . then there's no way I would have gone anywhere near him. I hate the thought of getting in the way of someone's relationship.'

'Well, I'm soon to be divorced which I know, on paper, may not be the best catch . . . but I am very much a free agent.' He held his breath, waiting for her to respond.

She smiled and moved closer, leaning towards him and kissing him softly.

Reuben kissed her back, all the tensions and questions that had been hanging between them disappearing. When they pulled apart, she rested her forehead lightly against his.

'Sorry to spoil the moment,' she said with a gentle laugh. 'But can I just go and freshen up?'

He cleared his throat. 'Of course. It's just through the hall and to the right.' He watched her, his gaze unblinking.

Jessica stood up and shrugged off the blanket.

'I'll be right back,' she said.

The butterflies he had in his stomach reminded him of being a teenager when he was awkward and fumbling and unsure of what to do. It had been such a long time since he had made moves on anyone. It was laughable to think he used to be described as a ladies' man because, at the moment, he felt like the absolute opposite. He wished he had consulted the guidebook on how to seduce someone romantically when you'd been out of the game for a while. But when Jessica walked back into the room, he immediately noticed the change of expression on her face. She was no longer looking at him with the longing of five minutes ago. Now she looked withdrawn and he wondered what had happened in the time it had taken for her to cross the hall. Had he left the bathroom in a mess? Were his pants lying on the floor or was there no loo roll? It didn't make sense. What *had* he done?

'You're going away for Christmas?' she said sadly, wrapping her arms around herself and leaning against the radiator.

His heart fell. The bloody suitcase. She must have seen it in the hallway. Why had he left it lying there in full view? He may as well have left a pile of travel brochures by the toilet as well. And some tubes of suntan lotion and a sombrero. He groaned inwardly knowing how it must look to Jessica.

'I saw your case,' she said, spelling it out.

He held up his hands. 'Okay, But if you look inside, you'll find it's empty. Just because my bag is out doesn't mean a thing,' he said, trying his best to make light of it. 'I can understand you being annoyed if I'd left my Speedos out.' His attempt at humour didn't work as Jessica looked at him as if someone had told her Christmas had been cancelled. 'Okay, I was thinking about a trip and I did say to your mum and Murray that I might go away. After everything that has happened with Belinda and my dad. And then you . . .' Reuben paused as if he was searching for the right words. 'Well, things between us had changed and so I needed to clear my head. But I haven't booked anything . . .'

'And are you going to now?' she said quietly.

Reuben stood and crossed the room towards her, overwhelmed by the rush of desire he felt. 'Now, there is nowhere I would rather be than in this room with you.'

Standing close, his eyes searched hers as he rubbed his thumb across her bottom lip. 'I'm definitely not going anywhere.'

She shivered. This time she reached up to press her lips against his. He kissed her deeply back.

She put her hands against his chest. 'Are you sure about that? she said, her focus not wavering.

'Yes,' he said, his voice thick with emotion. 'I realise that I can't escape everything. And I don't want to. Because it doesn't matter where I go, you're always on my mind and in my head.' He leaned in and slowly grazed his lips over hers. 'I've been wanting to do that ever since I first saw you at the bakery that day . . . Jessie.' He could feel her smile against his lips.

'So why didn't you?' she whispered.

'Because you didn't know who I was and then I thought *you thought* I was still your brother's annoying friend. I didn't know if you felt the same way.' He took a step back and looked straight into her eyes.

He smiled at her cautiously and then chanced it with a wink. 'I'm very much a bachelor. Who has no idea what to do any more.'

She reached for him and laced her fingers through his, then lightly kissed him on the lips. 'I'm sure you'll figure it out.'

He shook his head. 'Or you can show me.'

'Just one more thing,' she said, trying but failing to hold him back slightly.

'What's that?' he said, dipping his head to leave a trail of kisses along her collarbone.

She tugged at his hands until he looked at her again. 'Spend Christmas with us in Rowan Bay.'

His heart lurched at the longing he felt for her and he reached to push away a few strands of hair from her face, which was full of hope as she waited for him to reply. 'I would love to spend Christmas with you and your family, Jessie. I just hope your brother doesn't thump me.'

She burst out laughing. 'Something tells me you'll be okay. One other thing I need to ask you, though, which could be a deal-breaker,' she said.

'What's that?' He frowned.

'Please tell me you don't own a pair of Speedos.'

He laughed. 'No, that was supposed to be a joke.'

'It was terrible. So, you'll put the suitcase away then?' she said firmly.

He smirked as he watched her smiling eyes. 'I will put it away right now.'

'There's no rush,' she said, pulling him closer again.

CHAPTER THIRTY-NINE

Jessica opened her eyes, momentarily confused as to where she was. She took in the cornicing on the ceiling and the wooden floors. Then she felt Reuben's arms wrapped around her and he kissed the top of her head. They were still curled up together on the sofa in his flat where they had been since he'd rescued her from Zander. In a panic, she sat bolt upright.

'Hey, what's wrong?' he said.

'What time is it?' She grabbed her bag and looked at her phone, then sighed in relief. 'I thought I'd slept in.'

He chuckled. 'If you're worried about missing your curfew then don't worry. I messaged Murray to let him know you're here and okay and that I'd bring you home later. He was going to let your folks know.' He pulled her back towards him. 'We have loads of time. Don't worry.' He paused for a moment. 'No pressure, but you can stay over.'

She groaned as she felt his stubble graze her mouth and found herself kissing him again. Never before had kissing felt like this. The pressure of Reuben's lips sent sparks of excitement through her body. 'I wish I could but I can't.'

Reuben sat up this time and looked at her, confusion in his eyes.

She chuckled. 'Don't worry. You haven't lost your touch. It's just that I need my beauty sleep.'

He lazily raised an eyebrow. 'I beg to differ.'

She sniffed. 'I've got an early shift at the bakery in the morning. I need to be up before four.'

'Ah,' he said, pushing his sleeve up and glancing at his watch. 'That's okay. I'm happy to get up to take you then.'

'If you're sure,' she said softly, sinking into his arms again. 'I don't want to move.'

'Me neither,' he said, tightening his grip on her. 'But I don't want to be a bad influence on you.'

'As if,' she said, before kissing him again.

* * *

The early morning sky was dark but clear and Jessica looked up at the stars as Reuben drove her home to Thistle Cottage so she could change before her shift. The snow had continued to fall overnight and everything was covered in a white blanket although fortunately the roads had been cleared. It was beautiful and Jessica was the most alive she had felt in such a long time. She couldn't quite believe what had happened in the last twenty-four hours. Especially the stuff with Zander. She frowned as she realised that she would need to call Ivan to tell him, although she was quite sure Zander would already have beaten her to it. He would have made up some story to ensure she was to blame. It would have to wait until later. She still couldn't believe he'd behaved in the way that he had. She was also hugely relieved that Tim's wife had backed off. She was now starting to realise just what a huge and constant strain it had all been for months. But when she looked at Reuben, all the unpleasant thoughts around what had happened disappeared. The last thing she expected to do when she came home to Rowan Bay was to fall for the neighbour. He glanced at her, which made her smile, then reached his hand across to cover hers. 'What will you do now?' she asked.

'After I've made sure you're safely home, I will return and put away my case,' he said. 'Then go to bed and dream about you.'

She felt a ripple of excitement at the way he was looking at her. His eyes were dark and smouldering and she wished he could just keep driving until they could be alone together in a remote cabin in the woods. She sighed in contentment. 'Shall I let my mum know that you'll be joining us on Christmas Day then?'

He nodded. 'Aye. Thank you.'

'And will I tell her what changed your mind?'

He chuckled. 'Yes. The thought of her delicious Christmas dinner.'

She rolled her eyes and playfully smacked him on the arm with a chuckle.

All too soon, Reuben was following the road into the village and making his way to Thistle Cottage. He pulled into the lane and stopped outside, turning the engine off.

'Are you going to mention anything about this to your mum?' he said, reaching over to clasp her hand.

She chewed her lip for a moment as she thought. 'Let's just keep it to ourselves for the moment. It would be nice if we can enjoy this even for a short time before everyone else knows.'

He grinned. 'I'm sure they'll find out soon enough.'

Jessica unclipped her seat belt and turned to look at him. 'Let's hope there are no curtain twitchers watching us kiss goodbye.'

He cupped her face in his hands and looked at every inch of her face. Then he kissed her.

'That was . . . nice,' she said coyly.

'Not sure that was quite the reaction I was going for.'

She paused. 'You'll need to try harder the next time. Thanks for the lift. And thanks for everything. I don't know what I would have done if you hadn't appeared.'

'I'm sure you would have been okay. You're a very capable woman. But I'm very glad I decided to go into town and could help.'

'Me too.' She brushed his lips with hers. 'I'd better go, otherwise I'll be late.'

'I'll call you this afternoon,' he said. 'Hope work goes well.'

'Drive carefully,' she said, kissing him one last time. She watched as he drove away, unable to wipe the beam from her face.

CHAPTER FORTY

Jessica quickly changed as quietly as she could and then trudged down the snowy lane to wait by the bakery door for Struan to open up.

'Morning,' he said gruffly, hurrying along to her, his keys jangling.

'Good morning,' she said cheerily.

He eyed her suspiciously. 'You're awfy happy for this time of the day.'

She grinned. 'That's because it's Christmas soon and it's been snowing.'

'It's bloody freezing,' he grumbled, unlocking the door. 'Come on then, two more shifts to go and that will be us for a good few days.'

She was very glad he had taken the decision to close early on Christmas Eve and not open again until the thirtieth. That meant no early morning alarm calls for five mornings which would be bliss. Especially if she could enjoy some of them with Reuben.

'I'll even put on the Christmas tunes for you today. As a treat.'

Jessica laughed. Struan had banned all Christmas music in the bakery as he said it made him feel completely un-Christmassy. 'I used to quite like that Mariah Carey woman,' he'd said to her and Gillian the other day. 'Then that bloody song, "All I Want for Christmas" was in every shop I went into from October onwards and that was it. Killed it for me. I just can't look at her in the same way.'

Gillian had looked at Jessica. 'I'm sure she's devastated,' she said drily. 'I'm not sure you would necessarily have been her type anyway, Struan.'

He looked affronted. 'You never know. Lots of American women go for Scottish men. Look at *Outlander*. That's all the rage in the States.' He stood there looking quite indignant in his baker's overalls and hat.

'I don't like to break it to you but *Outlander*'s main star is Sam Heughan,' said Gillian.

Struan had shrugged. 'And? What's your point?'

Jessica couldn't help laughing. 'I think what she's trying to say is that she doesn't really think *he* is representative of your average Scottish bloke.'

Struan had harumphed and gone out back muttering to himself.

Now as they switched on the ovens and got ready to bake for the day ahead, Struan turned on the music. The first song to play was "Have Yourself a Merry Little Christmas" and they quietly got on with the baking, the soft hum of festive music filling the kitchen. Neither Jessica or Struan said much, quite content in their shared routine that they had grown used to over the past couple of weeks. Jessica loved the sound of the mixers, the beeping ovens and the scent of cinnamon that filled the air.

'Well, good morning,' said Gillian, running in a couple of hours later looking flustered. 'Sorry I'm a bit late. I meant to try and come in a bit earlier to help, but I slept in.'

'Hey, Gill, don't worry it's all in hand. And now it's the twenty-third of December, Struan says we are *finally* allowed to have Christmas music on in the bakery.'

'Yes, I can hear that. Though not the most obvious choice, is it?' She crinkled her nose in disgust. 'Is that *Luther Vandross*? I didn't know he even had any Christmas hits.'

'He has lots. And there is nothing wrong with Luther,' said Struan firmly. 'At least he can sing, unlike the young numpties of today.' He turned and disappeared through the back.

Gillian shrugged. 'I suppose it makes a change from Slade and Shakin' Stevens.'

Jessica sniggered. 'I've a feeling this could be a whole compilation of Luther's Christmas songs.'

Gillian groaned. 'Well at least it shows he's not a complete Scrooge. *And* he keeps telling me how much he loves the gingerbread house. Struan never praises anything. I think you're maybe making him *lighten* up a bit in his old age.'

Struan wandered through from the back. 'I'll pretend I didn't hear that. Anyway, look what I've got.' He held up three red Santa hats. 'I've even got us some special hats for when we open.'

'Have you been talking to my dad?' said Jessica, remembering his Santa suit. She wondered when he was planning to wear it. She wouldn't be surprised if her mum had hidden it away so that he never wore it.

'Just trying to inject some festive cheer into the workplace,' he said drily. 'Let's get to it. We have a village to feed and standing about here chatting won't get the bread baked.'

Gillian rolled her eyes at Jessica. 'What has happened to him? He's never bothered with anything Christmassy before. See what I mean? I am putting it all down to you. You've definitely changed him. For the better.' She paused as she heard the next song start and had to stifle a laugh as Struan strutted around the kitchen snapping his fingers and wiggling his hips. 'I may have spoken too soon.'

He looked over at her. '*What?* It's "The Mistletoe Jam (Everybody Kiss Somebody)". How can you *not* want to dance?'

'Erm, quite easily,' said Gillian. 'That's one of the worst Christmas songs I've *ever* heard.'

Jessica grinned at how much she loved working with them both. In that moment she felt as if the magic of Christmas was taking hold.

The next hour passed quickly as they worked together to make sure all the loaves and pastries and cakes were ready for when they opened the doors just after eight.

'You're looking very pleased with yourself this morning,' said Gillian, looking at her quizzically. 'Anything you want to share?'

Jessica shook her head and feigned innocence. 'Just happy to be at work with you both.'

'Hmm,' she said suspiciously. 'I don't think I've ever *glowed* in the workplace. But, okay, if you insist. I don't think you're telling me the entire truth,' she continued knowingly, 'but that's okay. You can tell me in your own good time. But if I'm honest, you look like you've had sex.'

Jessica managed to keep her expression blank. She did want to tell Gillian about Reuben but she also didn't want to break their promise to each other to keep things between just them for now. She wondered if Gillian would be surprised.

Gillian looked at her, eyes wide open. 'Did you have sex last night?' she said in a stage whisper.

Jessica shook her head. 'No.' She could feel her cheeks flushing bright red, but before her expression gave her away totally Struan reappeared just at the right time.

'Right,' said Struan. 'That's us just about ready to open. Make sure you're wearing your hats.'

'Can I make a suggestion?' said Gillian.

'Of course,' said Struan. 'Though it depends what it is.'

'Then I would suggest you change the music. Luther's been on a loop for a while now and he could do with a wee rest. So could my ears and you also don't want to scare the punters away.'

He nodded and scratched his chin. 'Fair point. Let's see what else I've got.'

Gillian shook her head. 'This could go anywhere,' she said, wincing as she looked at Jessica.

They braced themselves as they waited for Struan to select his next song. 'Oh,' she said, as Mariah Carey's "All I Want for Christmas" started to play. 'That was unexpected.'

'I've decided to give her another chance,' he said, walking back through. 'It is Christmas after all. And it's snowing.'

'I'm sure Mariah will be delighted,' said Gillian.

Jessica frowned as she saw her dad standing at the door. She hurried over. 'Hi, Dad. I wasn't expecting to see you here so early. We're not quite ready to open.'

His face was white. 'Oh, Jess, love. I couldn't get hold of you on your phone and I didn't want to wake your brother.'

She felt panic setting in. She never had her phone to hand when she was at the bakery. 'What is it? What's wrong?'

'It's your mum. She's had a fall. I don't know what to do.'

'Where is she now?'

'At home. She told me to come and get you.'

Jessica looked at Struan. 'I need to go. Sorry, Struan.'

'Off you go, hen, and don't give it another thought. Me and Gillian will be fine. You go and make sure your mum is okay.'

She pulled off her apron and hat and ran through the back to grab her coat and bag.

Gillian hugged her. 'Call us and let us know if we can do anything.'

'Thanks, I will. Come on, Dad. Let's go.'

CHAPTER FORTY-ONE

Jessica walked as briskly as she could back to Thistle Cottage, mindful that her dad was trying to keep up with her, the road was now a bit icy and he was already in a bit of a state. 'What happened?'

'She slipped going down the stairs this morning. I don't quite know how. I just heard a thump and then a yelp and I went down to find her in a heap.'

Jessica winced at the thought. 'What did she hurt?'

'Her arm. She said it's sore to touch. I got her up and she's sitting on the sofa. But she's very quiet and I'm worried. It's unlike your mum to not say much. I tried making her a cup of tea. But she didn't want one and she wouldn't eat the toast I made her. That's when she asked if I could come and get you. She didn't want to bother Murray in case they were all still asleep.'

Jessica nodded. 'I'm glad you did come and get me and I'm sure she'll be okay. Don't worry, Dad.' She was now becoming more concerned about him — his face was grey. She wasn't used to seeing him in such a tizz.

They got to their lane and Jessica quickened her pace and pulled her key from her bag, unlocking the door. 'Hi, Mum,' she said, running in to see her mum sitting on the sofa. 'Dad told me what happened. How are you feeling?'

'Much better now that you're here. Honestly. He's been making such a fuss, which has made me feel worse.'

Jessica turned to see her dad coming in the door behind her. 'Dad, will you go and put the kettle on while I just see how Mum is doing?'

He nodded and looked over at Catriona with a small shrug. 'Can I get you a cuppa, love?'

'That would be nice. Thanks, Gus.' She waited until he'd disappeared and looked at Jessica. 'I'm only saying that to give him something to do. His tea is awful.'

'What happened, Mum?'

'It was my own silly fault. I was wearing socks and slipped down the stairs.'

'*Mum* . . .'

'I know. How many times did I tell you and Murray not to run down the stairs wearing socks when you were kids? Serves me right. I feel like a right old fool.'

Jessica wanted to give her a big hug but wasn't sure what hurt right now, so instead gently patted her on the back. 'Don't be silly. It's one of those things, Mum. But Dad did say he's worried about you as you've gone very quiet. He said your arm was sore.'

Catriona looked over at the kitchen door to make sure he wasn't standing there and lowered her voice. 'He was fussing and that stresses me out.'

Jessica shook her head kindly. 'Never mind that. How is your arm?'

'It's very sore,' she said. 'I really do think it might be broken.'

'Okay. What should we do then? Do you want me to call the doctor? Or take you up to the hospital?'

'There's no point in phoning the doctor. You'll be held in a queue and be there all day and lucky if you get an appointment three weeks on Tuesday. They'll likely need an X-ray anyway. Do you mind just running me up to Larbert? I'm sorry, dear. Sorry to be a pain. Especially with it being so cold and snowy out there.'

'Oh, Mum,' said Jessica tenderly. 'There's no need to apologise. Of course I'll take you to the hospital.'

'Hospital?' said Angus, who appeared at that moment with a tray of mugs. He clattered it onto the coffee table and the tea sloshed over the rim of the cups.

'Honestly,' said Catriona sharply. 'There's no need to panic. Jessica will nip me up to the hospital and get it checked out. I'm sure it's just a sprain.'

Angus stood up tall. 'Righto. I'll come too.'

Jessica felt her mum's pointy elbow in her ribs. She was clearly making the most of her good arm. 'Dad,' she said decisively. 'I think it would be better if you stayed here. You can let Murray know what has happened. And it might be better if I go anyway.'

'Yes,' said her mum. 'She wants to come and check out the doctors.'

'Do I?' said Jessica, puzzled.

'Yes. There might be some handsome doctors there. Didn't you say that you knew a doctor there?'

'Um,' she said uncertainly, now realising her mum really didn't want her dad to come along. 'I'm sure I did.'

'There's also a parcel being delivered this morning. Someone needs to be here for that.'

'Well, okay, if you're sure. But I'm really not all that happy about not coming with you.' He scratched his head.

'Dad,' Jessica said soothingly. 'Don't worry. I'll call you as soon as we know what's wrong and I'll take good care of Mum.'

'Hmm, make sure you do. Don't get all distracted by the first man in a white coat to come along.'

Why was she even having this conversation? The only man she wanted to talk to or look at was Reuben.

'Right, come on then, Mum. Let's go. Can you manage to get your jacket on, do you think?'

Catriona stood up and winced. 'I don't think I can, love. It's awfully tender.'

'Let's just get your shoes on and get you in the car and I can pop a blanket over you. At least you're dressed.'

She managed a small smile. 'I know. I would have been the talk of the village if I'd still been in my pyjamas.'

As they made their way outside, her dad fussing around them, Jessica unlocked the car and made sure her mum was as comfortable as she could be. She then got in and started the engine. Lowering the window, she said, 'I'll call you as soon as we're there and have seen someone.'

'Thanks, dear. Look after her.'

'Go back inside now and warm up. You've had a fright too.'

'Oh, Jess . . .' said her mum, her voice trailing away.

'Is it painful, Mum?'

'Well, yes, it is but it's not that. The timing of it is awful. It's Christmas Eve tomorrow and I've got so much still to do.'

Jessica reached over and patted her mum's knee. 'Let's just see what the doctor says. One step at a time.'

CHAPTER FORTY-TWO

Later that day, Reuben tried to call Jessica's phone again, but it was switched off. He knew she was working at the bakery until lunchtime. Maybe she had been asked to stay on later as it was busy. He was longing to speak to her and hear her voice. In the meantime, he thought he would call Catriona and find out if there was anything he could take with him to help with Christmas Day.

'Hi, Angus,' he said when he picked up the phone after just one ring. 'It's Reuben.'

'Oh, Reuben, I thought you were Jessica. I'm waiting for her to call. She's at the hospital.' Angus was talking quickly and sounded very flustered, which wasn't like him at all.

'What do you mean? Why's she at the hospital?' His mind immediately started to flood with questions as he wondered what had happened. Had she had an accident at work or fallen ill suddenly?

'It's Catriona. She had a fall earlier and hurt her arm. Jessica's away up to Larbert with her. I'm just waiting for her to tell me what's going on. They wouldn't let me go with them, you see. Said something about Jessica wanting to check out the doctors or something like that.'

Reuben frowned. That didn't sound right but then Angus didn't sound like himself at all. He was clearly worried and very anxious. 'Does Murray know? Is he with you?'

'I'm supposed to tell him but I didn't want to wake him up and I'm meant to stay in for a parcel.'

'Okay,' said Reuben. 'I'll phone Murray now and let him know what's going on. I'm sure he'll be with you soon.'

'Thanks, son. I'd better get off the line in case they're trying to get hold of me.'

'Bye, Angus.' Reuben ended the call and grabbed his jacket and car keys and let himself out of his flat. As soon as he got into the car, he called Murray to fill him in. 'Sounds like your dad is in a bit of a state. He didn't want to disturb you in case you were still asleep.'

'Thanks for letting me know. I had no idea. Mind you, we did end up sleeping in a bit later this morning. Well, after a five o'clock start with the wee one. I'll go and check on him now. You said Jessica would call when there's news?'

'Yes, that's what your dad said. I tried her phone earlier and it's switched off. I'll head over now anyway, in case I can do anything to help.'

Murray sighed. 'Thanks, Reuben. I appreciate it. See you when you get here.'

Fortunately, the roads had been gritted but the traffic was busy and Reuben could feel himself getting frustrated as he tried to manoeuvre his way out of traffic, ignoring the horns being honked behind him. He tried calling Jessica's number again and was surprised to hear it ring.

'Reuben,' she said, sounding out of breath. 'I was just about to call you. Give me a second. I've just come outside and it's freezing.'

'Take your time,' he said. 'I've heard about your mum. How is she?'

'She's broken her arm. She's in a lot of pain but putting on a brave face. I think she's more annoyed at the timing of it all. As you can imagine. We're just waiting for her to have a plaster cast put on. I'm not sure how long that will take.'

'Oh, Jess, I'm sorry. Have you updated your dad yet?'

'I'm just about to phone him. He's been in a bit of a state. I've never seen him look so flustered.'

'He's just worried about your mum,' said Reuben softly.

'I know and she hates it when he fusses, which is why she wanted me to go to the hospital with her.'

Reuben laughed. 'Nothing to do with you wanting to check out the hot doctors then?'

Jessica groaned. 'That was my mum's idea for an excuse. She was trying to get my dad to stay at home. *Honestly.* Now my dad thinks I'm just here to check out the talent. Which I'm not by the way.'

He chuckled softly. 'Murray should be with your dad now and I'm heading over, too. Are you okay?'

'I am now,' she said huskily. 'I'll update Dad and then go and grab a coffee. I'll phone you later on. I'm not sure how long we'll be here for.'

'Sure. Phone me if you need anything at all.'

'I will.'

'And Jess . . .' He hesitated, unsure what to say without sounding cheesy or creepy.

'I know, Reuben,' she said. 'I can't wait to see you too.'

CHAPTER FORTY-THREE

After speaking to her dad and reassuring him that her mum was okay, Jessica had a quick debrief with Murray. 'We could be here for a while but hopefully she won't be kept in overnight. I don't think that would land well with her. She's champing at the bit to get home. The best thing you can do is keep Dad calm as he's been freaking out, and I'll find out from Mum if anything urgent needs doing at home. I'm sure between us we can manage to pick up the turkey from the butcher's and rustle up Christmas lunch. How hard can it be?'

Murray tutted. 'Don't let Mum hear you say that. But honestly, she is always running about after everyone else. It's time she just did as she was told and looked after herself. I agree. We can take care of Christmas.'

'Exactly,' said Jessica. 'And I haven't yet told her but Reuben is going to be joining us after all. I'm sure he and Carolyn will muck in.'

'That's great. So, he's not going away after all then . . . Mind you, I didn't think he would.' He paused. 'It sounds like there are more interesting things to keep him in Rowan Bay.'

He was trying to wind her up but she refused to take the bait. 'He's keen to see his dad on Christmas Day and I'm sure he wouldn't mind seeing you either. Though I don't know why,' she said, jokingly. 'Your chat stinks.'

'He's actually just off the phone and is heading out here now. Keep in touch, sis, and let me know if you need us to come and get you. I know you've been up since the crack of dawn and may not want to drive back.'

'Thank you. And maybe Lexi and Carolyn could be a good distraction for Dad in the meantime? Get them to take him down to the loch and skim stones or something? Tell them that I always beat you at it.'

He chuckled. 'I'm not sure she needs to know that at this stage in her life. There is still room for me to beat you. Anyway, you're right, Lexi will put a smile on his face for sure. Phone me later and take care.'

'Oh, I almost forgot. If things get bad with Dad and he needs a distraction then ask him about his Santa suit. I'm sure he'd love to put it to good use.'

Murray groaned. 'I'll leave it until we're desperate. I don't even want to start to imagine what Dad would look like in a Santa suit. Doesn't bear thinking about.'

After ending the call, she walked back to the small cubicle where her mum was waiting. 'Everyone is up to speed now and you've to do as you're told and just get better. You've to be a good patient.'

'But Christmas dinner . . .'

Jessica did feel sorry for her mum. She was always so capable and healthy and hated even catching a cold. She always loved being the host and it wasn't often she had her family around her. And now she was stuck in this cubicle in pain, just two days before Christmas. 'Look, Mum, please don't worry. It will all be fine. Murray and I will make sure it's all sorted and you can tell us what to do. Think of us as your task force and you're the team leader who is delegating from the sofa. And we will all be there to keep Dad calm.' She paused and reached for her mum's hand. 'You know he only gets in a flap because he's worried about you.'

She nodded, clearly upset at the whole situation. 'I know, dear. He means well. But when he flaps it makes me more anxious and then I get stroppy.' Her eyes pricked with tears.

Jessica tilted her head at her mum. 'Dad knows you don't mean it though.'

She shook her head. 'We're not as young as we once were. We keep needing to remind ourselves of that. What on earth was I thinking wearing socks to go downstairs.'

'You're hardly decrepit, Mum. You just slipped. It could have been me or Dad or anyone. *That's what slippers are for,*' she said, mimicking what her mum always used to say to her when she was spotted in just stockinged feet. 'Look, hopefully they will get a cast on you soon and then we can get you home. Then you can sit with your feet up and relax.'

'I'm not sure I know how to do that any more,' admitted her mum.

'Well maybe this is a gift and a reminder to slow down,' suggested Jessica. 'Just sit on the sofa with Lexi and make the most of the time you have with her.' She reached over and carefully gave her mum a hug. 'You're always running around helping everyone else. Now let us help you.'

'Thanks, dear,' she said with a sniff.

Jessica passed her a tissue. 'Would it make you feel better to know that we also have an extra guest for Christmas dinner?'

She was immediately intrigued. 'Oh, who is that then?'

'Reuben's going to join us after all.'

She tried to clap her hands together in delight but couldn't. 'Ouch. That's great news, dear. That has cheered me up no end. Oh, I am glad he's decided to come and won't be on his own in some random holiday resort.' She lowered her voice. 'And I'm so glad he's decided to divorce that woman.'

'You knew?' said Jessica in surprise.

She nodded. 'Yes, he told me the other night when he came over. Before Murray arrived.' She tapped her nose. 'But I don't like to gossip. I knew he would tell you when he was ready. Anyway, for what it's worth, I think he's made the right decision. I never really liked her. Can you pass the water please, dear?' She took a sip from the small cup of water that Jessica gave her. 'And let him know he's very welcome to stay with us. It's the least we can do given that the Stewart family has taken over his house.'

Jessica nodded. 'I will do.' She watched her mum's mind go into full organisational mode.

'You need to make sure the sofa bed in the love room is ready for him. And that he has clean towels . . .' Her mum stopped talking suddenly and stared at her expectantly. 'Unless there's anything else you need to add? Is there anything that I should know?'

'Nothing at all, Mum. Nope, not at the moment. And I promise, I will make sure the love room is ready to go. Though let's call it the reading room or the spare room. That sounds a bit more *appropriate*.'

Her Mum gave her a knowing look. 'I think love room is much more apt, don't you think?'

Jessica shook her head in exasperation and managed to stifle a grin.

CHAPTER FORTY-FOUR

It was Christmas Eve and even though she had spent most of the previous day with her mum at the hospital, Jessica didn't want to miss this morning at the bakery. Especially as it was Christmas Eve. After her mum's cast had been applied, the doctor had decided she was good to go as long as she promised to take things easy.

'Of course I will,' she'd said sweetly. 'I will do as I'm told and my daughter is here to look after me.'

The doctor nodded and smiled, glancing over at Jessica. When he left the room, her mum looked at her.

'What?' said Jessica.

'He seemed a nice young man, didn't he? Bit of a looker?'

Jessica shook her head in despair. 'I'm not sure you can say stuff like that any more, Mum. But, yes, I'm sure he's very good at his job.'

Catriona had raised an eyebrow and looked at her in that infuriatingly knowing way that she did. 'At least it's something to tell your dad.'

Jessica was grateful that Murray and Reuben had come to collect them. She was exhausted and wasn't quite sure she would have been able to keep her eyes open on the drive home. Murray had driven their parents' car back and Reuben had taken Jessica and her mum.

'Now, Reuben,' Catriona had said from the back seat of the car, clearly back in the swing of things now that the painkillers had started to work. 'Please do come and stay with us so you're not waking up on your own in Glasgow. I've told Jessica to get the love room ready for you.' Jessica's cheeks flamed and she knew she couldn't risk making eye contact with Reuben.

He kept his eyes on the road ahead and cleared his throat.

'Mum means the reading room upstairs. Where she keeps all her romance books.'

'I'm a real sucker for a good romance book,' he said diplomatically. 'You can perhaps recommend one to me?'

Jessica had looked round at her mum, who sat there looking the picture of innocence.

'Of course I will, dear. So that's a yes then? You'll stay?'

'Thanks, Catriona,' he said grinning. 'That's really kind of you. I would like that. Is that okay with you, Jessie?' He winked at her.

Once back at the cottage, they had made sure Catriona was comfortable and settled on the sofa with a cup of tea and Angus next to her. Reuben and Jessica sat at the kitchen table.

'You look tired too,' said Reuben. 'Are you going to go to bed and try and get some rest?'

'I will,' she said yawning. 'I need to go to work tomorrow and I don't want to let them down. I do feel like I could face plant right here at this table.'

'Come on,' he said huskily. 'You go and get some sleep. And I'll head off.'

She stood up, dragging her feet. 'And you'll stay with us tomorrow?' She wasn't too tired to notice the playful smile tug at his lips.

'In the love room? How can I resist.' He pulled her close and kissed her, only moving away when they heard Angus move around next door.

It hadn't taken Jessica long to fall asleep and she had slept well, dreaming of Reuben and waking with a smile on her face.

* * *

The time at the bakery had flown and there was only an hour left until closing time. Gillian and Struan had both greeted her with a hug when she arrived first thing, clearly grateful she was back and that her mum was okay.

'I hope we've got enough to last us until lunchtime,' said Struan. 'There's some more loaves out back but not many.' He surveyed the counter display which was starting to look sparse. 'The cinnamon buns are all away and there's only a few mince pies left.'

'Yes,' said Gillian, who appeared with another tray of buns and pies. 'But you've forgotten that we decided to make an extra batch in case. And anyway, folk will start coming in for their sausage rolls soon and pies.'

Struan, wearing his Santa hat again, nodded in agreement.

Just then the door opened and Iris, who ran the bottle tombola at the Christmas fair, came in with a woman who looked around the same age as Jessica and Gillian. She wore an orange woollen coat over a pair of blue dungarees and she had a knitted hat over her long, dark hair.

'Good morning,' said Jessica, pleased to see Iris.

'Hello, dear,' said Iris, her eyes twinkling. 'How are you? I heard about your mum and her broken arm. How is she?'

'I know,' said Jessica. 'But she's okay. We're here to look after her and she's been told to rest and make the most of it while she can. I've left her in the capable hands of my dad this morning.'

'It's lovely you're home to be with her. *And* I saw Reuben earlier at The Wee Bookshop,' she said knowingly. 'He said he's spending Christmas with you, too.' She gave Jessica a wink.

She could feel her cheeks redden, and Gillian was now looking at her strangely.

'Who's this then?' said Jessica quickly.

'This is my granddaughter, Flora,' Iris said, smiling proudly at the woman standing next to her.

'Nice to meet you, Flora. Are you here for Christmas?'

Flora nodded and grinned.

'That's so nice for your gran.'

Iris beamed. 'Yes, it will be nice to have some company. Otherwise, it's just me and the boys.'

Jessica looked at her in confusion. 'The boys?' Had she missed something? Did Iris have lodgers or new men in her life?

'Scrumpy and Sidney,' said Iris as way of explanation.

Jessica remembered she had mentioned them at the Christmas fair.

Flora chuckled and cleared her throat. 'They're Gran's rescue parrots,' she explained.

'Ah, I see,' said Jessica with a laugh. 'I did wonder who you were talking about.'

'Did you think I'd found two new men for myself?' She chuckled. 'Sadly not, but I do love them dearly. You should pop in and see them sometime before you go back to London. They would love to say hello.'

'She's not joking about the saying hello bit,' said Flora. 'In fact, some of their chat is quite interesting.'

Jessica nodded at her with a smile and then the realisation of all of *this* coming to an end soon started to dawn on her. She turned away as she felt tears spring in her eyes and busied herself restocking the counter.

'Oh good,' said Flora. 'Gran has been telling me about these cinnamon buns and I thought you had sold out and we'd missed them.'

'You're in luck,' said Gillian warmly.

Iris looked at Jessica conspiratorially. 'Are these ones yours, dear?' she said in a whisper.

Jessica nodded.

'Don't tell Struan, but yours are way nicer than his.'

240

'Thanks,' said Jessica, grateful for the compliment. 'I won't say a word.'

After they'd left the shop, she knew she was being watched. She turned to find Gillian leaning against the doorway of the kitchen with her arms folded. She raised an eyebrow. 'Care to share anything with me?'

'What do you mean?'

'You didn't tell me Reuben was spending Christmas with you,' she screeched.

Jessica tried to shrug nonchalantly. 'He's not just spending it with me. It's all of us. Mum didn't want him on his own.'

'Mm-hmm. And you?'

'I'll do whatever will keep my mum happy.'

Gillian waited for Jessica to expand, and when she didn't, she tutted in frustration. 'I know you, Ms Stewart, and I know when you're not telling the truth. Something is afoot.'

Jessica feigned innocence. 'Is Millie excited about Santa coming later?'

She rolled her eyes. 'Don't think I don't know what you're up to. Trying to change the conversation, not very subtly at all. But, yes, since you ask, she is. We've been on the final count-down for what seems like weeks. Let's just say that I don't think I'll be having a lie-in tomorrow morning.'

Jessica grinned at her. 'That's the best part of Christmas. Being small and getting up really early to open your presents and eat chocolate and then going back to bed.'

Gillian nodded at her. 'Is that what you and Reuben plan to do too?'

Another flurry of customers came in the door at that moment.

'Looks like I've been saved by the bell,' said Jessica good-naturedly.

Less than an hour later, Struan had turned the sign to say *Closed* and he sighed. 'Phew. Girls, thank you so much. I couldn't have done any of it without you. You have both worked so hard.' He choked back a sob which had Gillian looking at Jessica with a panicked expression. Struan had never shown any sign of emotion, just general grumpiness since she'd met him. The last couple of days he had really relaxed and been happier around them.

'Are you okay?' said Jessica kindly.

'I'm fine. Just a wee bit emotional. And tired.' He cleared his throat. 'Anyway, look, you two head away and I'll finish off here. You've got your families to go and see to. Have a very happy Christmas both of you.' Then he handed them both a Christmas gift bag. 'Just a wee something from me to say thank you.'

Gillian flung her arms round him and Jessica joined their group hug, too. 'It's been fun, Struan. Thanks for letting me help out.'

He shrugged and adopted his grumpy face again. 'That's fine, doll. Enjoy your time off and we'll see you again on the thirtieth?'

Jessica nodded. 'And you enjoy time with your sister in Stirling.'

He rolled his eyes. 'Aye, can't say I'm looking forward to it but at least she'll be doing the cooking.'

'We will really miss you when you go, Jess,' said Gillian.

Jessica nodded, a lump forming in her throat. 'Come on, let's not get teary yet. By the time I go back to London, you'll be ready to see the back of me.' She gave Gillian a hug and a couple of small packages for her and Millie.

Gillian looked genuinely touched. 'Thank you,' she said. 'It's been just pure brilliant having you around.'

They pulled on their coats and hats and Jessica turned on her phone to see a message from Freda, thanking her for the present she'd sent. There were also several missed calls from Ivan. *Oh shit.* With all the drama of her mum's broken arm yesterday, she had completely forgotten that she should have called him. She was quite sure that Zander would've already been in touch and tried to throw her under the bus. She said a final goodbye to Gillian and then, with a clammy shiver, she dialled Ivan's number.

CHAPTER FORTY-FIVE

It didn't take long for Ivan to answer. 'Hi, Jessica,' he said briskly.

'Ivan.' She steeled herself for the barrage that she was expecting to hear. But as she walked up the high street towards home, she realised she didn't actually care that much what he said to her. She knew she hadn't done anything wrong. She waved at Moira, who was standing in the window of The Bay, and then smiled at Emmet, from the sauna, as he cycled past with a cheery wave and grin.

Ivan cleared his throat. 'I've had Zander on the phone and, well, I owe you an apology. I didn't fully appreciate just how much of an arse he was. I'm sorry that I didn't take on board what you said previously to me about his behaviour.'

Jessica was taken aback. That wasn't what she had been expecting Ivan to say at all. 'What did he say?'

'He called me like a bleating lamb to tell me he had bumped into you in Glasgow and you had insisted he join you for a drink. As soon as he said that I knew he was lying. You're on leave for God's sake and he's probably the last person on the planet you would choose to have a drink with.'

'I see,' said Jessica, wondering if he was going to expand. She crossed the road and could smell the comforting scent of a wood burning stove in the air.

'He said you'd acted very inappropriately and had crossed the client line with the things you said to him.'

'Is that right?' said Jessica, now intrigued to hear more about the story Zander had spun.

Ivan sighed. 'I will spare you all the grizzly details. But suffice to say I am sorry I didn't do something earlier and I'm also very sorry for any additional stress this has caused you. Especially when you're supposed to be having a proper break from work.'

'Thanks, Ivan. I suspected he'd call you and make out it was all my fault. But he pretty much accosted me at the café I was in and then wouldn't leave me alone. Fortunately, a friend turned up at the right moment. He was totally out of order. I can safely say I won't ever be working with that man again.'

'I know, and you won't need to.'

Jessica snorted, wondering which one of her poor colleagues was going to have to deal with him next. Freda would be sure to give him short shrift too.

'I've told him to take his business elsewhere.'

'Really?' said Jessica, stunned. This was *unheard* of.

'Yes. His behaviour has been totally unacceptable and I know you can handle yourself but not everyone in this firm can. I can't have him behaving like this around you or any of the younger associates. We're supposed to be employment law experts. He makes a complete mockery of that. In fact, he's lucky that we're not taking any action against him.'

Jessica's shoulders sagged in relief. She was so glad she didn't have to try and fight her corner again and that Ivan had actually defended her. 'Thank you, Ivan.'

'Don't mention it. Okay, I'd better go and leave you to your Christmas preparations. And I had better go and start my shopping otherwise Martha will quite probably kill me.'

Jessica laughed. It wasn't often that he mentioned anything to do with his personal life. It was only rare slips like this that gave her a glimpse into his private life and his long-term girlfriend, Martha. 'I hope you have a good Christmas, Ivan, and thanks for phoning to tell me.'

'Bye, Jessica. See you in the new year.' He ended the call.

The new year was in just over a week. She pushed the thought aside for now. In the meantime, she would focus on Christmas.

CHAPTER FORTY-SIX

Reuben loved watching Jessica play with her niece and the doting look she had on her face whenever she was around her. She was sprawled on the lounge floor at Primrose Cottage helping Lexi build a tower with wooden blocks. Murray had just come in from a walk with Carolyn, thankful they could make the most of willing babysitters.

'Hey, Lexi,' called Carolyn, and she laughed as she was ignored by her daughter. Lexi's face was a picture of concentration as she tried to balance another block on their tower.

'Oh!' she squealed in excitement.

'I know,' said Jessica. 'It's the highest we've got yet.' She glanced up at her brother, whose face was pink from fresh air. 'Did you know when I was a wee girl, your daddy knocked down everything I built.'

Lexi frowned and looked at her dad in disbelief, her eyes wide.

'As if I would do such a thing,' he said brightly. 'Jess, try not to destroy my reputation with my daughter just yet.'

'Reubs,' said Lexi, shyly pointing at the blocks.

Reuben crouched down next to her and handed her a block. She looked at it. Her tongue stuck out the corner of her mouth as she focused on where to put it. Then she turned round and handed it to Reuben. 'You go.'

'Try not to mess it up,' said Murray drily.

'No pressure then,' he said, looking at Jessica and gingerly adding it to the top. It wobbled slightly.

Jessica pulled a face. 'What do you think, Lexi? Can we try one more?'

She giggled and clapped her hands. 'Daddy do it.'

Murray groaned. 'What could possibly go wrong?' He knelt down on the ground and assessed his options. 'What do you think, Reuben? You're the architect.'

He shrugged. 'Don't ask me.' He laughed at Carolyn, who stood watching, a nervous look on her face.

'Rather him than me,' she said.

'Okay. Let me try this then.' Murray carefully leaned over and carefully placed the block on top of the towering stack.

They all watched, with bated breath, as it wobbled and jiggled and then tumbled to the ground.

'Daddy,' said Lexi. 'Silly Daddy.'

Reuben shook his head at his friend. 'Indeed.'

As Lexi and Jessica started to build the tower again, he glanced at the clock. It was nearing four o'clock and he wondered if, in fact, he should head off and leave them all to enjoy Christmas Eve together.

'What's the plan tonight then?' said Murray.

Reuben looked over at Jessica, who was deep in concentration.

'Are you not going to stay with us in Rowan Bay and help put things out for Santa and the reindeer?' said Murray with a wink.

Lexi looked up at him. 'Cawwots for reydeer. Biccies and milk for Santa.'

Murray grinned. 'And you need to make sure you go to sleep even though you're very excited,' he said softly to her. 'So that when you wake up in the morning it will be Christmas Day.'

She beamed at him, stood up and excitedly danced round in circles.

'Come on, poppet,' said Carolyn. 'Why don't we go up and see Granny and Grampa for a wee while before tea?'

'Okay,' said Lexi and ran to the kitchen to fetch something.

Jessica looked over at him. 'You are staying with us tonight, aren't you? Have you got your stuff with you?'

He nodded, slightly embarrassed that he was so prepared. 'Yes, my overnight bag is in the car.'

Murray raised an eyebrow at him and smirked. 'The love room awaits you.' Murray stood up and looked over at Carolyn. 'I'll come with you to see Mum and Dad.' He then waited until she and Jessica were out of earshot in the kitchen with Lexi, before placing a hand on Reuben's arm. 'Just remember, the third stair from the top still creaks and Jessica's door also tends to squeak. You know . . . just thought I'd mention it.'

Reuben breathed a sigh of relief. There was obviously no need to worry that Murray was going to be annoyed about him and Jessica getting together. He was practically encouraging it. But he didn't want to say anything that would confirm things either way. 'I don't know what you mean. I'm a total gentleman, as you well know. I'm just here to enjoy Christmas with you all.'

'What was that?' said Carolyn as she and Jessica came back through with Lexi.

Reuben smiled pleasantly at Carolyn. 'I was just telling your husband that he is a very lucky man. I don't know how you put up with him. He's a complete pain in the neck.'

'Thanks, mate.' Murray linked his arm through Reuben's. 'I always know I can rely on you to say the right thing. And that is why I have missed you. It's great to be back.'

'The bromance is back then?' teased Jessica.

Murray shook his head in exasperation.

'You guys go ahead and have some time with Mum and Dad,' Jessica said to Murray and Carolyn. 'Reuben and I will come up in half an hour or so to get food in the oven. Just make sure Mum doesn't try and do anything. You know what she's like even with a broken arm.'

'Will do,' said Murray, pulling on his jacket. He gave them both a look. 'See you soon.'

As soon as the front door closed, Reuben turned and pulled Jessica towards him, kissing her hungrily on the lips. 'I've been wanting to do that all afternoon,' he said.

She smiled at him. 'I know. Me too.'

'By the way, I think your brother knows about us.'

She hooked her hands around his neck and leaned up to kiss him again. 'He doesn't. He's just teasing you.'

He levelled his gaze on hers. 'Does it bother you if he does?'

She crinkled her nose for a moment then looked up at him. 'Not in the slightest. But I quite like all this subterfuge. It feels a bit *naughty*. Let's just try and keep it our secret while we can.'

CHAPTER FORTY-SEVEN

Jessica realised some secrets were not meant to last. Especially when her big secret, Reuben, was in such close physical proximity. It was Christmas Day and she had woken up with a grin on her face when she realised that Reuben was lying next to her. Ironically, he wasn't in bed with her because they'd had a night of wild passion but because they'd sat up late chatting.

'Hey,' he said, looking at her with a smile. 'Good morning, Jessie. Merry Christmas.' He leaned across to kiss her.

She groaned. 'So much for us keeping this under wraps. I just hope you don't come face to face with my mum at my doorway.'

He chuckled. 'I know, and there we were having such a reckless and thrilling night too. My chat was so scintillating that you fell asleep mid-sentence.'

She giggled. 'I'm sure this is a first for you, Reuben Campbell. Have you ever just slept in bed with a woman without actually sleeping *with* her?'

He rolled onto his side and tucked the pillow under his head, his eyes twinkling mischievously. 'I think you've got the wrong impression of me. What makes you think that I was ever that type of guy?'

She looked at him incredulously. 'Because you absolutely were. And you know it. You were known as the Lothario of Rowan Bay.'

He looked at her in disbelief. 'I wasn't that bad, was I?'

'Yes,' said Jessica firmly. 'You were known as a total ladies' man.'

He looked sheepish and chewed his lower lip. 'What can I say? I am a different and better human being now.'

She wriggled closer to him so their faces were just inches away. 'I do hope so.' His dark eyes swept over her and she grazed her lips against his.

Reuben kissed her deeply back, then gazed at her. 'I wish we could stay like this all day.'

'Me too,' she said, her heart starting to race as he moved to kiss her again.

Then they heard clattering and banging downstairs.

'What on earth is that?' said Reuben as he sat up suddenly.

She chuckled. 'That's our cue to get up. That is the sound of my dad, as it'd better not be my mum, emptying the dishwasher.'

'Noisy,' he said, yawning. 'Sounds like he is launching it from ten metres away.'

'Yup. That's why I started helping at the bakery. There's never a chance of a lie-in when you're here. Just wait. It will soon get noisier.' Sure enough, the radio was switched on and then the blender.

Reuben laughed in disbelief. 'You're not joking.'

Jessica shook her head. 'Nope. Dad has taken to making Mum smoothies to boost her energy levels. And deplete my sleep levels. Let's get up. There's loads to do and I'd better go and check on Mum. She's not a fan of the smoothies.' She gave him one last lingering kiss, a promise of more to come.

* * *

After breakfast they sat by the tree in the front room of Thistle Cottage and exchanged gifts with Jessica's parents. Catriona handed them both a stocking and Jessica smiled when she saw the look of surprise on Reuben's face. His was a red felt stocking with little jingle bells sewn into the cuff.

'I made it at the craft class,' she said proudly. 'We couldn't leave you out, Reuben. You're part of the family too.'

'Thank you,' he said, clearly touched.

Jessica watched him as he looked down at the stocking as though he wasn't quite sure what to do with it. She could tell he was overwhelmed and she gave him a reassuring smile when he glanced up and caught her eye.

After opening their stockings, they all took turns exchanging gifts. Her dad looked delighted as he unwrapped whisky truffles and a bottle of whisky, inspecting the label, a Lagg Single Malt, with an approving nod. 'This is great, dear. I've been wanting to try this one for a while.'

Her mum's face lit up as she unwrapped her chocolates, the necklace and blue silk scarf. 'These are just lovely,' she said, holding the necklace up. 'Jessica, will you help me put this on now, love? It's a bit tricky with my arm.'

'Of course I will, Mum,' she said, thrilled she liked it. It was these simple moments, of giving and being with family, that reminded her what Christmas was all about.

Reuben had given Catriona and Angus a case of their favourite Portuguese red wine which they were delighted with. He was equally pleased with the navy merino wool scarf they gifted him. Jessica's parents gave her vouchers for the newly opened spa in the village and a bottle of her favourite perfume.

Seeing that her parents were desperate to go to Primrose Cottage to see Lexi, Jessica insisted they go ahead first. She didn't want Lexi to be over-excited if they all descended at the same time. She and Reuben would go a bit later. It also meant they could get ahead with some of the Christmas dinner preparations while her mum was safely out of the way.

'Are you okay?' she said to Reuben when her parents had left. They were sitting in the front room by the tree. The lights cast a warm glow on the room and the log fire crackled and sparked.

Reuben nodded. His voice was low as he spoke. 'The stocking was so kind of your mum. It made me feel like I really belong. I haven't felt that way for a long time.'

She leaned over and kissed him. 'You do belong, Reuben, more than you think. You've always been welcome here. A little *too* welcome,' she said teasingly.

He smiled as he kissed her back. Then he stood up. 'Wait there a minute,' he said, before disappearing upstairs.

'I know we're not really doing presents,' he said, as he appeared holding out a small, wrapped parcel. 'But I got you a wee thing.'

Jessica was surprised but also touched. 'You didn't have to.'

'I know, but I wanted to and it seemed like the ideal gift.'

Her eyes widened slightly as she took it, surprised and touched all at once.

'The minute I saw it, I thought of you.'

She opened the package and grinned when she saw what was inside. '*The Perfect Christmas Romance*,' she said her eyes sparkling with amusement. 'How did you know I love a good romance novel?'

He chuckled. 'Because your mum told me . . . I thought this was perfect and it would also go nicely in the love room upstairs.'

'Thank you,' she said, kissing him again then smiling. 'I think we must be on the same wavelength with presents.' She stood to walk across to the tree. 'Either that or we shop at the same place. The new bookshop must be doing a good trade.' She reached down and plucked up the last parcel from under the tree. 'Merry Christmas, Reuben,' she said handing it to him.

'Thanks,' he said, and carefully peeled back the wrapping paper to reveal a book. He turned it over in his hands, his eyebrows raised at the blood-red text on the cover. '*The Snowman* by Jo Nesbø. I've a feeling this isn't going to be a festive or romantic read.'

'I believe you like a good crime book, right?' She had asked her brother's advice earlier in the week.

'I do, as long as it doesn't keep me up at night,' he said with a grin.

'Well, if it does you can borrow my romance novel.'

Reuben chuckled. 'Sounds like a plan. As long as you don't tell anyone.'

Jessica grinned. 'Worry not. Your secrets are safe with me. As long as you do as you're told.'

He raised an eyebrow.

'Oh, I almost forgot,' she said reaching for a small package under the tree. 'This is just another wee thing, that made me think of you.' She smiled as she watched him unwrap the millionaire shortbread chocolates.

A smile tugged at his lips. 'My favourite. Thank you.'

'Right, come on,' said Jessica. 'Let's get the turkey in the oven and the veg prepped before Mum and Dad get back.'

'Okay, chef. I'm all yours,' he said with a smirk.

'Let's get to it then,' she said, grabbing his hand and pulling him towards the kitchen, her heart fluttering with joy.

CHAPTER FORTY-EIGHT

Judging by Lexi's excited face and the piles of presents in the front room, Santa most certainly had been to Primrose Cottage. There was a singing teddy bear already mid-serenade, a purple scooter — still waiting to be assembled, a football, crayons, books and a toy guitar. Lexi was wide-eyed and beaming while Murray and Carolyn looked quite startled.

'It was an early start,' said Carolyn, yawning. 'I think I need more coffee.'

Jessica laughed as she glanced at her brother who looked as though he was ready to lob the singing bear out the window. 'No wonder Mum and Dad went home for a wee rest.'

'Yes, I think we must have worn them out. Or at least the bloody bear did,' Murray said drily. 'I think it will be having a rest soon, too, if I get my way.'

'Think you're going to need a shipping container to get this back to Melbourne,' said Reuben.

'Indeed,' said Murray. He was smiling now at Lexi, who had picked up the guitar and was trying to play it.

'Mum and Dad wanted to get her a keyboard,' said Jessica. 'Things could have been a whole lot noisier.' She looked at her brother who looked alarmed at the suggestion then relieved that they hadn't actually got it. 'Which is why we've brought you some small and thoughtful gifts,' teased Jessica. Although she and Reuben had brought their presents separately, she knew what he had for Lexi.

They sat down on the rug near the tree and she reached into the gift bag beside her and pulled out a carefully wrapped parcel, passing it to Lexi. 'This is for you,' she said with a smile.

Lexi's small hands tore at the gold and silver paper excitedly. When she pulled out the fairy costume — a swirl of sparkles and delicate lilac chiffon — she squealed. 'Fairy dress,' she announced to the room. She immediately started to twirl the wand around and point it at them all.

'And here is another wee thing for you, poppet.' Jessica passed another gold package to Lexi who immediately opened it. She grinned when she saw what was inside. 'Book.'

'Not just any book. It's a Katie Morag book,' said Carolyn excitedly when she saw what it was.

The Katie Morag books were about Katie, a feisty, red-headed girl who lived with her family on the magical Scottish Island of Struay.

'And she looks a bit like you, Lexi, doesn't she? She has the same colour hair as you and me too,' said Jessica. Then she looked at Carolyn and Murray. 'I just thought I'd keep my niece in touch with her Scottish roots. And the woman in the new bookshop recommended it. Even though she's maybe still a wee bit young. But if she likes it there are loads more. And I know you love reading to her.'

'I do. Thanks so much,' said Carolyn. 'That was so thoughtful of you.'

'Tank you,' said Lexi throwing her arms around Jessica.

'You are welcome, Lexi, and maybe I can begin to read it to you later?'

Lexi clapped her hands together in delight.

Then it was Reuben's turn to give Lexi her gift. He passed her a small parcel, wrapped in shiny red paper with a green bow.

Lexi unwrapped it carefully and giggled when she saw what was inside. It was a pair of bright, noisy maracas which she immediately started to shake vigorously.

'A brave choice,' Jessica said, grinning at him. Then she caught sight of her brother across the room. He shot Reuben a *look*.

'Thanks so much, you're a real pal,' said Murray sarcastically. 'Just what every household needs.'

Reuben chuckled. 'You're very welcome. Between that, the guitar and the singing bear you could have quite the band.'

'Maybe the keyboard would have been useful after all,' said Jessica teasingly.

They sat for a while laughing and drinking coffee, while Lexi tried on her fairy costume and danced around in front of the tree. After the adults exchanged their gifts, Jessica noticed the time. 'Oh-oh,' she said. 'Time to get back and check the turkey. I don't want to be responsible for ruining Christmas dinner. And mum will start getting twitchy and try and do it herself given half the chance.'

'I'll come shortly and give you a hand,' said Murray glancing over at Lexi and Carolyn who were both yawning. 'I think I'll let you two have a nap.'

'I'd better head off and see my dad now,' said Reuben glancing outside. 'But I won't be long. Then I'll be back to help.'

They gathered their things together and made the short walk back to Thistle Cottage, Reuben reaching for her hand. She glanced down, surprised but pleased, and gave his hand a squeeze. Jessica smiled, content, looking forward to the rest of the day. It was turning out to be the perfect Christmas Day.

CHAPTER FORTY-NINE

Later that afternoon, everyone sat round the table at Thistle Cottage. Reuben had just arrived back from the visit to see his dad. Jessica knew he was apprehensive about going, and although she had offered to go with him, he had insisted she stay at the cottage. Jessica knew he was right — if she turned her back for five minutes, her mum would soon be trying to regain control of the kitchen which was not a good idea given her general state and the weight of the turkey that needed to be taken out of the oven. She wasn't sure she could rely on Murray to do it on his own. Reuben had come back with a smile on his face and said his dad had seemed much brighter and chattier than usual. Jessica had instinctively hugged him, not giving a second thought to what her parents might think. Although her dad was oblivious, she caught her mum giving her one of her looks.

'Did he like the present you got him?' Reuben had bought his dad an old-fashioned turntable.

'He loved it,' said Reuben with a huge smile. 'His eyes lit up as soon as he saw what it was. He couldn't wait to get the Elvis record on.'

'That was such a thoughtful gift to get him,' she said.

Reuben shrugged bashfully. 'I know how much he has been enjoying music and the positive impact it's had on his mood. I just thought it might bring him a wee bit of joy.'

Jessica sat next to him and watched him laughing at something her dad said as he topped up their glasses with wine. He looked so much more relaxed now that he had spent time with his own dad and the visit had gone well. Reuben looked so at home here and she hoped he realised how much he belonged.

Lexi sat at the top of the table next to Murray and Carolyn. Angus was across from Catriona, who was tucked in against the wall so she didn't try and serve or clear up, and Jessica and Reuben had positioned themselves at the other end of the table so they had easy access to the kitchen stove.

'I'd just like to make a toast,' said Angus, standing up and banging his knife against his glass. Lexi then copied him and banged her spoon against the table. 'That's it, Lexi,' he said with a chuckle.

Murray looked over at Jessica and winked. Their dad had mentioned his Santa suit a few times and whether he should wear it that day. They'd convinced him not to. 'You don't want Lexi thinking that you're Santa,' said Murray. 'You might confuse her.'

'True. I never thought of that,' he said. 'I'm sure it will come in useful some other time.'

Murray and Jessica had looked at each other, shaken their heads and laughed. 'Oh, Dad. I'm sure it won't go to waste. Maybe save it for the Christmas fair next year?' suggested Jessica.

Now, wearing a Christmas jumper with a herd of reindeer which had flashing red noses, he stood with his glass in the air.

'Dad, that jumper looks like an emergency access site. That's some amount of red flashing lights,' said Murray.

Catriona tutted. 'I did say it was quite garish. But you know your dad. He doesn't listen.'

'I don't think that's entirely true, dear,' he said. 'I could have had *another* costume on you know.'

'True,' said Catriona, taking a swig of wine with her good hand. Even though her broken arm had slowed her down, she was still able to perform the essential tasks.

'Anyway,' said Angus rolling his eyes. 'I just want to say that I am so happy you're all here to celebrate Christmas. Your mum and I are very proud of you all and it's been a real treat to have you, Murray and Jess, both back in the same country for once and in Rowan Bay for Christmas.'

Jessica slipped her hand under the table and clutched Reuben's. He laced his fingers through hers and squeezed her hand tight.

'Carolyn and Lexi and Reuben, you're part of this family. Thank you for being here and making this Christmas so special for me and Catriona. Especially given her incapacitated state.'

She tutted. 'Angus, I'm not drunk. I've just been slightly slowed down by this caster plast.'

'Aye, okay love. I meant incapacitated due to your broken arm and *not* the amount of bevvy you've downed today.' He raised an eyebrow. 'I think you mean plaster cast by the way. Rather than caster plast.'

'Whoopsie,' said Catriona, shaking her head and laughing.

'Anyway, Merry Christmas. Wishing you all happiness, health and love.'

Everyone else raised their glass. 'Merry Christmas.'

'And talking of love,' said Catriona, looking over at Jessica and Reuben. 'Will you two stop with the pretending?'

'What do you mean?' said Jessica, flustered.

Catriona chuckled. 'Don't think we haven't noticed something is going on. I know you're trying to act as though you're just old friends but friends don't look at each other in the way that you two do.'

Jessica didn't dare look at Reuben.

'You're embarrassing them,' said Angus. 'But your mum is right.' He paused to look at Reuben. 'Even I've noticed it and you always say I can be a bit slow on the uptake.'

'Calling her Jessie was a bit of a sign,' said Murray drily as he turned to Reuben. 'You're like a big teenager. Trying to wind up the girl you fancy by doing the thing that annoys her most. Honestly.' He chuckled loudly.

Jessica and Reuben tried to feign innocence but they, too, burst out laughing.

'Apart from anything else,' said Angus, 'you're holding hands under the table. That's what me and your mum did when we were courting.'

Everyone started laughing and Lexi started banging her spoon against the table.

Reuben held up his hands in defeat. 'I don't think we'd make very good undercover agents, would we?'

'No,' scoffed Murray, 'that's safe to say.' He smiled at them.

'I think you guys are great together,' said Carolyn, her eyes full of warmth.

Jessica turned to look at Reuben and reached for his hand. This time above the table so everyone could see. It was a Christmas that she would never forget and Reuben was the most wonderful and surprise gift.

CHAPTER FIFTY

One Week Later

All too soon it was Hogmanay, the final day of the year. Lily and Gillian had both texted several times to make sure Jessica was coming to the New Year's Eve party at the Rowan Bay Inn. She had reassured them she would be there, but hadn't yet told them that Reuben would be her plus one. She thought she would leave that as a surprise. Though something told her Gillian would be anything but. She was sure Gillian knew exactly what had been going on. That was the gift of a friend who knew the real you.

That afternoon she and Reuben were curled up on the sofa at Primrose Cottage watching a movie. She still couldn't believe how comfortable she felt wrapped in his arms and had to pinch herself as a reminder that this wasn't a dream. As she looked up at him, his mouth curled into a smile. He cupped her chin in his hand and kissed her, his stubble grazing against her face. She didn't think she would ever tire of being with him. Their connection was different to anything she had experienced before. As clichéd as it was, he felt like home. The days between Christmas and New Year seemed to slow down and

Jessica felt as though it was only her and Reuben who were lost in this magical pocket of time. Murray, Carolyn and Lexi had gone to Edinburgh for a few days to visit family, and her dad had insisted that he would take over the caring duties for Catriona so Jessica could have a break and make the most of her time with Reuben. They had pretty much spent their time holed up at Primrose Cottage, making the most of each other's company without any distractions. With the bakery also closed, Jessica was enjoying the slower pace of life, hiding away without any expectations or pressure. She had no idea what lay ahead but what she did know was that she felt hopeful and excited again about the future.

'You look very thoughtful,' he said huskily in her ear. 'What are you thinking about?'

She squeezed his arms which were wrapped around her waist. 'London,' she said, turning to see the look of confusion on his face.

'What about it?' He untangled his arms from her and turned her round to look at him properly.

They had talked about how they would make things work between them. Reuben said he was happy to visit her in London but Jessica knew that wasn't enough. She didn't want to have a long-distance relationship with him. She was ready to come home for good. Even if Reuben hadn't come onto the scene, life in London as she knew it was over. She didn't want to go back to that way of being.

'I've decided to resign.'

Reuben grabbed the remote control and paused the movie. 'You've what?' He shook his head incredulously.

She nodded and pressed her lips firmly together. 'I've made my mind up.'

'That's a really big step, Jessie. I'd hate you to rush into anything.' He stroked the hair away from her face, his eyes full of tenderness. 'You need to do what's right for you.'

'Please don't try and talk me out of it and don't take this the wrong way, Reuben,' she said with a chuckle, 'but even if we weren't seeing each other, I would still want to come home.'

'Cheers,' he said jokingly. His gaze roamed across her face. 'What will you do though?'

She shrugged. 'I could do consultancy work . . . let's face it, everyone needs employment law advice these days. And I want to help with the bakery buyout. I don't think I'll be sitting around twiddling my thumbs. It just feels like the right time for me to move on and do something different.'

He nodded, his expression thoughtful as he listened.

'And it will be good to be nearer my parents. Murray and I have been lucky that they've been so healthy. But you saw what my dad was like when my mum broke her arm. He went to pieces. I'd like to be closer to home.'

'You shouldn't feel responsible for them though. They wouldn't want that,' he said, leaning in to kiss her. 'They're still fit and healthy.'

She sighed in contentment. 'I know that. As I said, it's been on my mind for a while. But I feel like I *belong* here back in Rowan Bay. Obviously, the fact you're here is like the cherry on the cake.'

He raised an eyebrow. 'That's not something I've ever been compared to before. But I will take it as a compliment.'

'What I meant to say is that I love you.' Jessica's hands flew to her mouth. *Why on earth did she just say that?* 'I mean I love being with you.'

Reuben's eyes were now twinkling with mischief and he pulled her hands away from her mouth so he could kiss her again. 'I know what you mean and it might help you to know that I think exactly the same.'

She smiled coyly at him then glanced at her watch. 'We'd better go and get ready for the party.'

He nodded then grinned lazily at her. 'There's no rush is there? Let's just stay here a wee while longer.'

She grinned, knowing exactly what he had in mind, and she pushed him back and shifted her body closer to his, laying a trail of kisses on his neck. He shifted beneath her and she leaned in again, brushing her lips against his. Jessica had come to Rowan Bay to hide away from everything and find solace and peace in her home village. Yet she'd somehow managed to find love when she least expected it.

Reuben put his finger on her lips for a moment. 'Do you know what, Jessie? I *never* make New Year's resolutions, but I think you're changing my ways.'

'What's your New Year's resolution?' she said, intrigued to hear what his answer would be. The moment was charged with emotion as she waited for him to expand.

'To take a chance, Jessie . . .' His lips curved into a playful smile. 'With you.'

'I think your most important resolution has to be never to call me Jessie, ever again,' she said firmly. 'Or you can forget your chances, mate.' But a spark of excitement and hope rippled through her. 'Let this be your final warning,' she murmured.

'That's a deal,' he said, taking her face in his hands and kissing her softly.

THE END

ACKNOWLEDGEMENTS

As always, I would like to thank the Choc Lit and Joffe Books team for their wonderful support. Producing a book is a team effort and I couldn't do any of this alone. But most of all I would like to thank my very wonderful editor, Becky Slorach. Thanks for being you and always helping to make my books so much better! I would also like to say a huge thanks to the brilliant Sarah Tranter who did a fabulous job as always. Thanks also to Jasper Joffe, Kate Ballard, Tia Davis, Elane Retford and Sharon Rutland. I'm thrilled that Jarmila Takač has designed another wonderful cover for me. I am also hugely grateful to all the ARC reviewers, book bloggers and everyone who reads my book in advance.

Loch Lomond is a place close to my heart, thanks to my dear friend, Tricia Thompson. I have so many treasured memories of spending time in Drymen, Rowardennon and Milarrochy Bay with you and your family, especially your wonderful mum, Ali. Thanks also to my other Loch Lomond pal, Alex McEwan, who lives on the opposite side of the loch. I've so appreciated your support and humour as I've written this book knowing that you are on the end of the phone if I need you! Thanks also to Nicola Martin and Anouska Woods for letting me pick your brains for some character development. And a special thanks to my early morning swimming pals, Sandra Duguid and Lindsey Thomson. Those cold dips kept me sane while editing the book!

A special thanks as always to my mum, my family and other friends for their love and support, too. Finally, thanks to Claudia and Grace for answering all the questions that I ask you in the name of writing research. Hopefully one day you'll read these books!

THE CHOC LIT STORY

Established in 2009, Choc Lit is an independent, award-winning publisher dedicated to creating a delicious selection of quality women's fiction.

We have won 18 awards, including Publisher of the Year and the Romantic Novel of the Year, and have been shortlisted for countless others. In 2023, we were shortlisted for Publisher of the Year by the Romantic Novelists' Association.

All our novels are selected by genuine readers. We are proud to publish talented first-time authors, as well as established writers whose books we love introducing to a new generation of readers.

In 2023, we became a Joffe Books company. Best known for publishing a wide range of commercial fiction, Joffe Books has its roots in women's fiction. Today it is one of the largest independent publishers in the UK.

We love to hear from you, so please email us about absolutely anything bookish at choc-lit@joffebooks.com.

If you want to receive free books every Friday and hear about all our new releases, join our mailing list here: www.joffebooks.com/freebooks.